SPARTACUS

AND THE CIRCUS OF SHADOWS

PRAISE FOR SPARTACUS AND THE CIRCUS OF SHADOWS

"As an author, there's a moment when noble emotions such as "admiration" and "respect" for a fellow scribe cross over into outright, green-eyed jealousy. And, about midway through reading Molly E. Johnson's page-turning debut *Spartacus and the Circus of Shadows*, my appreciation for her quirky, breezy style quickly gave way to wanton prose-envy of the worst kind. The "E" surely stands for either "Effortless," "Eclectic," or perhaps "Eunice"... I can't be sure. Only someone with the middle name of Eunice, like a creepy secret hidden at the nougaty center of their name, could create a charming outsider such as Spartacus Zander, AKA "Poop Lip."

As exotic as his name is, Spartacus grounds the fantastical events of his story in a deeply affecting and relatable way. His insights and feelings at being a runaway in a difficult situation at a difficult age hold your metaphoric hand as Johnson leads you, circuitously, to the inevitable big showdown at the Big Top. But it's the various roadside attractions and delightful deviations along the way that make her story sparkle like the creepy-shiny eyes of a carnie. Seriously: your mind will do advanced yoga moves at the story's twisting twists and—at times—stomach-turning turns. But I'm a better person for every mile spent with Spartacus on his darkly comic road trip. And, if you're from inner- or even outer-Portlandia, you will derive extra joy from the numerous inclusions of various beloved landmarks, twisted like a helium-filled balloon animal into Johnson's wonderful story."

— Dale E-for-Eunice Basye
[Author of the demonically delightful series *Heck: Where the Bad Kids Go*]

"I couldn't put it down. Literally. Never pick up a book while eating honey glazed ribs. But, if you are going to be stuck with a book for a few days, I advise you to make it *Spartacus and the Circus of Shadows*."

—Dr. Cuthbert Soup
[Author of the hilarious road trip tale, *A Whole Nother Story*, and (N)others]

SPARTACUS

AND THE CIRCUS OF SHADOWS

MOLLY E. JOHNSON

RAINTOWN PRESS
PORTLAND, OREGON

Spartacus and the Circus of Shadows
Text © 2011 by Molly E. Johnson (www.mollyejohnson.com)
Illustrations © 2011 by Robin E. Kaplan (www.thegorgonist.com)
For interactive games and other cool stuff: www.circusofshadows.com

Published by RainTown Press, Portland, Oregon's premier independent press dedicated to publishing classic and original literature for middle grade and young adult readers. RainTown Press does not advocate lemur-napping, hitchhiking, fire eating without a license, or the use of the alias Casey Moe. All stunts in this book are performed either by highly-trained professionals or ridiculously lucky amateurs. Do NOT try this at home.

RainTown Press • 1111 E. Burnside St. #309 • Portland, OR 97214
Or via the web at: www.raintownpress.com

Library of Congress Cataloging-in-Publication Data available.
LCCN: 2011936734
First Edition, October 2011
ISBN (Hardcover): 978-0-9840500-0-0
ISBN (Paperback): 978-0-9840500-1-7
ISBN (Electronic): 978-0-9840500-2-4

SYMPATHY FOR THE DEVIL
Words and Music by MICK JAGGER and KEITH RICHARDS
Copyright © 1968 (Renewed) ABKCO MUSIC, INC.,
85 Fifth Avenue, New York, NY 10003
All Rights Reserved   Used by Permission

Printed in Canada
The title type was set in Hiroshige Std
The text type was set in Sabon LT Std

To Z:

For sending the tornado,
the tattoo artist,
nineteen-dozen parentheticals,
and
twenty-eight hyperboles
to their
alternate dimensions.

I'll always trust you to kill my darlings.

YMEFL—LYBRYSSM.

PROLOGUE

A CLOWN CAN BE A scary thing. And a clown posing as a cop can be even scarier. And a mob of clown cops? Let me tell you—you haven't experienced real fear until you've been chased and cornered by a mob of pale, grinning clown cops.

From my spot on the catwalk (a ridiculous fifty feet in the air), I could see all the performers coming out onto the stage below me—the mime-faced muscle men, the wiry contortionists, those creepy, spindly-legged skeleton guys—like this was some big, end-of-the-show curtain call. The ringmaster looked up at me with a smug smile, like everything was going according to plan. Sharkman stood by his side, gnashing his knife-sharp teeth. The circus orchestra was sending insane music blatting through my head, so loud I could barely think.

Right below me, twenty or so fake cops climbed both sides of the scaffolding, crazy smiles pasted on their faces. I only had a few seconds before they'd be up on the catwalk with me.

I had two choices, and they were both bad: I could dangle from the catwalk and jump down onto the diving board ten feet below... or I could stay right where I was and wait for Bartholomew's goons to reach me.

One more look at the advancing clowns and I knew I wasn't staying.

Ten feet isn't that far, is it?

I told myself not to look down.

Don't look down.

Looking down would be a very bad idea.

I lined myself up with the diving board before dropping to my stomach. Then I inched my way backward off the edge, letting my feet dangle below me. I'd never been so high off the ground before, and there I was, blindly lowering myself off a fifty-foot catwalk, about to do some sort of reverse pull-up. And I'd never been able to do a *normal* pull-up.

Don't look down.

I got to the point of no return, where I was more in the air than I was on the ledge, legs kicking. I knew I was right above the diving board—all I had to do was let go and I'd land right on it. It wouldn't be so bad.

I looked down.

And lost my grip and fell.

For the brief moment I was in the air, the music paused and I heard the audience's combined gasp over my own.

I landed on the diving board to wild applause, the cymbals crashing in triumph. I clung to the board vibrating beneath me.

"Go, Spartacus, go!" someone in the audience shouted.

Morons. They were all morons.

Shaking, I clambered to my feet and looked up at the catwalk where I'd been hanging a few seconds before. The clown cops were already there, shaking their oversized, foam billy clubs at me. I hoped the guns strapped to their uniforms were equally fake. They wouldn't hurt me in front of the audience, would they? I didn't think so, but maybe they could cover it all up as being part of the show.

Bartholomew was crafty like that.

"Please! I'm not part of the circus! This is real!" I shouted to the audience, waving my arms, feeling pathetic. But the music and the crowd drowned me out.

I looked down at the water tank so far below me and, as if the situation wasn't bad enough, Sharkman ran across the stage and took a flying leap into the tank. He then started swimming around in darting circles so all I could see was his dorsal fin above the water. You had to hand it to him; he really did look just like a shark.

Down below, the clowns started climbing the ladder to the diving board. I only had a few seconds before I would be cornered again—and this time, there was only one way down.

"They've got me surrounded," I whispered. That was something I'd always wanted to say out loud, but until that moment, I hadn't realized that that's one thing you *never* want to say.

So I cried out again, a pathetic "Help! This is real! I'm not with them!" It all felt like a dream—no, a nightmare. It had finally reached the point of weirdness where you know you've got to be waking up any moment. You've just got to.

Everyone was on their feet, wildly cheering. It was like Bartholomew had seen this coming and planned the whole commotion. And then someone from the audience shouted it.

"Jump!"

And then again, from more voices: "Jump, kid!"

Were they insane?

I looked down at the tank. It might as well have been a glass of water at this height. I frantically shook my head. Jumping would be crazy. I wasn't my mom. I wasn't a performer.

The clowns on the ladder were almost up to the diving board. When they got there, they were going to take me backstage to do who knows what. Erase me. Bump me off. Rub me out.

"Jump!" shouted someone else. Soon the whole audience was chanting it: "Jump! Jump! Jump!" The noise was deafening.

This wasn't a dream and I wasn't about to wake up and find myself at home in bed. This was really happening.

I gulped the thick summer air as I considered everything that had led me to this moment. To what was looking more and more like the end of the line.

The fat lady singing.

The grand finale of Spartacus Ryan Zander.

CHAPTER 1

I'M GOING TO START RIGHT at the beginning, the day mom left home to become The Amazing Athena, World-Famous Human Cannonball.

Sure, first there were the epic fights, the Month of Silence, and the time Dad set Mom's hula-hoops on fire. But going into all of that would just make you think Mom ran out on Dad. But trust me—none of that stuff is important.

Dad and Will (my older brother) took her departure pretty well. And by "pretty well," I mean they seemed to think we were better off without her. Will was convinced she'd left Dad for another guy—maybe a circus performer. Her absence was a touchy subject with Dad. Sometimes when I tried to bring it up, he wouldn't talk to me for days.

She went missing the same day I started the seventh grade. I came home that afternoon to find the house looking *a little odd*. (Those were Dad's exact words to Grandma: "The place looked a little odd." Personally, I think a better way to put it would be "the place was *destroyed*.") When Will opened the front door, water started pouring out onto the porch. The front hall's bathroom sink was overflowing, flooding the entryway.

Will slogged through the water to turn off the sink while I checked out the living room. The couch's smoldering, smoking cushions smelled like burnt lemon custard, like they had been lit on fire and then doused with a pitcher of lemonade. Our old box television had been knocked to the floor, and there were footprints high up on the wall.

Then there was the kitchen. The blender was running and the dining table was on its side with only three legs attached. (We never did find the fourth one.) Six steak knives stuck out of the pantry door in a perfect vertical line. The bottom knife pinned a note at eye level, scrawled in handwriting that didn't quite look like my mom's.

The bottom half of the note was torn off in a jagged line, like someone had tried to erase the rest of her message. I wanted to tear the note down and crumple it up, but instead I just slid to the floor and sat there staring up at it and trying to blink away the pressure building behind my eyes.

"What are you doing?" Will hadn't noticed the note yet and he was peering down at me. "Poop Lip—wait, are you crying?"

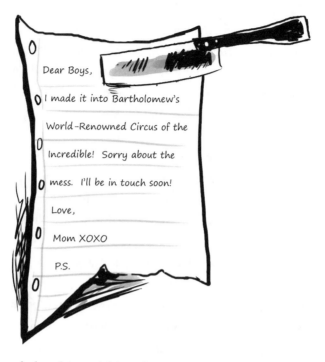

Dear Boys,

I made it into Bartholomew's World-Renowned Circus of the Incredible! Sorry about the mess. I'll be in touch soon!

Love,

Mom XOXO

P.S.

I scowled at his smirking face. Poop Lip. One unfortunately-placed freckle—not a mole, a *freckle*—one concentrated cluster of melanin, one overly-pigmented spot just above my lip and, thanks to Will, nearly every kid at Brenville Middle-Senior High School called me Poop Lip. The town we live in is small and Will's reach was long—even the old man at the gas station once called me Poop Lip. I just stared at him. I couldn't think of anything to say.

I guess I was lucky that at least my dad, my teachers, and Eli Carson, my best friend (and next-door neighbor), called me Ryan, which is my middle name. I go by Ryan because my first name isn't exactly normal, but I'll get to that tragedy later.

When dealing with Will, you need to follow two simple rules: rule number one is you never question him. Not unless you want to walk away bruised and possibly wedgied. And rule number two? Never show weakness. Not even if your mom destroys the house and then abandons the family.

I wiped my nose before standing up. I realized I was shivering—maybe I was cold from the windows being left wide open. I pulled the note from the pantry door and handed it to Will.

"Mom left," I told him. "With the circus. She's gone."

Will skimmed Mom's note. He looked even angrier than usual. "Of course she's gone," he said, kicking a can of green beans so it skittered across the floor. "How long has she been trying to get out of here?"

Will had a point. Even though I was the only one who knew Mom was serious about becoming a circus performer, anyone could see she wasn't happy. Brenville wasn't big enough for someone with her talents. But even though I knew she wanted to lead a more exciting life, I always thought that, if she left, she'd take us with her.

I never thought she'd leave me behind.

Dad got home a few minutes later and the three of us just stared at the mess and the note and then—get this—no one said anything. Every time I started to speak, to ask what we were going to do, Dad glared and Will elbowed me in the armpit. Can you imagine? No, you can't, because it's not normal. But then again, no one in my family is normal.

So, instead of talking, Dad went upstairs to shower, Will called in a pizza, and then we sat and ate dinner in front of the broken TV, as if Mom trashing the house and leaving with the circus was the most normal thing in the world.

IT'S COMMON SENSE THAT IF someone goes missing and your house looks like a tornado went through it, you call the police. Dad didn't. He made a few late night phone calls that I couldn't quite hear through the heating ducts, but he must have decided to take the note at face value and leave it at that.

Maybe he was just relieved to be rid of her. Whenever he found her doing something "weird" or "crazy," they fought like stray cats. Like when he came home to find her teaching me how to throw knives. Or when she dyed her hair orange and red so that it looked like flames. Or when he got a call from the neighbors complaining that she was leaping from fence post to fence post in front of their house. Or the time, on a family picnic, she somehow got on the back of a wild elk and rode it for a whole twenty yards. (And that was just the stuff Dad *knew* about.)

Brenville is a small town. If you stand out at all, you may as well start your own reality TV show because everyone is going to know everything about you anyway. So the neighbors talked. And Dad? Dad just wanted to be invisible.

The day after my mom disappeared, Eli told me the Story of the Black Van. Eli had been home sick on the first day of school (which he's been getting away with every year since the third grade) and happened to look out his window to see a black van pulling up in our driveway. An unmarked van—it definitely did *not* have *Bartholomew's World-Renowned Circus of the Incredible* scrawled across the side like you'd think it would if it was there doing anything normal. No, it was a plain black van with tinted windows. It didn't even have license plates.

Eli watched what happened because he thought the van was weird—and because he didn't have anything better to do. He said it was there for exactly forty-two minutes and that there might have been some crashing and banging coming from inside the house. He never saw Mom, but he did see two creepy men heave a big black bag into the back of the van right before it left, tires squealing down the street.

"One of the guys was all pale and really tall," Eli explained. "He was like a vampire version of Conan O'Brien. The other guy was like a Mr. America, weightlifter type. Built like a brick house. Man, I can't believe they kidnapped your mom!"

Yeah, he said it just like that. No build up, no saying it in a *Do-you-think-this-is-possible?* kind of way. Just *bam!* Dropped the bomb without even thinking. Of course, he argues over who actually said it first, but this is *my* story and I can say with utter certainty that I am pretty sure it was Eli.

Will was dribbling his soccer ball around the lawn like nothing had happened when I ran to tell him about the Black Van. He snorted but didn't look up.

"So what you're saying," he said, dancing around the ball and breathing hard, "is that you and The Eel think she was kidnapped?"

Pow!

I jumped as Will kicked the ball hard against the fence. It always hit the same spot. He'd put one toe on it, fake left, fake right, then:

Pow!

"Maybe," I said, trying to sound more casual than I was. Will made me nervous. But then, Will made everyone nervous. I think he even made our parents nervous.

"Why would a circus kidnap somebody?" Will asked.

"Maybe so they don't have to pay them?" I ventured.

"That's the stupidest thing I ever heard."

Pow!

I flinched again. He was kicking the ball really hard. Harder than usual. But I wasn't going to let it drop.

"What about the bag, though?" I asked. "It was big enough for a person."

"Maybe it was her makeup," he said. I worked up enough confidence to glare at him. "What? Seriously! They wear a lot of makeup in the circus," he said, before firing the ball again.

Pow!

The look on Will's face made it clear that, unless I wanted him to get *really* angry, the conversation was over. So I kept quiet for a while, but it never really left my mind.

It wasn't just the house being destroyed and the Black Van and the large-enough-for-a-person bag. There was more. Much more.

A few weeks later I started getting postcards from my mom. Postcards with secret messages, saying things like "Help me" and "I'm in trouble."

No matter how ridiculous it seemed, it was true—my mom really had been kidnapped by the circus.

EVEN BEFORE THE POSTCARDS BEGAN arriving, Eli and I had started researching Bartholomew's Circus. What we found wasn't very reassuring.

Sure, the main website for Bartholomew's World-Renowned Circus of the Incredible was kind of underwhelming. They only had a few pictures and a schedule that listed just a handful of shows. Eli and I knew from other websites that the circus performed a lot more often than that. Plus, the postcards from Mom came from all over the country. So that was weird.

But Wikipedia had more information on Bartholomew. There had been an incident where three trapeze artists had died (getting weirder). We couldn't find many details about that, but according to Wikipedia, it was an accident. Then there was a tiger mauling where another guy almost died. There had been some accusations of animal cruelty, but they were dismissed as coming from angry ex-performers.

That wasn't even close to the weirdest (and worst) stuff, though. We found a site, IHateBartholomewsCircus.com, where everybody and their brother seemed to have a story about how evil the circus was—they claimed that Bartholomew had sold his soul to the devil, that he used dark magic to entertain his audience, and that he'd even helped fix the 2005 Tour de France.

Obviously I wasn't the only person who had come to the conclusion that something was strange about Bartholomew's Circus. It all sounded too crazy to believe, but if even some of it was true, it didn't bode well for my mom.

I wasn't really surprised that Dad didn't take my kidnapping theory seriously. Adults seem to lose their ability to think about anything strange or out of the ordinary. But Will, who knew evil inside and out, should have sensed that something was off.

Over the next ten months, I showed him the twenty-five postcards Mom sent me, including the ones with the secret codes. Those were the strangest. Every new one I got, I brought immediately to Will. I've never seen anyone laugh so hard.

"How could it be more obvious?" I fumed, shoving the postcard from Last Chance, Colorado in his face. "Read it."

"Come *on,*" he said. "Circuses don't kidnap people. Don't be a moron."

"Just read it," I repeated. "Read it and tell me she isn't asking for help."

And so he read it out loud:

Hello Spartacus!
Everything is going really good!
Lots of fun people to meat and
Places to see.
My cannonball thing is going really grate.
Everyone thinks I'm the best they have ever seen!
  Love,
  Mom

"First of all, do you think Mom is that bad a writer?" I asked him. "She's trying to get my attention. I mean, look how she spelled *meet.*"

Will scowled, squinting at the card and then back at me.

"You really think there are hidden messages in these things, *Smarticus?*"

I wanted to think that maybe he was hiding his fear to protect me. That maybe, deep down, he saw how weird and scary the whole situation was.

But when I pointed out that the first letter of each line, going from top to bottom, spelled "HELP ME," he laughed so hard, he farted.

"Why would she write that in there, huh?" I asked.

"It's a coincidence!" he exclaimed, after containing himself and wiping a tear from his eye. "Look, you know how a hundred monkeys pounding on a hundred typewriters for a hundred years—"

"Yeah, yeah. They'd write a play," I said, rolling my eyes. I hated his guts right then.

"Yeah. Everyone knows that. It's a scientific fact," Will explained. "But it doesn't mean anything. Besides, what about the other postcards? She sends you some without all the... what did you call them?"

"Clues," I huffed, pulling the card out of his hand and tucking it back in an envelope with the others.

"Whatever. Some don't say anything secret, though, right? Why would she do that?"

I thought about it for a minute, and then shuffled through the envelope until I found one I liked, the one with the skull of a triceratops on it. It was from the Academy of Natural Sciences in Philadelphia.

There weren't any clues on it—at least none that I could find. Why was that?

"Maybe to throw Bartholomew off her track?" I suggested as Will snatched it out of my hand and began to read,

"*Dear Spartacus,*" he began, speaking in that high lady-voice he used when he imitated Mom—or any girl, for that matter. "*You don't know how much I miss you and your lovely brother Will. Will is the best brother you could—*"

"Give me that! It doesn't say that!" I lunged for it but he hopped up onto the sofa he'd been sitting on and, holding a hand over my face, jumped up and down while continuing to "read."

"*The best brother you could ask for. In fact—*oof! Watch it, Poop Lip!—*In fact, I've told your father to give your allowance to sweet William for the next four years and*—Ooh, Poopy, now you've done it!"

The scuffle we had doesn't need to be recounted blow for blow, so let's just cut to me, back upstairs in the safety of my room, tending my bruises and taping the postcard back together. (Will had turned it into confetti and stuffed it down my pants.)

As I taped the last piece into place, I had to admit Will had a point. Why would only some of the cards have clues and not the others? And why would the ones without clues make it sound like she was having a great time? I had to sit there and think about it for a minute before it made sense: the ones *without* clues were the ones she wrote and sent to make it appear like everything was normal, just in case they were being read. And even though she was sending the cards *with* clues secretly, she still put them in code.

BEFORE WE GET ANY FURTHER, I suppose I should address the whole "Spartacus" issue. Mom was pretty smart, but she seemed to have forgotten that when it came to naming me. I don't think it crossed her mind that a child growing up in a town the size of Brenville might not do very well with a name like Spartacus Ryan Zander. Then again, her name was Athena, which is just as ridiculous, so maybe I should blame *her* parents—but then again, we never saw her parents. Mom never explained why. It'd just always been that way.

When I asked her why Will got a normal name and I got Spartacus, she just kissed me on the head and said in that airy way of hers, "In time, Spartacus. In time."

The name didn't bother me for the most part, except when we had a substitute teacher, or when it was report card time, everyone was reminded that I wasn't only Ryan, or Poop Lip, but also Spartacus. So then I'd get teased for another few weeks about that. It was ridiculous.

Mom was the only one who called me Spartacus. At least in a serious, not-making-fun-of-me way. And I never minded. It never sounded weird when she said it.

Dad thought the name was just as stupid as I did. He started calling me Ryan as soon as I was born, hoping I'd "turn out normal." Even when Mom told him that Ryan wasn't my name, he'd say "Ryan" right over the top of her "Spartacus" until they were both yelling my names back and forth over my crib. As I got older, it continued...

"Spartacus, please pass the peas."

"Ryan, pass your mother the peas."

"Spartacus *heard* me, Phil."

"Ryan. The peas. *Now*."

I TRIED TO TALK TO Dad about the postcards, but he refused to even read where they were from, let alone help me decode the secret messages. When I tried to show him the maps that tracked her erratic movements across the country or the connections to other kidnappings I saw on the news, his response was—well, you know those people who can crack their knuckles without even touching them? Yeah, Dad's one of them. Two or three cracks from his fingers and I'd clam up for a day or two. But I kept trying. I mean, this was my *mom*.

As it turned out, Dad's limit for putting up with conspiracy theories was two and a half months.

He was doing bills at the new dining room table when he saw me standing in the doorway with the map and postcards. I was trying to get up the nerve to sit down next to him, hoping he'd finally show some interest.

His groan was so loud, dust flew off the light fixture.

"No more of this," he growled before I'd even said a word. "You hear me, Ryan? No more postcards, no more random connections, *nada*. If I see another map with even a pushpin in it, I will tear it up and make you eat it like cereal. Got it?"

I heard Will snicker from the family room, but I ignored him. I was just starting to *think* about saying something when Dad shut his eyes and sucked air in through his teeth. Then, with his eyes still closed, he pounded both his fists on the table.

"Not (*bang*) another (*bang*) word (*bang*)!"

I ducked out of the kitchen before he could open his eyes and light me on fire with them.

After he shut me down, I tried calling the local police station a few times... and then a detective called our house and told Dad I had to stop calling them. I was grounded for a full week. That gave me free time to do some more research and draft a few letters to the FBI. But all I got back was an FBI baseball cap and a letter written from the point of view of a cartoon dog. A lot of help they were.

Nobody listens to kids. I was officially on my own.

I SPENT ALL WINTER COBBLING together a rescue plan. But before I can explain my plan, I need to tell you about one of Mom's weird talents.

One weekend, when Dad was gone on a business trip, I heard Mom's voice calling for help. It took me a few minutes to trace it to Dad's study, but even then I couldn't find her because there was nowhere in the room she could be.

Then I realized her voice seemed to be coming from inside Dad's filing cabinet. I opened up the top few drawers first, but still nothing.

I thought I was going crazy, until I heard my mom's voice say, "Lower."

She was in the very bottom drawer. A single drawer. It was amazing to see her unfold herself out of a little pretzel to become my mom again. I mean, I wouldn't have thought it was possible if I hadn't seen it myself.

"Don't tell anyone about this," she'd said, putting the papers back inside. Like anyone would believe me. But I knew what she really meant: "Don't tell Dad."

So I came up with the idea of using a suitcase the size of a small dog carrier—with wheels. I knew she could fit into that; it was bigger than the filing cabinet drawer. My brilliant, if simple, plan was to get to the circus, call the cops ahead of time (using myself, the Missing Kid, as bait, since the kidnapping of mothers obviously isn't something they care about), get backstage, and get Mom into the suitcase. Then I'd just wheel her out, lost in the crowd of kids and families. I'd take her straight to the cops waiting outside. Mom would tell them everything—and we'd bring Bartholomew down.

The rescue mission was planned for June, right after school let out. I figured there was no point in getting in extra trouble for missing school. I knew leaving was going to get Dad riled up, but I figured if I came home with Mom, there was no way he could ground me.

The one thing Eli and I had to go on was Bartholomew's website. Even though the schedule was incomplete, it listed two shows coming up in June. One was in California. As far as we knew, this was the closest they'd ever be to us in

Brenville, Oregon. Even though we knew they'd probably be performing in other places, this was the only one we could actually plan for in advance.

Eli's cousin was going to drive me to Bend, which was a bigger city about two hours away, where I'd "resurface," as Eli put it.

"You can't just get a bus from Brenville," he explained. "You have to go dark for a bit of time and pop up somewhere you don't belong. They'll never track you that way." Did I mention Eli watches a lot of spy movies? But it made sense. So, once I was in Bend, I'd catch a ride to California. Eli would set it all up using this ride-share website we'd found.

While Eli helped me prepare, Mom's postcards got more and more desperate. The one from Imalone, Wisconsin (where she'd underlined a bunch of random letters in the message that, when put together, spelled out "bring help") made me realize that she didn't mean for me to come alone. Eli was out though. He wasn't known for being brave—in fifth grade he'd peed his pants crossing a four-lane highway. I mulled it over and over (and over) until finally deciding Will was my only hope. After all, he was tough, she was his mom, and we were brothers. That had to count for something, right?

Look, I know what you're thinking—Will would have refused to go with me. But I was certain that if I could just get him to really look at all the evidence (and see that I was going with or without him), he'd have to say yes. It was just the matter of finding the right time to ask. But when your house is a war-zone, there really isn't a "right time." And so the right time still hadn't come when Will pulled the Worst Prank Ever on me.

I'm not talking about when he used a syringe to inject my unopened yogurt with a laxative. Or the time he convinced me the house was haunted by writing messages on mirrors (and in my food) before finally putting a very alive squirrel in my room in the middle of the night. No. Those were just jokes. Teasers. Child's play. They were nothing compared to what he had planned for me.

What I'm trying to say is that Will (and by default, Dad) left me no choice but to go it alone.

CHAPTER 2

BRENVILLE WAS JUST A BLIP on people's trips across Oregon, trips to bigger cities that had bright lights and things to do. We had a place to rent movies, but that was really about it when it came to entertainment. Other than the pool.

Brenville had a real Olympic-sized public pool with the full ten lanes and a thirty-three foot high dive. (Years ago, some rich guy had the pool built and donated it to the town because his kid wanted to swim in the Olympics. He didn't, of course, and they eventually moved away.) During the summer, pretty much every kid in town lived at the pool. As far as we were concerned, the high dive was *it*. The whole chilidog of existence.

No one under eighteen was allowed to jump off the high dive, so that was the surest way to achieve Brenville fame. Everyone talked about doing it, but Will was one of the only kids who broke the rules and actually did. A few others just ran up as quick as they could and did cannonballs, trying to soak everyone. But Will was an honest-to-god diver. He took his time before springing off the board and slicing into the water like a knife.

I didn't know how he got so good. Maybe he was a natural performer like Mom. Seeing him up there on the board, hearing all the other kids *Oooh* and *Aahh*, was one of the few times I was proud he was my brother.

Everyone wanted to dive like Will. I'd even been up on that diving board once to check it out, thinking maybe I'd try a cannonball. But thirty-three feet is really high. Like ridiculously high. I figured you had to be kind of crazy, like Will was, to want to try something like that.

I must have mentioned the high dive a few too many times at home, though, because Dad seemed to get it in his mind that I *really* wanted to do it. Actually, I would have been quite happy living the rest of my life in Wimpdom. I could have grown to be an old man of forty, with kids of my own, and not have felt the least bit sad I'd never jumped off the high dive.

But, according to Dad, if I wanted it so badly, I should just do it. See, just because Dad thought Mom joining the circus was unacceptable, that doesn't mean he was against doing crazy things. My mom bungee jumping off the overpass? Frowned upon. Me risking my life jumping from like a -mile in the air? Yes, perfectly fine.

I think he was just upset that one of his sons was defective. With Will being the fearless weirdo he was, and my mom being what she was, I should have been less afraid. It's like my fear of diving represented all my shortcomings, wrapped up in one perfect, shameful package.

"So, did you go off the high dive today or what?"

Almost every summer dinner conversation began this way.

During the last week of school, while I was focused on my rescue mission, Dad focused on the high dive with even more excitement than the year before. He was like a dog with a bone and he wouldn't let go. This summer would be the Diving Summer. He actually said that: "Diving Summer." That's when I felt like I needed to speak up.

"Dad, I know this is important to you," I half mumbled to both him and my plate. "But it's not to me."

While I said this, he just shook his head in a mixture of sympathy and disgust. Mostly disgust.

"I just don't get you, Ryan," he said. "You're thirteen now, a teenager. I mean, really, it's not that high."

I bit my tongue. Yeah, falling thirty-three feet through the air was easy. That's why there were so many Olympic high divers around.

"Besides," he continued. "You can't go through life being afraid of things. When I was a kid, I was scared of—well, I was scared of…" Dad looked thoughtful. "Well, I could *imagine* what it would be like to be scared of, like, say, the dark or something. But I wasn't of course. I'm just saying that I know what it would be like."

There was no point in telling him that I wasn't going to do it. So I kept quiet and that seemed to be the end of it, at least for that night.

But that wasn't the end of it.

The next day, Will "accidentally" ran over my binoculars while Speed Mowing the lawn. Before I got a chance to tell Dad, Will cornered me and said he really felt bad about it. He said he would teach me to dive, to be just like him. He said we could sneak into the pool late at night so no one would know I was practicing.

"You'll be famous," he said. "The girls are gonna go nuts."

So I said yes, almost without thinking. One of my main reasons was that I thought if we bonded with the diving stuff, Will would be more likely to listen to the Rescue Mom Plan and come with me. It was the day before the last day of school, and I was set to leave in one week.

And I really needed Will to come with me.

But, to be honest, I was also kind of interested in the "girls are gonna go nuts" part. Well, there was really only one girl I wanted to go nuts. Her name was Erika Dixon. Erika had gone to school with Eli and me since the second grade, and I could barely remember a time when I didn't have a crush on her. She was pretty and smart and popular. She also smelled like cinnamon all the time, which made no sense to me, but might have explained me liking her so much because cinnamon is my favorite spice.

Oh, and Erika never called me Poop Lip. Even after the time in fifth grade when I burnt her dress with Eli's homemade arc welding science project (which he got a D on because of the danger level). So she wasn't rude to me even after I lit her on fire, which was a plus. However, when I *wasn't* burning her stuff, she didn't have two words to say to me. So, as much as I was thinking about my up-and-coming rescue mission, I have to admit my mind might have been on Erika a teeny bit... and the fact that she'd have to notice me if Will really did come through and teach me to dive.

But I'm sure you've already guessed that I shouldn't have said yes to Will, right? Shouldn't have trusted him, shouldn't have gone to the pool, shouldn't have hoped I was on the brink of a brand new brother?

You'd be right.

But he *seemed* sincere. He *seemed* apologetic about my binoculars. He *seemed*—well, like Dad might have put him up to it. So the very same night he offered, the night before the last day of school, I went with Will to the pool.

Will knew how to sneak in through a weak part in the fence. He even knew where the light controls were. It was like he owned the place.

"You got to just get used to the height first," said Will when we got to the pool. After ten minutes of coaxing, I finally went up the ladder. All the way to the top, past the normal boards. Thirty-three feet in the air. When the time came, I only jumped so Will wouldn't push me in.

We just did regular jumps off the high dive. More like just falling off the board. Once I got comfortable with that, Will got me diving off of the side of the pool. Real diving, where I was facing straight down with my hands in front of me like a wedge. And I was pretty good. I have to say, I might even have been a natural. At first, Will thought it would take me a few days to learn, but I moved so quick he decided I should do the high dive that night.

So we moved up to the nine-foot diving board. That came pretty easy. I just had to overcome my natural urge to chicken out and go straight back down the ladder.

Then came the fifteen-foot board, which wasn't that much scarier than the nine-foot, except there was a lot more water to swim through to get to the surface.

Then, finally, back up to the high dive again. My hands were sweaty as I looked down all that way to the pool. Doing a real dive was a lot different from just falling off the board. I hesitated for a long time before going off. Will was right beside me, giving me pointers. He was actually encouraging me. And so I did it.

You know how some people are born to be good spellers or fast runners or chess masters? I was born to do the high dive. I was that good. I was going to go to the Olympics. I was going to be on cereal boxes.

"You're like Greg Louganis," Will said, shaking his head in awe as we walked home from the pool in the dark.

"Greg who?" I asked. I was walking on clouds. Will rolled his eyes.

"You know, Louganis? Like the best Olympic diver ever?"

My grin hurt my cheeks.

"Everyone is going to be talking about you after tomorrow, Ryan," Will said.

Ryan? I thought. I almost tripped. *What happened to Poop Lip?*

"Trust me," he said, a big grin on his face. "Even Erika will remember you after tomorrow."

And then he ruffled my wet hair.

Ruffled. My. Hair.

The clues were everywhere. I should have known something was up.

THE NEXT DAY, AFTER THE last class on the last day of school, I stuffed everything from my locker into my backpack and raced home through the summer heat. I sort of wished Eli had been around for moral support, but he was already away at a week-long computer camp. (Dad thought that it was ridiculous that Eli got out of school early for "nerd camp.")

At home, I was scrambling to find my swim shorts when Will appeared in the door, tossing his own shorts at my head.

"Here, you can wear mine," he said with a smile on his face (or was it a smirk?). "You're gonna be awesome."

I gulped at him, standing there, looking calm as a clam, nothing like how I was feeling. I was suddenly really afraid. Not like last night. Something didn't seem right. I was getting a pain in my gut.

"Maybe we should wait until another day," I said.

"Don't worry so much, Poop Lip," he said. He stopped when he saw me flinch. "I mean, Ryan. I saw you last night. You're a natural."

He kept up the pep talk and never left my side while I got ready to go. As we were walking there, he kept giving me pointers: hands out to your sides before you jump. Only two bounces or you'll look like you're scared. Remember to breathe until the last possible second. Don't plug your nose.

"And another thing, once you start the jump—"

"You have to finish it. No matter what," I finished for him. He looked at me in surprise.

"Mom told me that, once," I said, blushing. I didn't elaborate—Will thought Mom's circus stuff was dumb. He just nodded his head, kept a firm hand on my back, and, before I knew it, we were at the pool.

Thousands of kids were there. Well, maybe not thousands. But every kid from Brenville Middle-Senior High, as well as a bunch of younger kids from the elementary school.

Holy crap. I stiffened.

"I invited a few people," Will shrugged. "Don't even go into the pool first. Just dive in. Trust me, the kiddos will go nuts."

"Where's the Lifey?" I asked. The lifeguard's chair was empty.

"Probably taking a leak," answered Will, but I still didn't move. I just stood there in my brother's swim trunks that came down to my calves, suddenly shivering in the ninety-degree heat. Will finally gave me a shove.

"Come on, Ryan. You can do it."

I stumbled forward and thought about how much I needed Will to help me rescue Mom. If I could just survive this, I thought, then Will would take me seriously when I told him about my plan. As I reached the ladder, the kids noticed and started whispering to each other.

I saw Erika Dixon, just a few feet away. I nodded awkwardly at her, having nothing to say, as usual.

"He's gonna do it!" she whispered to her friend. She actually sounded impressed. It should have made me braver, more determined, but it just made my heart pound more—like in a heart-attack kind of way.

I hesitated before putting my foot on the bottom rung of the ladder. I hesitated at the top of the ladder and again at the middle of the board. I hesitated until there was no more room and the board ended. My toes curled over the edge with the sandpapery grippy stuff cool under my feet. Standing at the end of the board, I thought of my mom and all the crazy things she'd done. In comparison, this was nothing.

Kids outside of the pool pressed into the chain link fence and those in the pool swarmed into bunches in the shallow end, making room. All of their faces were turned up to me, mouths open. I suddenly felt very, very important. It actually felt... well, it actually felt pretty good.

Too bad I actually had to dive and couldn't just quit while I was ahead.

My brother looked very small from up there, standing shoulder-to-shoulder with some older guys, blocking the restroom door. I could hear the Lifey shouting inside.

The weirdest thing, though, was that, for just a moment, I thought I saw my mom. She was standing next to the pop machine, wearing this weird, red cape that billowed in a breeze that wasn't there. I shook my head to get a hold of myself and when I looked again, she was gone.

It was a sign. *Today the pool, tomorrow the world.*

I took a deep breath and did it. Really. I didn't back down. I didn't run away.

I. Did. It.

CHAPTER 3

I JUMPED OFF THE BOARD, and my body went into the shape of a perfect arrow, slicing through the air and into the deep water.

Cheers erupted as I came back up to the surface of the water, swam to the edge of the pool, and climbed out to take my bows. I was entirely out of the water, facing my adoring crowd, when I realized something was wrong.

Everyone was suddenly quiet, for one thing. Erika was a few feet away, staring at me, eyes wide in amazement. Or was it some other emotion? She actually looked kind of afraid. Our eyes locked for what seemed like a minute, but was probably only a split second.

That's when a kind of group gasp came from the crowd.

That's when everybody's heads swiveled to the pool, where a wadded up piece of red cloth was swirling just below the surface. All heads turned back to me. I could feel my eyes growing as big as pie plates as I took in the situation from wherever my inner Ryan had run to.

And that's when I looked at Will in the corner, a big stupid grin slowly taking form on his face.

Thousands of kids, all still and quiet, watched in horror as Will's elastic-waisted, two-sizes-too-big swim trunks floated to the surface of the pool.

AFTER THAT, I COULD HAVE stayed in my room all summer. Maybe for all time.

I was in a state of permanent embarrassment, with a full-body blush radiating heat like a terrible sunburn. I could still hear the sound of the kids laughing as I ran to the shower room. I could still see Will's crooked smile.

Will. He had done it all on purpose. The diving practice, the kind words, giving me his shorts that were too big—it was all a big set-up that I should have seen coming. It was my fault for forgetting that he was pure evil.

Before this, the most embarrassing thing that had happened to me was in fourth grade when I'd spilled my lunch tray in the cafeteria and slipped on the mashed potatoes. It had been bad. Everyone had laughed at me. I'd tried to stay home sick. But that was nothing compared to this. How was I ever going to recover after the whole town had seen me—well, *naked?* Yes, naked. There was no other way to put it. And I didn't even like taking my shirt off at the beach!

I thought briefly about the possibility of being home-schooled. But who was going to teach me? Dad? That wasn't going to happen. Maybe I could convince Dad to send me away to boarding school? No, it was hopeless.

I was lying facedown on my bed when I heard Dad's car pull into the driveway. He was hardly through the door before I heard Will's voice filtering up the stairwell. The only things I caught were: *"Can't believe he…"* and *"Outta there so fast…"*

I thought I heard a small chuckle from Dad.

I buried my face in the pillow when Dad came up the stairs to my room.

"Hey!" he called through the door. "Big diver, you in there?"

He came in without waiting for me to answer. I kept my eyes squinched shut, still as a rock. A Ryan Rock, I thought. Here I'll lie, until the end of time. Still, silent.

"Hey, kid, you okay?" he asked, pushing at my covered leg with his toe.

"Yep," I said, louder than I'd meant to. "Fine."

Archaeologists will someday use a mallet and chisel to break me open and find a petrified boy inside, scrunched up in a ball.

"I… uh, I heard what happened at the pool today," Dad said. "Jill in accounting told me about it. Her daughter was there."

He sat down on the end of the bed, but I said nothing else. I kept hoping he'd realize that his son had fossilized and just leave.

"I'm glad you dove, Ry," he said, sounding sincere, but… "But maybe it's time we buy you some shorts that fit—no more of this 'room-to-grow.' I heard you gave them quite a show!"

His forced chuckle died quickly.

"Look, let me start over," he said slowly, but I interrupted him with a mumble he couldn't make out.

"Turn over, Ryan. I can't understand you when your head is in the pillow."

"They were *his* shorts. He did it on purpose," I said, sitting up to face him. Dad looked surprised at my puffy eyes.

"Don't be so dramatic, Ryan. You're gonna live through this. It's not the end of the world."

My fingers clawed into the bed at this. Because, really, it kinda *was*.

"Dad, he planned the whole thing."

"Look, Ryan," he stood up, the amused sympathy in his voice turning to exasperation. "You're going to stop this right now. I don't know why you think that—"

"No, Dad," I said, jumping up to face him. I'd finally had enough. I was a time bomb, seconds from exploding. I was a volcano, about to burst hot, burning lava. I was that two-liter of soda that Eli and I shook for a full hour before throwing it into the street where it shot seventy-five feet into Eli's yard, barely missing Mark Twain, his cat.

"I've had enough of Will's..." Should I have dared? I dared. "I've had enough of his *shit*."

"Ryan!"

"*Shit*, Dad. *Shitola*." Boy, I was on a roll and I hadn't even gotten started yet.

"*You* lose *your* own shorts in *your* messy bedroom and suddenly *Will* is to blame? I don't believe this."

"You never take my side, no matter what he does!" My voice rose with each word, until it cracked in that way I hated. There I was, arguing like an adult and suddenly *crack!* I'm a kid again.

"You're pushing it, Ryan," Dad said in a warning tone.

"Don't you think me—*naked*—in front of every kid in town is pushing it?" I bellowed. I was an out of control train. I had jumped the tracks. "He *hid* my trunks so I'd have to wear—"

"Oh, he did not," he snapped back.

"Yes, he did!"

Dad scowled and looked at his feet, but I wasn't done.

"*Mom* would never take Will's—" I started, but that was the wrong way to begin a sentence.

"Enough!" Dad roared so loudly that I took a step back. He looked like one of those sharks you see on the Discovery Channel, waiting to tear apart a diving cage like it was a gingerbread house. All mouth and teeth.

"Are you going to listen or what?" he growled.

My face was throbbing with anger. Nothing is worse than when a parent tells you to listen and you know whatever they're going to say won't matter one bit. But the sooner you shut your mouth and pretend like you're listening, the sooner you'll get your chance to tell them why they're wrong.

"So you finally went off the high dive!" Dad was practically shouting. "It was about time, too. I thought I was going to have to throw you off myself. And you don't even thank your brother for helping you? You can't blame everyone else whenever things go wrong. Just like your mother leaving—there's not some big conspiracy around it. She's accountable for her own actions, just like you are. When are you going to take responsibility for your mistakes? Poop Lip, it's time to grow up."

I was silent. He'd said It. My own father had called me Poop Lip.

"I'm done here," Dad said, heading for the door. "I don't want to hear from you for the rest of the night, got it?"

He slammed the door behind him.

AFTER THAT, I WASN'T MUCH interested in lying hopeless and ruined on my bed. I had enough anger to fuel a rocket to Neptune. I called up Eli at eCamp.

"I heard about the pool," Eli said. "That's rough."

"You heard about it?" I sputtered into the phone. "It just happened! And you're all the way at camp!"

"It's all over Facebook, Ryan. You're lucky there weren't any pictures."

"So pretty much every single person in Brenville—"

"And all their friends and relatives," Eli interrupted helpfully.

"Right. Oh, man," I said, lying down on the floor, my face in the carpet. Maybe I wasn't done being wrecked.

"I think leaving now is your best bet," he said. "Without Will."

"Mmmph." I turned my face so I was looking under my bed, where my plans were in a tidy stack next to my winter boots.

"Come on, Ryan, a man can't go on living like a normal person after something like that. But if you rescue your Mom, nobody's going to remember how you completely self-destructed and humiliated yourself in front of all your peers. Everybody might even forget they saw your—"

"*Mmmph*," I interrupted, closing my eyes.

"Look, I can find out where she's performing now," he said. "We don't have to wait for California. You know how people scalp those tickets online. Just let me do some searching…" He trailed off and we were silent for a moment. I could hear him clicking away at his computer.

"You really think we're ready?" I finally asked.

"Come on, we were ready months ago," he said. "You know, I'm kinda glad this happened. Get you off your—"

"Shut it!" I exclaimed, jumping up. "Never be glad this happened to me. Ever. I'm barely alive."

"Easy, there," Eli said. "I take it back. Geez. Hey! I found it."

Please not the east coast. Please not the east coast.

"Not bad. They're in Albuquerque right now."

"Albuquerque? As in *New Mexico?*" I mean, sure, it was great that she wasn't in Florida or something, but New Mexico? I knew I was going to have to travel a bit but this was ridiculous. That was like… what? How far?

"It's okay," Eli assured me. "It's basically like California. And really, what's the difference to you, right?"

"I guess," I said. "When are the shows?"

"They've got shows tonight and then Friday and Saturday. You can make the Saturday show for sure."

"What about Carl?" I asked.

"He said he was ready whenever. So he'll pick you up tomorrow at five in the morning. He'll drop you off in Bend at this Internet café he knows about, which is probably the last Internet café in North America. Anyway, they have computers. Then we'll rendezvous online." He always said it like it was spelled: *ren-dez-voos.*

"Then what?" I asked. You had to press Eli or he wouldn't tell you anything.

"Then I'll find you a way to Albuquerque," he said. "Trust me."

"Right."

"Just leave it to me. I'm gonna get to work on the logistics tonight—oh, and remember your suit. You never know when you'll need a nice suit."

"Want me to pack a set of martini glasses, too?" I asked, looking out the window as the sun set. It was starting to feel less like a game now. It was starting to feel real.

"Ha. Funny. No seriously, bring the suit. You can be anyone in a suit."

He had a point.

TALKING TO ELI ALWAYS GOT me back on track. Sometimes I thought I was going crazy making my rescue plans, but Eli always reminded me how much sense it all made. Really, if it wasn't for him, I don't think I ever would have put all the pieces together.

I went under my bed and grabbed my packing list, which I'd been working on for months. Then I got the rolling suitcase and laid it open on my bed.

First, I packed two t-shirts (both black), jeans, a blue hooded sweatshirt, and the dark suit and tie I'd worn in a wedding a month ago (I had been the oldest ring-bearer ever). Then, I packed the essentials: a heavy-duty flashlight I'd gotten at the army surplus store, a magnifying glass (for making a camp fire), some rubber bands (they're just very useful), my pen with disappearing ink (for secret messages), two pairs of underwear, my camouflage paint, a stethoscope, a ball of string, a mini screwdriver set, all the postcards, five issues of *Captain Fantastic*, and—

I was running out of room.

Once when Will had the flu, I felt sorry for him, listening to him barf all night, so the next day I brought him a stack of my comic books to keep him company. He looked grateful at the time, but later, he filled in every "o" and zero with colored markers and gave Captain Fantastic boobs and a mustache in every single frame. I'm saying this so what I did next won't sound so terrible.

After making sure the coast was clear, I snuck into Will's room (which Eli and I called the World of Fartcraft). The smell of Will's room used to be enough to keep me out, but I'd gotten one of those hospital masks the last time I was at the doctor's. This let me explore the room whenever I wanted, so I knew it inside and out.

I grabbed his compass and pocketknife from his desk drawer. Then, I took his map of the U.S. from the back wall of his closet and his Boy Scout manual from his night stand. Who relaxes before bed by learning knots and trapping? Only masterminds in torturing brothers, that's who.

Next on my list was Will's new pair of black sneakers. I found them in his closet. He hardly ever wore them, just on special occasions. I needed them because they were black and I figured they'd help me blend into the dark.

Back in my room, I packed these new items and then prepared for the Moment of Truth. How much money had I saved?

In the back of my closet there was a place where the carpet didn't quite meet the wall. If you knew just where to tug at it, a small square would come up, exposing a cubbyhole underneath. Mom had shown me this hiding place last fall, just before she disappeared.

"Don't tell your Dad," she'd whispered. "I thought that you could use a place to keep secret things. Stuff you don't want your brother to find."

I reached in the cubbyhole and brought out this little golden bug thing. Mom called it a scarab. She'd mailed it to me a few months ago, saying she'd seen it in Mexico and thought of me. Then I took out this photo of her in her human cannonball suit, standing beside the big white cannon. The scarab and the picture were the only two things she'd mailed me, except all the postcards. Seemed kinda sappy to pack them, but I guess it felt like I was bringing her with me.

Then I got out the metal box where I kept my money. I'd been saving my allowance since September. Who knew how much I'd been able to stash away? A few hundred dollars—maybe more? I was thinking I had at least enough for a bus ticket to wherever Mom was.

Then I counted it.

Thirteen dollars and eighty-seven cents.

I hadn't been planning on taking Will's money. I'd planned on him coming with me and bringing it himself. But plans change. And I wasn't exactly feeling friendly toward my brother.

Back in Will's room, on a shelf, next to his trophies, was a single book: *Shakespeare: The Collected Works*. The book didn't have any real pages, though—it just had an empty, carved out space in the middle. Will was an idiot if he thought it was a secret. I mean, he was smart, but he hated to read and everyone knew it. Inside was all the money Will bragged about saving from his past two years of raking pine needles. I took it all.

Back in my room, I counted it. Seventy-four dollars.

It would have to do.

I finished packing and settled into my room to wait.

And wait.

AT THREE IN THE MORNING, I was in the pantry, silently cramming as much food as I could fit into my green backpack. I snagged a bag of chips, a six-cup pudding pack, some fruit bars, some beef jerky, a can of spaghetti, and three bottles of root beer. In my head, all I could hear was *I'm gonna do it, I'm gonna do it.* My internal chant must have been too loud because at first I didn't hear Dad come down the stairs.

I was still in the pantry when a slice of light appeared in front of me. I froze. There, no more than three feet away, stood Dad in his underwear, swigging cranberry juice from the carton in the refrigerator light. If he turned even six inches, he would see me, and I'd be as good as toast.

Backing against the pantry wall, I noticed I was still clutching the cookie bag in my hand... a single muscle spasm in my pinky finger would crinkle the plastic and send me straight into the depths of summer grounding and yard work.

The plastic felt damp in my hand. *Why was my hand sweating?*

I held my breath as Dad polished off the juice and tried to squash the carton with his bare hand (he failed). The suitcase and my sleeping bag lay at his feet, in the shadow of the counter.

Dead. I was dead.

Dad turned away, letting the fridge door swing open as he gazed out the window. The light from the fridge crept into the pantry slowly—moving as the fridge door opened further—to my toes, then up to my knees. The plastic crumpled slightly in my hand.

Dead, dead, dead, dead.

He suddenly slapped the fridge shut without even a glance in my direction. His feet were at the top of the stairs when the cookies slipped from my hand and fell harmlessly to the floor.

That was close, I thought and then smiled to myself, letting my breath out in a *whoosh.*

"Almost *too* close," I whispered.

I'd always wanted the chance to say that out loud.

I put on my backpack and, as an afterthought, grabbed Will's black baseball cap off the table, pulling it low over my eyes. After glancing around the kitchen one last time, I finally whispered, "This is me leaving." I paused, waiting for something to stop me.

Nothing did.

I eased the door open and stepped out into the summer darkness. I stood on our back porch for a moment. I was nervous. But more than anything, I was excited. I didn't know how far I'd have to travel, but I'd get there. Nothing would stop me from coming back with Mom.

Absolutely nothing.

Three houses down I realized I'd forgotten the suitcase and had to run back home.

But after *that,* nothing could stop me.

CHAPTER 4

I KNEW THE POLICE WOULD start looking for me as soon as Dad reported me gone. Dad had a weekly poker game with Officer Barton, so there might be a little more publicity than for any other teenage runaway. Besides, it was a small community—anyone running away would be a big deal.

From watching cop shows on TV, Eli and I knew the police would check my phone records first. I could have taken Will's cell phone. It would've made everything really easy, but Eli insisted I shouldn't. He said the cops would be able to track me with it. But at least I wasn't traveling blind; I had Eli in my corner. And since he was away at computer camp, he was online twenty-four seven. And the best part? No one would be able to get to him and make him talk before Mom and I got back home, safe and sound.

Well, in theory.

In reality, Eli can't keep his trap shut, which was why I hoped he'd be untouchable at eCamp. He might be a great friend, but he's definitely a squealer. Eli's dad is always calling my dad, fuming about one thing or another, like that Eli said a curse word he said he'd learned from Will. Will would get in trouble (not for saying it, but for saying it around "that Carson kid"), and then take it out on me.

"Pay it forward," Will would say, giving me his usual Tattled-On Revenge: a dead-arm, a dead-leg, and a rug burn on some delicate body part, like my face. I didn't want Eli to feel bad so I never told him, but *sheesh*. You'd think he'd catch on sooner or later.

I JOGGED LIGHTLY DOWN THE sidewalk, past all the neighbors' dark houses. Every thing was quiet. I didn't hear a single car engine or a dog barking—not even a cricket.

I hurried through the main strip of town, dodging in and out of the shadows. The last thing I wanted was to be taken home by the cops only a few minutes after leaving. Luckily, I saw them before they saw me. A squad car was parked under the buzzing fluorescent light at the gas station, but I had luck on my side. Officer Barton was leaning back in his seat, asleep, all slack-jawed and snoring.

It was easy to slip out of town after that. There are only about ten buildings on the main strip. Once you get past the gas station, Brenville just… stops. It doesn't dwindle off into suburbs or a park or something, it just plain ends. The only thing at the end of town is a green sign that says, *Next Gas: 194 mi.*

I couldn't help but grin—I was doing it.

The plan was simple enough: just be out around milepost three no later than 5 AM. I walked down the right side of the county road. It felt strange being out there all alone in the dark. I still had two hours before the rendezvous with Carl, which meant I needed to hide from any cars until then. I knew I'd hear anybody coming long before they'd reach me, but I was still jumpy. I hoped if someone went by, I wouldn't look too suspicious, what with my backpack, suitcase, and sleeping bag. Maybe they'd think I was a Boy Scout, working on a survival merit badge or something like that.

Dad was always getting on me about becoming a Boy Scout, but I never wanted to do it. It was like the diving: even if I wanted to do it, it kind of became a bummer if he was into it, too. He was always telling me I had to "take advantage of all this wilderness" and that "I'd regret it when I was older."

Dad always went on about how great the area was but I didn't think it wasn't anything special. Brenville is in something called the high desert, which is like a desert but without the sand. It's just really brown, with these weird, scraggly trees that don't look like normal trees you see on TV or in magazines. In the summer, it gets really hot during the day and really cold at night. In the winter it's just cold with snow drifting across the flatness. The one cool thing was that there were all sorts of animals, like lizards and scorpions and mountain lions and rattlesnakes. My favorites, though, were the coyotes (maybe because they scared Will when we were younger). As I trekked along, I heard them start up, making that *row-oooh-ooh-ooohh* sound they sometimes made near our house. On the blacktop road, in what felt like the middle of the night, they sounded like ghosts.

51

The coyotes seemed to be moving away from me. Soon, I was alone again.

I shivered.

I REACHED MILEPOST THREE WITH about twenty minutes to spare. There wasn't a car in sight—well, at least I didn't see any headlights yet. I stepped off the road and sat down behind a large rock to drink a morning root beer. Then I heard an engine in the distance. If it was Carl, he was way early. I felt a pounding in my chest as I jumped to my feet.

At 5 AM, it's still dark, but it's not too dark to see details. As the lights came over the horizon, I saw it was a truck, not a car. And as it got closer, I saw it was an old, beat-up Chevy truck hauling... what were they? I squinted in the dark. Were they *chickens?*

But the truck went on by and my heart slowed. Coincidence? Probably. I was about to sit back down when the truck lurched to a stop, maybe fifty yards past me.

So it was Carl after all? And my ride was... *in a chicken truck?*

I guess it was possible. Eli didn't tell me much about Carl, but knowing Eli, his relatives were probably capable of being or doing just about anything.

As I walked in the dim light toward the truck, I let out a slow breath. This was it. The Moment of Truth.

I waited behind the truck for Carl to make his move. Greet me, open the passenger door, or something. I could see his plaid-shirted elbow in his side-mirror, but he wasn't getting out.

Strange.

That's when it hit me: *Carl was pretending to be on his phone.* I could see him in his big side mirror, under the glow of his dome light, looking in the glove compartment with his phone to his ear. If he didn't talk to me, he could say he hadn't stopped for me. He could tell the cops, "Nope, I didn't even *see* him."

Which meant he wanted me to ride in the back.

Well, it was better than walking. I lobbed my suitcase and sleeping bag into a gap between the cages, sending the chickens into an even louder fit of clucking. I had my hands on the pick-up gate, getting ready to pull myself up into the truck—and that was the same moment that Carl chose to drive away.

I WASN'T REALLY MUCH OF an athlete. Except for my new-found talent for diving, I couldn't really do much else in the physical activity department. I've been told I run like a wounded cow. But I *am* fast when I need to be.

Sprinting behind the chicken truck, I just barely kept my hold on the slick tailgate. Soon, the toes of Will's brand new shoes dragged along the asphalt—and we were picking up speed.

"Carl! Slow down!" I called out, but I don't think he heard me over the squawk of the chickens.

I could already see the headline about my death:

RUNAWAY DRAGGED MILES BEHIND TRUCK; OLDER BROTHER FINISHES HIM OFF FOR DESTROYING SHOES

Feathers blowing in my face and legs flailing, I grabbed on to a bit of rope tied to the tailgate. Begging it not to snap, I used all the strength in my skinny arms to pull myself up. I got one foot on the bumper, and then the other. The chickens sounded like they were cheering me on as I got a leg over the tailgate—and then the truck jolted like Carl had run over a tree stump.

My "Ohgodohgodohgod" mixed right in with the loud clucking as I fell, headfirst, into the truck bed.

We drove on as I struggled to get off my face and upright. The chickens really seemed to be going nuts (but then again, I didn't know how they usually acted in the back of a speeding truck). I got situated just in time for the truck to hit another big bump, this one causing my sleeping bag to bounce right by me, out the back of the truck.

"*No, no, no, no!*" I hissed, but it was gone.

Perfect. Just perfect.

"Carl!" I tried to yell to get him to stop but he couldn't hear me. And there were too many chicken containers in the way for me to get to the window to get his attention. *What a maniac,* I thought.

I pulled myself, the suitcase, and my backpack down low between the tailgate and the chicken cages, where it wasn't as cold. At least I still had Will's hat.

Just a little tip: if you ever need to hitch a ride in the back of a truck, a chicken truck isn't exactly the most luxurious choice. As we reached full cruising speed, the truck bed became a quaking, earsplitting, *reeking* tornado of feathers. And not just big feathers either, but little downy ones that got caught in my nose and mouth and eyes. I chose to believe that chicken crap doesn't blow in the wind, but I may have been wrong.

I got as comfortable as I could and watched the sun rise while we wound our way northwest, putting more and more miles between me and Brenville. In the back of the truck, I shivered, and it wasn't just the wind. My stomach was a lump of guilt and fear. And not just because I'd stolen from Will, though that was part of it.

I was starting to realize the seriousness of what I was doing. Yes, serious was the word. I imagined Dad talking to me, looking very disappointed. Maybe even sad. "This is a serious thing you've done, Ryan." And it was. Look at me—I'd almost been killed already and I hadn't even been gone three hours.

But did I have a choice? I remembered the diving board incident and my cheeks reddened. I thought of the look on Erika Dixon's face as I stood in front of everyone, naked. I couldn't go back. Not now. Having Mom back would be the only thing that could make Brenville bearable now.

So I was doing it. For better or worse, I was doing it.

This was either the start of something really great or the beginning of the end.

THE CHICKENS NEVER REALLY CALMED down. I had thought they were just excited by my clumsy arrival, but apparently that's just how chickens act.

As we bumped down the road, I squinted my eyes against the feathery chaos and watched them through the crook in my arm. Some were hunkered down together, others lay on the floor of their cages like they were dead, which I guess they might have been. There was this really fat, one-eyed hen wedged into a corner, her lumpy butt poking through the bars of the cage. Over the course of the drive, we had a few staring contests and she won every time. Chickens can stare. I hadn't known that before, either.

After a few hours, I checked my watch and saw that we were already an hour late. I was supposed to be in Bend at 8 AM and it was already 9. Maybe because Carl was driving so slow. Or maybe because of all the chickens—maybe they weren't very aerodynamic. I guess it didn't matter too much. Eli was going to be online all day.

Finally, I felt the truck slow. We made a few turns, went over a few bumps, and then we came to a stop. The engine shut off, and the truck door opened and then slammed shut.

I peeked my head up carefully. I wasn't sure we were there yet. I didn't want to just jump out if we weren't in the right spot.

We were parked in front of a small bakery... which, I guess, is kind of like a café. I chucked my suitcase out and leapt from the back of the truck. I tried my best to swipe the feathers off of my shirt and pants, but they were everywhere. Inside and out.

I looked around for Carl. Even if he was playing it cool, maybe I could at least give him a quick wave.

"Did you just jump outta my truck?" a voice hollered and I dropped my suitcase as Carl walked toward me. Or who I had *thought* was Carl. But Carl wouldn't be surprised I was in his truck.

And Eli's cousin probably wasn't a fifty-year-old Mexican man, either.

Uh-oh.

CHAPTER 5

MISSING CHILD ALERT
for Greater Oregon Area

Spartacus Ryan Zander

I TOOK A STEP BACK, eyes wide. My mouth moved but nothing came out. Nothing understandable, anyway.

"Uh, um, well, no, I was... I was just looking at your chickens," I stammered desperately.

"You just jumped outta my truck!" He was walking toward me, looking kind of shocked, like he didn't know what to do about it.

I snatched up my stuff and sprinted away from the chicken-truck driver as fast as I could and kept running until I was sure the driver wasn't following me. I found myself on this small-town street with buildings that had these weird western fronts. I felt like I was on the set of a cowboy movie or something.

I was obviously not in Bend. Bend did not look like this. Well, of course I wasn't in Bend. The truck driver wasn't

Carl so he wouldn't know to drop me off in Bend. Suddenly the extra hour it had taken to get here made sense.

You're a real genius, Ryan.

I looked at my watch. It was 9:30. I was more than an hour late for my online meet with Eli and I was in the wrong town. Right in front of me was a big, two-story building with a plaque that read *Sisters Library*. So at least I knew where I was. I was in Sisters. I knew a little bit about that town. They had a big rodeo every year—one of the biggest in the country. A couple years before, Mom had tried to get a job as a rodeo clown here. She said she had a really good audition, but she thought they didn't choose her because rodeo clowns were usually men. Dad just said, "Thank god."

At least the library was open. I glanced around to make sure the chicken truck guy wasn't watching me and then went inside.

The library was bright and cool inside. There were only a few people so early in the morning. I went straight to the computers and logged into the secret email account I'd made specifically for the rescue mission—nothing from Eli. It had a chat feature, but he wasn't online. I checked my watch again. 9:35. Where was he? He was *always* online.

I sighed and looked up "Sisters, Oregon" online. (What a weird name for a town.) I saw that I'd overshot Bend by about twenty-five miles.

Perfect, Ryan. Perfect.

While waiting for Eli to come online, I browsed Bartholomew's website. It looked the same as ever, like someone had made it and then forgot all about updating it. Simple and boring. A single page with a couple of pictures and small white text on a black background. The text looked like little kid handwriting. Eli and I found it weird that there were no fancy graphics, no way to buy tickets, no promotions, nothing. I mean, even I could have made a better page. It was definitely not the website you'd expect for a circus as well known as Bartholomew's. It was like they thought their name spoke for itself:

Bartholomew's World-Renowned Circus of the Incredible!

Come See the Most Marvelous, Miraculous, Stupendous, and *Spectacular* Circus in the World!!!
See *Captivating* Contortionists!
Gasp as *Extraordinary* Tiger Tamers TAME Tigers!
(and other Dangerous Creatures!)
Witness the *Death-Defying* and altogether *Unbelievable* Human Cannonball!!
It's Dramatic, It's Splendid, It's Fantastic, and it's Sensational!
ALL ROLLED INTO ONE MEMORABLE NIGHT!!!

And there, at the bottom of the page: *Shows.* I scanned it, wanting to see if there'd been any changes. The list of cities, dates, and times were the same as they'd been for the past few months. I scrolled back up and the picture of the circus tent caught my eye, as it always did.

The picture was taken at night, with a full moon rising up behind the huge tent. You could only see the front of it, but it looked like it was the size of a football field. The top of the tent had a tall, blue-and-red striped dome. The material looked pretty heavy-duty. I hoped Will's pocketknife would cut through it, like I'd planned.

There were two lines of people leading up to the entrance booth. The weird part was you couldn't see anyone's face.

There must have been a hundred people in the picture and *nobody* was turned toward the camera. You'd think at least one person would have been turned around when they took the picture. But no, everyone was facing forward like they were hypnotized by the circus. Like Bartholomew had cast some kind of magical spell on them. The picture always gave me the chills if I sat and looked at it too long.

ELI STILL WASN'T ONLINE. I sighed so loudly that the guy on the computer next to me glanced up. I tried to pretend I was frustrated because the mouse was broken.

Eli was going to have to find me a different ride to Albuquerque. I'd screwed it all up. I mean, *a chicken truck?* In what alternate reality would Eli's cousin be driving a chicken truck? I tried to stop blaming myself. I mean, the guy did pull up and stop next to me. How many people would be stopping right in that spot at 5 AM?

It was just pure bad luck. And maybe a bad sign. Well, if you believed in stuff like that.

I looked to see how far the ride was from Bend to Albuquerque. When the page loaded, my jaw dropped: twenty-three hours! That was like twice as far as it was to California!

I remembered Eli saying, "It's okay. It's still basically on the West Coast." Why did I ever listen to him?

And he still wasn't online to help me. Getting even more frustrated, I pounded my fist on the desk. A few people looked and I reddened.

"Sometimes you have to unplug the mouse to get it started again," said the guy next to me. I nodded and did it just to avoid looking crazy.

I turned back to the computer, drumming my fingers against my knee. *Come on Eli.*

IT MIGHT BE HARD TO believe, but there are actually a lot of people trying to get into the circus. They send out these audition videos showing off their talents, hoping a circus will respond and give them a chance to apply in person.

I know this because Mom showed me her own circus audition DVD before she sent it out. This was about a year before she disappeared. I was the only one she showed it to; I was the only one she trusted. She told me to keep it a secret, which I did. I never even told Eli about it until after she was gone.

The video was amazing. I mean, over the years I'd gotten a few glimpses of what she could do. I knew she was good at gymnastics. I knew she could throw knives. I knew she wasn't scared of wild animals. But the video was the first time I got a glimpse of *all* the stuff she was capable of. I'd heard of people walking on hot coals before. But I'd never seen someone do it on their hands, blindfolded, while carrying a watermelon between their knees. That would have been impressive no matter who it was, but the fact that it was my mom made it totally unreal.

When she showed it to me, I felt like I was dreaming.

So I knew that my mom wanted to join the circus. But I'm sure she didn't expect to attract the attention of someone like Bartholomew. I'm sure she didn't expect that a black van would pull up one morning and throw her in a sack and haul her off. And I'm sure she wouldn't have done it if she'd known he'd never let her see her family.

She'd never have signed up for that.

Eli and I had heard about something called "Stockholm syndrome," which was this weird thing where people fall in love with their kidnappers. My mom was strong, so I didn't really think she could succumb to something like Stockholm syndrome, but Eli thought that could be why she sounded so happy in some of the postcards. I argued that she was probably using the happy postcards as a way to fool anyone who was watching her. Either way, Eli cautioned me to be ready, though, just in case. I hated to admit it, but it was possible. Who knows what can happen to a person who's been trapped and stressed out for so long?

I CHECKED THE EMAIL ACCOUNT again and saw that Eli had finally logged on. We'd agreed ahead of time: no real names. I was "Funkspiel" (which was German secret agent jargon or something). Eli chose "Peter Parker" (because he loves Spiderman).

PETER.PARKER: *What happened?*
FUNKSPIEL: *I messed up. Got on chicken truck.*
PETER.PARKER: *Why?*
FUNKSPIEL: *I thought it was Carl!*
PETER.PARKER: *Oh boy. Where are you?*
FUNKSPIEL: *Sisters.*
PETER.PARKER: *Oops. Close, but no cigar.*
FUNKSPIEL: *Can we continue with Plan A?*
PETER.PARKER: *Too late. You missed the ride.*
FUNKSPIEL: *Great. What now? Walk home?*
PETER.PARKER: *No. Plan B. One moment...*

A few minutes passed. Nothing from Eli.

A few more minutes. I was getting impatient.

FUNKSPIEL: *What's Plan B?*
PETER.PARKER: *Hold your horses!*

I was rolling my eyes when the librarian walked by me with a stack of papers. He taped one of the papers to the side of the nearby printer. I didn't have to squint to see that it had a picture of me on it. It was my school yearbook photo from the year before, the one with me blinking. And below that:

MISSING CHILD ALERT
FOR
GREATER OREGON AREA

SPARTACUS RYAN ZANDER, 13 YEARS OLD
5'5" WITH BROWN HAIR, BROWN EYES,
MOLE ON UPPER LIP;
LAST SEEN IN BRENVILLE, OREGON
AT 10:00 PM
POSSIBLY WEARING STRIPED PAJAMAS.

I was angry for a split second (it's not a mole, it's a *freckle!*). Then I saw that the librarian was putting the posters up at the end of every other bookshelf. I watched as a few people wandered over to look at the them.

This was not good.

I pulled Will's hat down low on my face and stared at the computer screen. I was just a student doing research. Doing homework. But wait—school got out yesterday. Was

I studying for summer school? I realized I hadn't seen any other kids in the library. Also, I had a suitcase and a back-pack. That definitely wasn't helping.

I pushed the suitcase under the desk with my foot. Out of the corner of my eye, I thought I saw a couple of people looking in my direction.

I typed quickly:

> FUNKSPIEL: *Got it yet?*
> PETER.PARKER: *One moment.*
> FUNKSPIEL: *No time. It's getting hot in here.*
> PETER.PARKER: *So take off all your clothes?*

Ha ha, Eli.

A blonde woman wandered over to a shelf of encyclo-pedias right behind me. I thought she was just pretending to browse, trying not to seem like she was looking at me. I pulled the bill of my cap even lower. I could barely see out from under it.

> PETER.PARKER: *1555 Northeast Forbes Road. Go out of the library, take a right and go 2 blocks. Then take another right and go 6 blocks.*
> FUNKSPIEL: *Then what?*
> PETER.PARKER: *Wait out front, by the road. Look neat. Put on your suit. Driver will think it's your house. Getting a ride to your grandma's funeral in Boise.*
> FUNKSPIEL: *My what? Albuquerque! Not Boise!*

What was I thinking, having Eli help me? This was crazy. Then, he read my mind:

PETER.PARKER: *You don't trust anyone, that's your problem.*

Great. A quote from the Spiderman movie.

PETER.PARKER: *Be there in ten minutes. Trust me! E.T. (End Transmission)*

I scrawled the address and the directions on a piece of paper. I looked up and saw the encyclopedia woman at the front desk, talking to the librarian. The lady touched her lip, right in the same spot my freckle is, and then they both looked in my direction. *Crap crap crap crap...*

I GRABBED MY BAGS AND headed toward the front door. My luggage suddenly seemed ridiculous. I was obviously a runaway.

The encyclopedia woman and the librarian got to the door before I did. They stood shoulder-to-shoulder in front of me. I tried to act normal, but I was forced to stop right in front of them.

"Excuse me. Young man?" asked the woman. I immediately turned and walked down an aisle of audio books. They followed at a fast clip, calling after me.

"Young man?"

"Spartacus?" the man called. I cringed. They even knew my terrible name.

I walked faster, head ducked, turning down random aisles. The ceiling was vaulted and up ahead, I could see an open-air second floor—and the stairs leading up to it. Right before I reached them, though, the librarian stepped out in front of me.

I abruptly turned left and followed an aisle that ran along right below the second floor of the library. I could see chairs and books and a railing maybe eight feet up. Best of all, I could see an emergency exit up there at the end of the building. If I could get up to the second floor, I was home free.

"We just want to help you!" came the man's voice behind me. He still hadn't moved from the stairs, blocking me from them. He probably figured I was trapped.

At the end of the aisle, though, I threw the suitcase up and over the second floor railing and, before anyone could stop me, I jumped onto the bookshelf and started climbing.

"Not the shelves!" the librarian shouted, running toward me. The blonde woman materialized from another aisle and tried to grab me, but I was already too high. As I climbed, I accidentally kicked a few books off the shelf, causing the librarian to yelp.

My heart was pounding in my chest. Besides the high dive, this was the craziest thing I'd done in my life.

At the top of the shelf, I turned and jumped to the second floor balcony. In the process, I knocked into a heavy mobile of the solar system, sending the planet Mars tumbling below me where it shattered on the ground. The librarian was already running up the second floor stairs, using the kind of words you never hear a librarian say under normal circumstances.

I climbed over the railing, grabbed the suitcase, and ran to the fire exit door. It said USE ONLY IN CASE OF EMERGENCY. I was used to following the rules, so I paused a second before snapping out of it. When I pushed it open, it set off a loud beeping.

"Stop!" called the woman.

I stepped out onto the fire escape and pushed the door shut behind me. I was ten feet or so off the ground and *there were no stairs!* There was just a rusty-looking ladder that I guess you were supposed to push down, but I couldn't see how.

Nice emergency exit, I thought, cursing under my breath.

I kicked at the ladder but didn't have time to figure the stupid thing out, so I threw my suitcase off the side and climbed out onto the edge of the fire escape. There was some sort of metal furnace box thing a few feet away and when the librarian burst out onto the fire escape, I had to drop. I landed on the edge of it but I couldn't keep my balance. I pitched off the side, landing hard on the ground next to my suitcase.

I looked up and saw the librarian on the fire escape and a few other people looking out the window nearby.

I knew I didn't have any time to feel sheepish. I picked myself up, grabbed the suitcase, and started booking it. I knew they were about to call the police—if they hadn't already—so I didn't stop running. I made a zigzag path to the address Eli had given me, taking shortcuts through parking lots and people's back yards.

MOM HADN'T ALWAYS WANTED TO be a human cannonball. According to Dad, she was actually pretty normal before I was born. She had a job in an office. She liked watching TV with him and baby William. But everyone knew it wasn't really me that changed her. It was the accident.

A couple months before I was born, Mom and Dad were driving back from Bend when their car was hit by a semi.

Dad was okay—he'd been wearing his seatbelt. For some reason, Mom wasn't. When the truck hit them, Mom flew right through the front windshield like—well, like she'd been shot out of a cannon. The paramedics found her twenty feet away, stuck headfirst in a snow bank. She went into a coma and everyone thought we were both going to die. There were lots of tears and hospital visits from everyone she knew. But then, four days later, she woke up like nothing had happened.

She was different, though. Will told me that she wanted to become a human cannonball because she had liked flying through the windshield so much. But that's just ridiculous. The doctors said some medical stuff about how head traumas can have weird side effects. Like after the accident, she could never sit still. She always complained that her back and her eyes hurt. She quit her job at the office and didn't even try to get another one. Then she got all these weird hobbies: hula-hooping, juggling, riding a unicycle. She got more... excitable. More reckless. She said, according to Will, that she "needed to live life to the fullest."

Dad talked about her like she'd become an entirely different person. One time, late at night, I heard him on the phone with Uncle Mike.

"It's like nothing's good enough for her. Not me, not the house, not even Brenville. I mean, how can all this open space be suffocating?"

So from everyone else's perspective, she'd changed. But for me, she'd always been weird and exciting. Maybe even a little cuckoo. But that was the only version of Mom I'd ever known. And I don't think I would have changed her if I could have.

As I JOGGED DOWN A neighborhood road, I thought about what had just happened. How were they onto me so quick? Eli had thought we'd have a day before my dad even noticed I was missing, and then maybe a few more days before there'd be any police looking for me. But maybe I underestimated how quickly Dad would know something was wrong. Maybe Will noticed his stuff missing immediately and told him. And maybe Dad got Officer Barton on the case, too.

It wasn't even ten, but it was hot. My back was covered in sweat because of the backpack, and I still had feathers caught in my shirt and pants. My clothes! I needed to have my suit on. I was going to a funeral, Eli had said.

I guess he was right about bringing the suit.

I was wondering whether I'd walked too far when I saw it: Forbes Road! I continued for two more blocks before I found the address: 1555 Northeast Forbes Road. It didn't look like anyone was home. The mailbox said *Moe*.

Checking my watch, I saw I had five minutes to spare—five minutes until what, I didn't have a clue.

I ducked behind the Moe's garage and threw on my suit. I skipped the coat, though—it was way too hot. I tried to straighten myself up a little bit, using the sweat that was already in my hair to smooth it down. Gross? Yes. But effective.

As I headed back around to the front of the house, I heard a sound like a huge chainsaw chopping through a hundred trees. Just when I thought it was as loud as it could get, it got louder.

I watched a big black motorcycle with a huge-normous bearded man on it pull up into the drive. That's when I realized that *this* was the ride Eli had gotten for me. And that's when I felt (for maybe the tenth time that day) as if I'd made a giant mistake.

CHAPTER 6

EVERYONE IN MY FAMILY HAD guts in their own weird way. Some bravery. Some sense of adventure. Not me. For whatever reason, I had none. When the motorcycle pulled up in front of me, all I wanted to do was run and hide.

The guy on the motorcycle cut off the engine.

"Casey, right?" he said, taking off his sunglasses. He was wearing a leather jacket and leather chaps over his jeans.

Casey? I just stood there frozen, not even blinking. Seriously, my stomach went cold, like it was filled with ice.

"Right?" he asked again, putting the death-machine's kickstand down. "You're Casey? Casey Moe?"

This couldn't possibly be Eli's ride. I started to back slowly away and, just before I sprinted down the street, he said:

"You don't trust anyone. That's your problem."

I paused. His eyes were black and unreadable.

"What did you just say?" I asked.

"You don't trust anyone. That's your problem," he repeated, and then explained. "Your dad said you might be nervous. He said if you heard that, you'd know it was okay."

I blinked and then nodded. *My dad? Did he mean Eli?*

"Sorry about your grandma," he continued. "Dying's never a fun business."

This was really Eli's ride. This wasn't some Carl/Chicken Farmer mix-up. I rolled my eyes—well, just in my mind. Apparently Eli thought it would be just peachy to ride with this guy.

"The name's Lloyd," the man smiled, putting out his leather-gloved hand. "Lloyd Lloeke." He said it like Loy-kee. When he smiled, his teeth shone white through his black beard. *Lloyd?* I marveled at his name as he shook my limp hand. He looked like a Rocky or a Rambo or something. I could even see him as a Mike or a Jim, but a *Lloyd Lloeke?*

"And you're Casey," he prompted. I just nodded. *Casey. Sure. That's me.*

"Boise's a long way for a funeral, but I bet your dad will be glad you're there with him," Lloyd said in a friendly way. I just kept nodding, trying to think of a way to get out of this. I wasn't getting on a motorcycle with Lloyd Lloeke. If I did, I was pretty sure we'd be going to *my* funeral in Boise.

"Here, let me get your bag."

That's when he stood up and I realized he was almost seven feet tall.

Lloyd didn't seem to notice the terror that must have shown clearly on my face—or maybe he was used to people being scared of him. He just picked up my suitcase and strapped it to the side of his motorcycle.

Next to this man, I felt like such an uptight nerd in my collared shirt and tie. His neck was as big around as a gallon of milk and his neck and arms were covered in tattoos. The one on his left forearm was a bunch of words on a big scroll.

While I was gawking, Lloyd brought a shiny black mixing bowl of a helmet down on my head.

"You can wear mine," he said, buckling it securely for me.

"Thanks." And that's when I saw he was bald. Very bald. His head was so bald that I imagined the air molecules squeaked past it as he rode.

"Don't let it blind you," he joked, noticing my stare while running a gloved hand over his head. "You okay wearing the backpack?"

"Yep," I answered.

"All right then," he said. "Let's get a move on!"

I wasn't sure what scared me more: Lloyd, or the motorcycle. I mean, even Mom called motorcycles death traps. And coming from someone who enjoys walking on high wires and shooting herself out of cannons, that's really saying something.

I willed myself not to be nervous. *Will* wouldn't be scared. He'd be hooting and hollering, itching to go for a ride. But I'm not Will and my mind was saying to run.

However, there was the teensy mission of rescuing my mom to think about. I wasn't going to solve anything sitting in front of a house in Sisters, Oregon. If I couldn't get on the bike, I might as well give up.

I took a deep breath, trying to use the Instant Calm Breath Method Mom had taught me. It's supposed to help you stop the body's flight-or-fight reaction (for me, it was more a flight-or-faint reaction).

Breathe in. Breathe out. Slow breaths...

"You okay, Casey?" Lloyd asked, looking concerned.

"Yep," I squeaked. "Fine."

"ISN'T THIS GREAT?" LLOYD SHOUTED over the roar of the Harley.

"Great!" I screamed back. I tried not to look at the landscape flying by all around us. Or at the bare pavement flying by a couple of feet below me. The bare pavement that would rip the skin off my bones if I touched it for even a second.

Instead, I focused my eyes on Lloyd's earrings. They were big circles with hollow centers that you could *see all the way through*. That somehow wasn't any more comforting.

"Nice day!" he said over his shoulder. "Makes you glad to be alive!"

"Yeah!" I said. "Alive!" I just hoped to be alive to see my next birthday. Lloyd twisted his head to get a glimpse of me, which didn't seem very safe.

"You're not looking!" he said. "Open your eyes!"

"Okay!" And I tried to look.

"Beautiful! Sun! Air! Fantastic! Who wants a car?"

Well, I did, for one.

"We're safe!" he said. "Completely stable!" With that, Lloyd swerved back and forth on the road.

"Don't!" I shouted.

"Sorry!" He straightened out. "Trust me! Best ride ever! Or your money back!"

After a half hour or so, I finally loosened up a little. I kind of had to, or my body was going to be seized by a full-body charley horse. I looked at the scenery, but wasn't all that impressed. It looked kind of like home, flat and brown. But the air felt good.

"Glad I could help you out!" he called over his shoulder.

"Yeah!" I remembered Eli's story about the funeral. But why was I going to Idaho? I mean, the real me, not Casey.

"You going to Boise anyway?" I called.

"Yeah! Always go there for my lectures!"

"Lectures?" I yelled back. Lloyd, with his tattoos and earrings, gave lectures? Maybe I'd heard him wrong. Lectures? Dentures? Sweatshirts?

"Comparative anatomy lectures! Osmoregulation! Tissue structure!"

At least that's what I thought I heard.

You can only shout so much on a motorcycle. We fell silent after that.

WHEN I WAS IN FOURTH grade, Mom slid down the flagpole from the roof of Brenville's post office. Dad's coworker's wife saw it happen and there was a lot of talk because of it. Dad really chewed her out for that one. After the yelling stopped, she said something to me that I never forgot: "It's okay when everyone else doubts you. It's when you doubt yourself that it gets hard."

Riding on the back of Lloyd's motorcycle, my own doubts about the rescue mission started creeping into my mind. I never admitted it to Eli, and I barely ever admitted to myself, but I couldn't help wondering if we were wrong about this whole kidnapping business. I thought of the way Dad looked at me like I was crazy every time I brought it up. I thought of how the cops completely ignored me. What if I'd somehow gotten it all wrong? As Will put it, who gets kidnapped by the circus? It was a ridiculous idea. I mean, I was the guy stupid enough to think that Will was teaching me to dive out of the goodness of his heart.

And it wasn't like they were keeping her hidden. There were all kinds of things online about the Amazing Athena. In the few months she'd been with Bartholomew, she'd set an honest-to-god Human Cannonball World Record for summersaults. That didn't make much sense if they were really keeping her against her will.

But kidnapping was the only thing that made sense, wasn't it? Maybe she was brainwashed. The postcards with the messages, the horrible rumors about Bartholomew, the black van, the near-destruction of our house, the fact that Mom hadn't come home to visit us: there was just too much evidence. There was no way I was wrong.

But what if I was?

LLOYD PULLED OFF THE MAIN road into a gas station's gravel parking lot. Everybody stared at our roaring motorcycle as we pulled in. He parked behind a car at the gas pump, and the bike shuddered to a stop. I hopped off, my stiff legs barely able to hold me up.

"Gotta get some gas and empty the pipes," Lloyd said. When he stretched his back, it sounded like someone shuffling a deck of cards.

After we had both used the restroom and got the tank filled, Lloyd bought two sodas and we went to a picnic table. It felt very, very good to be on solid, non-moving ground.

"Let's take a breather, huh?" he suggested, plopping down on the bench across from me and handing me a soda. "So, your name's Casey?" he asked, looking at me strangely.

"Right," I said, taking a swig from the soda. Yup. I'm Casey. Going to a funeral in Boise.

"Strange," he said. "Earlier, I called your name about five times and you didn't turn around."

Uh-oh.

"I, uh... must have been thinking about something else," I said. He nodded and let it drop.

I studied Lloyd's tattoo, the one with all the writing. I realized with a small shock that I knew the words.

"I like your tattoo," I said. I wanted to make small talk and distract him from the whole Casey issue. "My dad likes The Stones." I felt even cooler because I knew to call them "The Stones" and not "The Rolling Stones."

"You know 'Sympathy for the Devil'?" he asked, looking down at his arm. I nodded. Dad listened to that song all the time. I'd rocked out to that song a few times when I was cleaning my room.

"Reminds me to face my fears, you know?" he said, and he held out his arm so I could see the whole thing. "My dad wasn't easy to live with. He was—he was sometimes a bad guy. He died when I was seventeen. My brother and I went in and got matching tattoos. Sympathy for our dad, I guess."

I realized what he was saying: sympathy... *for the devil,* meaning his dad.

"You been to Boise a lot?" he asked, changing the subject.

"Uh, yeah," I lied hastily. "We used to visit our grandmother... grandma... in the summer."

"I like it there," he said, taking a loud slurp of his soda. "I took my mom there with me so we could see the Boise Opera. It was pretty good."

Lectures? Opera? Maybe I'd completely misread scary Lloyd.

A few hours later, and just half an hour outside Boise, Lloyd stopped on the wide shoulder of the road.

"Is everything okay?" I asked. Why were we stopping in the middle of nowhere? I felt a knot the size of a small grapefruit in the pit in my stomach.

"I think we've sprung a leak," he said, turning off the motorcycle.

"What do you mean?" I asked, looking at the ground below the bike nervously.

"Not the bike," he said. "Your suitcase."

He pointed a giant finger over my shoulder and I looked behind us. My postcards. Somehow, the suitcase had fallen open and the postcards were littered all over the road and the nearby field. I could see them blowing in the breeze on the road far behind us.

Without thinking, I took off in a dead run.

"Casey! Watch out!"

A truck I hadn't even seen barreled by me going about a hundred miles an hour. If I had run out another foot into the road, I would have been flattened. I only stopped for a second, letting that fact sink in. Then I started running again.

I snatched up a postcard from the side of the road, then another. *Minneapolis. Green Valley. Deadman Reach.* They were really all I had of Mom. Not just the ones with the clues, but the others, too. And her picture! The one with her by the cannon. I had forgotten about that, and now it was gone!

"Hey, hey," Lloyd said, coming up behind me, putting a hand on my shoulder. "You okay?"

"Yeah," I answered, wiping a palm across my cheek, hoping he wouldn't notice I was crying.

"Before you go running across that highway, you need to relax."

"I'm fine," I said, my voice cracking in the middle of the word. Then another huge truck blew by us, sending more postcards swirling. I moved to run after them, but Lloyd kept a hand on my shoulder, holding me in place.

"When you're more calm, you can go."

At first I was mad. Who was he to tell me what to do? But I didn't really have a choice, did I? And, after taking a few deep breaths, I did feel calmer.

"All right," said Lloyd, pulling his hand back. "I'll help you. They haven't gone too far."

I nodded. We made our way down the side of the road and into the field, picking them up as we went. *Winnipeg. Little Hope.*

"Want to talk about it?" Lloyd asked, stooping for a card.

"Uh, well, it's just that Mom is... well, she's in the circus. The postcards are the only letters she sends. I think... well, because she couldn't make it home for the funeral, I'm a bit... touchy."

And just like that, I discovered the secret to being an amazing liar. All you had to do was take the truth and bend it to fit. Why hadn't I ever thought of that before?

"The circus!" Lloyd called out. "No way. Which circus? What does she do?"

"She's the Human Cannonball for Bartholomew's Circus." At that moment I found the picture of my mom. The one with her in her human cannonball suit. I handed it to Lloyd.

"I've heard of them! Bartholomew's Awesome Circus of the Stupendous something-or-other, right? Man, I love that kind of stuff!" he said. He looked from the picture to me, and back again. "Spitting image, you two."

I nodded, not feeling like correcting him about the name of the circus. He was so fired up, it was hard not to smile. I had never heard anyone get so excited about my mom being in the circus.

I snagged another postcard. *Philadelphia.*

"Man! And you're named Spartacus to boot? Crazy," he said, shaking his head.

When he caught my shocked look, he held up his hands in surrender. "Sorry, I couldn't help but see the name." He handed me the postcards he'd picked up. I smiled weakly at him, then counted the cards. I was still missing two.

"*Audentes fortuna iuvat!*" Lloyd cried, raising his giant fist in the air. "'Fortune favors the bold.' Not that it was Spartacus who said that, but still. That's a wicked name, man."

I nodded stiffly and he seemed to realize we'd landed on another tough subject.

"I guess Casey is just easier to go by? Kids tease you?"

"Well, yeah… I mean, no," I said hastily. " I mean, *yes,*

they tease me, but it's not about Spartacus. Mom's the only one who calls me that. Dad... well, he doesn't like it. He makes sure everyone knows my name is... my name is Casey."

I was so close to saying "Ryan," it wasn't funny, but Lloyd thought the pause was just me choking up again and his face fell in sympathy.

"That's rough, kid," he said. "But it really is a great name. The movie *Spartacus* was amazing. I still know parts of it word for word."

"I've never seen it," I admitted. "I don't really even know who Spartacus was."

Lloyd dramatically threw his hands up in exasperation.

"*Never seen it?* And you're the hero in the whole thing?"

I shook my head. I picked up *Farewell, Arkansas*. Lloyd and I climbed back up the ditch to the road so we could check up there for the last missing card.

"Ever read any history books about him?"

I shook my head again.

"He was a great man," Lloyd said. "He was born a slave. With no freedom. But he didn't accept it. He got all these other slaves to lead a revolt against the ruling classes. There's this great line, when Spartacus is getting ready to face certain death. The guy goes, 'Are you afraid to die, Spartacus?' And Spartacus goes, 'No more than I was to be born.' Oh, man, I still get chills thinking about that line!"

"That sounds pretty cool," I said. "So does he become a king or something? He wins the war and becomes free?"

"Well, no," said Lloyd. "He gets crucified. Nailed to a cross. He dies a horrible death."

"Oh," I said, eyes wide, not sure what to say.

"But," Lloyd said, "the point of his story is that your freedom is worth fighting for—and even if you die trying, your effort gives others the inspiration to fight for themselves. It was true then—what was that, like 100 BC?—and it's still true now."

I paused for a while, absorbing this.

"But all this you've been saying, about how great he was, that's why I *should* be Casey," I said. "So no one expects too much from me."

"You have a point," he said, looking thoughtful. "It is a whole lot of name to live up to. I guess if my parents had named me Coolest Man Ever, it might have put a cramp in my style... but it's still an awesome name."

I felt a small smile creeping onto my face. Lloyd, the big tattooed biker, wasn't laughing at my name. And, even though I was sure I would never want to be known as Spartacus, his enthusiasm was sort of contagious.

"But you said the kids tease you?" Lloyd said as we headed back to the bike.

"We-ell," I said, kicking bits of gravel off the road and into the dirt. "Everyone calls me... well, they call me Poop Lip. Because of the... well, the—"

"The freckle," Lloyd said, shaking his head. "Clever. But rough, nonetheless."

"My brother made it up," I explained. "He's kind of the town bully."

"And this... this bully brother calls you... *Poop Lip?*" Lloyd was trying to hide a smile, like it was funny.

"Look, I really don't want to talk about it," I said, wishing I hadn't brought it up. Hearing that name again made me feel about two inches tall.

"Why don't you stand up for yourself?"

My heart sunk. No one understood. I told him glumly, "You don't get it. It's not that easy."

"No, I know it can be tough. I have a rotten big brother, too."

CHAPTER 7

I HAD A GUILTY SECRET. One I never even told Eli. I really
enjoyed decoding the secret messages Mom sent me. My
favorites were the anagrams—you know, the word scram-
bles? Mom knew this, so it made sense that she would feel
safe putting her cards in code, knowing I would be able to
figure them out. Out of all her postcards, the hardest one to
decode had been the one from Hell For Certain, Kentucky:

> *Dear Spartacus:*
> *Things still going real good. Got to learn how to*
> *tame a lion. Their alot of fun!*
> *–Mom*
>
> P.S. *Saw the movie "Sir Gene's Got Wit!" last*
> *nite—real good! You should see it.*

It took me a week to figure out that the movie title in the P.S. was the anagram. Once I saw it, though, it made immediate sense:

Sir Gene's Got Wit = *It's getting worse*

Part of me wondered why she was telling me this random stuff instead of important messages like "Meet me in Cincinnati on the 5th"? And I couldn't even write back to ask, since she was never in the same place longer than a few days. So many mysteries.

WE PULLED UP TO A house on the outskirts of Boise. The driveway and street in front of it were lined with cars. The mailbox said Geneva Moe.

"Are you ready?" Lloyd asked, handing me my suitcase. It took me a minute before I understood he was talking about the funeral.

"I guess so," I said. I had no idea what I was supposed to do next. Apparently, the Moes were *actually having a funeral*.

"Hold on." Lloyd said. He pulled out a notepad and pen and scribbled something down. He folded the paper and handed it to me.

"Keep it for later," he said. "For when you go home."

I shouldered my backpack and pressed down my hair. When I tried to give him money for gas, he waved it away. I was grateful.

"You're gonna be okay, Spartacus," Lloyd said, patting me on the shoulder. "Give me a call if you need someone to help you lead a revolution, okay?"

"Sure thing. It was nice meeting you," I said, reaching out to shake his hand. My eyes caught on a lyric on his tattoo. *Hope you guess my name.*

Spartacus. Casey. Ryan...

A large woman in a black dress came out the front door of the house and stood there, watching us both. Lloyd waved at her in a friendly way and I cringed. This was awkward.

"Good luck, Spartacus," Lloyd said. "I enjoyed the company. See you around."

Lloyd pushed me toward the woman, who was walking slowly toward us with a questioning look on her face. He seemed to be waiting for me to do something. With bravery I never suspected I had in me, I walked right up the sidewalk and hugged the lady.

"I'm sorry for your loss," I said into her giant, soft arm, remembering the line from a movie somewhere. She seemed to accept I was someone she knew and hugged me so tight I could hardly hear Lloyd's motorcycle as he pulled away.

ELI HAD EVIDENTLY TOLD THEM that I was the paperboy of Geneva Moe, the deceased. The large woman immediately herded me into a crowded living room full of mourners laughing, crying, and, best of all—eating. I was planted in front of the hors d'oeuvres table, from which I gratefully scarfed.

Now, to contact Eli and have him get me the heck out of here.

The first moment I was left alone, I snuck to the back door. I was almost in the clear when I heard someone call "Wait!" from behind me.

I turned, as nervous as an imposter paperboy, my foot still halfway out the door. The large woman staggered toward me under the weight of a monstrous bouquet of purple and orange flowers. And I mean monstrous. It looked like an entire bush.

"These just arrived, you dear, sweet, little man," she said, heaving the flowers onto an end table. "Spending all your paycheck on Aunt Geneva! I could kiss you." And she did. She leaned down and gave me a big, wet kiss on the cheek.

"Well, you know," I stuttered, completely confused.

"I'm going to get a vase," said the woman, heading toward the kitchen. I looked at the bouquet and realized what it was.

Eli.

Pumped up with adrenaline, I clawed through the flowers until I found the card. It was bright yellow, didn't have an envelope, and said, quite clearly:

> **R**emembering
> **Y**ou
> **A**lways.
> **N**avin (*your paper boy*)

Thirty seconds later, I was booking it down some rural road, card in one hand, suitcase in the other. On the back of the card, Eli had had the florist write directions to a nearby intersection. There was also a time written: 6:30 PM.

It was already 6:15.

Sometimes Eli surprised me with his cleverness. As I ran, I took back all the bad things I'd said about him. By 6:20, I was standing next to a boarded-up restaurant. The parking lot was empty, no one in sight.

I hoped I hadn't been too quick to forgive Eli.

Sweating after the run in the heat, I stepped to the side of the building and quickly changed out of my suit into my black t-shirt and jeans. I flapped the suit shirt and pants around in the breeze to dry out and then put them back in the suitcase. It's strange how James Bond always wore a suit, but stayed so clean, even while riding motorcycles and fighting bad guys. I was already seeing stains in the armpits of my white shirt.

I collapsed on the curb to catch my breath. The sun was getting lower and glinting off the passing cars. How long would I have to wait? I didn't even know what I was waiting for. A bus? A taxi to the airport? A helicopter?

Then I remembered the note from Lloyd. I pulled it out of my pocket and read:

> *Spartacus,*
> *Don't forget your name:*
>
> *"Maybe there is no peace in this world for anyone,*
> *but I do know as long as we live, we must be true*
> *to ourselves."*
> *—Spartacus*
>
> *If you're ever in Portland, look me up!*
>
> *Your friend,*
> *Lloyd Lloeke*

He'd put his phone number and email address underneath his name. I folded the note carefully and put it back in my pocket.

I checked my watch. 6:30 on the nose. I opened my backpack and ate one of my fruit bars, then started counting cars. My count was up to a hundred and eight when a black semi rolled into the parking lot. It had orange and red flames down the sides and silver fangs on the grill. Two exhaust pipes belched black smoke, and the windows were tinted so you couldn't see who was inside. The brakes squealed loudly as it rolled to a stop in front of me.

This wasn't looking good.

CHAPTER 8

I DON'T KNOW WHAT KIND of person I expected to jump out of the truck cab, but it certainly wasn't a small young woman. She was brown-haired, with dirty jeans, an orange shirt, and a green trucker hat. And did I mention she was very small? Like my size?

"You Aaron?" she said, yanking the bill of her hat forward on her head.

"Yeah, that's me," I said cautiously. I wished Eli would have at least stuck with one fake name so I'd always know who I was supposed to be. *Aaron. Remember it: Aaron.*

"I'm Hailey," she said, putting out her hand. She was stronger than she looked; her handshake practically broke my hand. She had a tiny voice with a Southern accent. And brown eyes that were so deep I felt like I could fall into them.

"Pleasure to meet you," she said, though it came out more like "play-sure to meetcha."

"H-hey," I stammered back. "Nice to, uh, nice to make your—" I couldn't speak. Something was wrong with my mouth. She was just so darn cute.

"Ready to go?" she asked.

"You're going to Albuquerque?"

"Nope, Santa Fe. Change of plans. But don't worry. You'll get there. Let's roll." She smiled at me with big teeth and then turned and vaulted into the truck. I went to the passenger side, worrying for a second about the "change of plans" she'd mentioned.

After struggling a bit with the handle, I got the door open. I crouched down and threw myself up on the seat like I was doing a high jump.

I looked over at Hailey. This… this *girl* was going to drive me? She was sitting on some kind of raised platform kind of thing. A kid's seat was basically what it was. She really wasn't any bigger than I was.

I buckled my seatbelt. The leather seats were surprisingly soft and the cab smelled like a mix of mint and citrus-scented perfume.

"Like I said, my plans changed and I've got to drop you off in Santa Fe," she said, putting the truck into gear. "But you'll be able to get a city bus from there to Albuquerque, no problem. I'll give you a few bucks if you need it."

"Oh," was all I said. I wasn't sure what to say. Would a bus even let on someone as young as me? But I didn't want to say that and give away too much information.

"How long is the drive?" I asked. Tonight was Friday. Tomorrow was Saturday. I had one chance at making it there by tomorrow night.

"Let's just say we've got a long night ahead of us," she said. She pulled the truck out onto the highway. "We're not stopping much, unless you have to pee."

Usually a girl talking about me peeing would have made me blush. But weirdly I wasn't that embarrassed by it. I thought of my high dive experience and wondered if living through something that bad could make it so you'd never be embarrassed by anything again. I thought of my dad at the dinner table one night, talking about the high dive, saying, "Whatever doesn't kill you makes you stronger." Could he have actually been right?

"Aaron," she was still musing. Even though it was my fake name, I felt something weird in my stomach when she said it, like when Erika would glance at me in class. I guess things like that don't change after all.

Pull yourself together, Spartacus.

Did I just call myself Spartacus? That was weird.

"You know, that's a terrible name to be tryin' to hide under."

"I'm not hiding," I said, a little too forcefully. "What's wrong with Aaron?"

"I ran away from home, too," she went on, ignoring my question. She looked thoughtful and knit her eyebrows under her hat. "I changed my name to Jane, 'cause everybody would be looking for a Hailey. I was sixteen when I left. How old are you?"

All of a sudden I was very aware of my short, bitten fingernails and Will's scuffed new sneakers. I sat up a little straighter.

"How old are *you?*" I countered.

She gave me a look. "You're never supposed to ask a woman her age! Don't you know that?"

I blushed a little bit. So much for not being embarrassed ever again.

"I'm twenty-two," she said.

"And I'm sixteen," I lied. She snorted, obviously not believing me. "What? I'm small for my age," I said, trying hard to look offended.

"I know how these lies work." She glanced over at me with a knowing smile. "So you're *thirteen,* then. That's a little young to be trying to make it on your own."

"What makes you think I ran away?" I asked.

"Whose parent would go on Craigslist to get their son a ride to the, what was it—oh yeah, the Geography Ultimate Fightin' Championships?"

It was really hard to hold in my laughter. "You mean the *Geology* Fighting Championships," I said. I couldn't believe Eli had used that as my story. It was a made-up event, a joke we'd come up with, and now Hailey thought that's where I was headed. Wow, it made me sound really nerdy.

Hailey gave me an incredulous look. "Okay, *Geology....* Whatever you say. It was such a stupid story, I had to pick you up, *Aaron,* but I don't believe it for a second."

"No, seriously. My team is already down there," I said.

"Okay, tell me what you do at this Geology Fightin' Tournament," she said with a smirk.

"Uh, I don't like talking about it before the competition. Gotta keep my head clear." When she laughed, it sounded like tinkling glass.

"You been travelin' long?"

"A day," I said, not thinking. "I mean, just a few hours. I got a ride from..." Where had I come from? I didn't know what I was supposed to say. How much had Eli told her? I was in over my head. I was getting the new story confused with the paperboy story and the story I'd had to tell Lloyd. *Navin. Aaron. Casey. Spartacus. Moe.*

When I looked over, Hailey was smiling to herself like she'd finally caught me.

But then, what did it matter if she thought I was a run-away? She didn't seem to care one way or the other.

"Did you ever go back home?" I asked her abruptly. "After you ran away?"

"Nope."

I thought about Hailey being out on the road. Never going back home. As mean as Will and Dad were, could I do that?

"Was your family terrible or something?" I asked, not even planning on saying it.

Hailey looked mostly serious, but still had that little, sly grin.

"Let me put it this way, kid," she said. "However bad you think your family is, mine was a hundred times worse."

There wasn't much I could say to that.

I watched the road fly away behind us in the side-mirror. We passed a few towns, the kind that you're practically out of before you even see the welcome sign. Patchwork fields turned into gray and black squares as the sun started to sink below the horizon.

After a while, Hailey put on this Spanish language-learning CD. She said she'd been learning Spanish for the past few weeks, trying to put all the time she spent on the road to good use.

"*Mira el campo,*" said a deep voice on the CD.

"Mira el campo," Hailey repeated, but she wasn't even trying to match the Spanish accent.

I pulled out a comic book and pretended to read, but really I was just happy to have a chance to think about the rescue mission. Bartholomew wasn't expecting me, so I wouldn't need a disguise inside the circus. I'd just need to blend in. But then there were the cops, too. Maybe I could use some makeup to cover my freckle? I could probably find some at a drug store.

"*Veo una vaca.*"

"Veo una vaca."

I had the knife to cut my way through the tent. Would I need rope? I don't know what I'd need it for, but it seemed like a useful thing to have. The circus would probably have some lying around if I needed it.

"*Esa es una gran cabra.*"

"Esa es una gran cabra."

My head began to feel heavy. I rested it against the cool window and watched the fields slide by. *Sleep would be really nice.*

I nodded off, thoughts of Bartholomew's Circus in my head.

BARTHOLOMEW HAD A CRAZY PAST. It was weird how you could find it all online and yet he was still allowed to roam the countryside, putting on shows and stealing people's mothers. He started out as Count Csizmadia Bartholomew. The story goes that Bartholomew came from some country near Russia that doesn't exist any more—one of those places that got all broken to pieces after a war or something. He went from being royalty to being exiled from the country. Maybe for kidnapping people—it didn't say.

On IHateBartholomewsCircus.com, it said that he arrived in the U.S. about twenty years ago, penniless, with only the clothes on his back. Right after he arrived, he got a job for a small circus. Some people said he started out shoveling lion poop. Some people said he started out as a juggler. Either way, in three years he'd worked his way up to be the circus's main animal trainer. People said he had hypnotic powers with the animals. He was known for doing this amazing performance where lions, tigers, and bears all performed together (which I guess was really hard to do usually). A couple years after that, the owner of the circus suddenly died and left the whole thing to Bart in his will. People on the IHateBart website said it was all really suspicious. The owner was only forty-five when he died, and people said he hadn't even liked Bartholomew.

Bart renamed the circus after himself and the show started growing. It went from being just Bart and a dozen performers to the hundred-person strong Bartholomew's World-Renowned Circus of the Incredible. While "world-renowned" was a bit of a stretch, they actually were pretty well known. They traveled all over America, and sometimes to Mexico and Canada. Even the people who hated Bart said he put on an amazing show. They said his show made you feel like a kid again, that children and old people cry when it's over. I was honestly kind of sad I wouldn't get to see Mom perform in it once before getting her out.

The tiger mauling and the death of the three trapeze artists were the only really public tragedies from the circus. But the IHateBart website was full of similar stories. There were stories about two workers from Bartholomew's who went missing and were never heard from again. The stories were all anonymous comments on message boards, so none of it was proven, but it still sounded pretty bad when you added it all together.

The other weird thing was that nobody knew any concrete details about Bart's real age or background. No names for anything: family members, schools, the boat he came over on. One of the stranger rumors was that he didn't have any wrinkles on his face. People said his skin was completely smooth, and this made it hard for people to guess his age. All the pictures we'd found backed up that story.

And even though he was the ringmaster and supposedly spoke five languages, he never spoke in public. He didn't grant interviews, but there had been a few articles written about him. There were several reporters who swore that they'd overheard him saying he hated children. But Bart never tried to clear the air.

Maybe the most bizarre rumor was that Bartholomew kept a plastic surgeon on staff—an old doctor who used to do work for the royal family in Bart's homeland. Some people thought that was why a performer who had gotten burned really badly was able to perform just a few months later with no visible scars. And why it was so hard to tell how old Bart was.

My dream as I dozed in the truck was that my mom's kidnapping was just another rumor that I'd read about online. I was showing the website to everyone but no one would listen, not even Eli. I was going to have to rescue her alone. She was performing in Sisters, Oregon, but I was naked and all I had was a motorcycle to ride, and when I got there, there were guards and she was tied up...

When I woke up, I had forgotten where I was until I saw Hailey sitting in the driver's seat. It was dark outside and there was a puddle of drool on my arm. We were stopped at a gas station.

"What time is it?" I yawned.

"Almost one," she said. "I'm gonna pee and get some food. You want somethin'?"

"I'll come in with you," I answered, looking forward to stretching my legs.

While the truck was being filled up, we made our way into the convenience store. Inside, the buzzing lights were bright and harsh after being in the dark truck for so long. Hailey used the bathroom and then got a cup of coffee and a box of crackers. I got a candy bar and a soda with Will's money (which felt pretty good).

"We got about five minutes until the truck is full," Hailey said. "Wanna look around?"

At first, I didn't know what she meant; we were at a convenience store. But then I realized it wasn't like most stores. This was an actual truck stop. There were public showers, places to nap, even a few computers (though I checked and the Internet wasn't working).

We were standing together, looking at the public notice board when I saw the poster, partially hidden under another flyer. I moved the top sheet out of the way. It was a picture of Lloyd, only the name wasn't Lloyd and he wasn't smiling. I gulped and read the details:

DAN LLOEKE, AKA "THE CUE"
CONSIDERED ARMED AND DANGEROUS. WANTED
IN FOUR STATES FOR BURGLARY, THEFT, ASSAULT,
AND MURDER. WANTED IN CONNECTION WITH
THE DEATHS OF THREE PEOPLE. HAS A ROLLING
STONES TATTOO ON RIGHT FOREARM.

I WISH I COULD TELL you that I remained calm when I saw the poster. I wish I could tell you I took it in stride and moved forward. That I bravely stared down Dan Lloeke's wanted photo and just shook my head in disappointment.

Anyway, that's what I'd *like* to tell you.

Instead, I'll tell you the truth, or at least part of it. I made this pathetic whimpering sound, threw up in the conveniently located garbage can, and slid down to the floor.

I had just become BFFs with a serial killer.

After Hailey helped me to my feet, I stood in front of the poster. The sweat on my forehead had nothing to do with the stuffy truck stop hallway.

"Are you gonna tell me what just happened?" Hailey said, looking between the poster and me. When I told her the truth, that this man had just given me a ride a few hours before, she hugged me tight in a way that almost made it all worth it.

Almost.

We took down the poster and headed back to her truck. I thought about how close I could have been to death. And not a hypothetical death, like the one I imagined when I worried about getting caught by Dad or dying from embarrassment after the pool incident. This was death, real death, staring me right in the face.

"Things aren't all fun and games on the road, darlin'," Hailey drawled in her tiny voice as she put the truck in gear. She sounded like she was somewhere between sympathetic and disappointed, which is a terrible tone to hear coming from a stranger, especially one you might possibly have fallen in love with. "You gotta to be real careful, because when you're a runaway, you ain't got no one lookin' out for you but you."

I was drinking my soda to get the vomit taste out of my mouth. I told her again: "I'm not a runaway."

"Mmm, okay, sugar," Hailey said, shaking her head.

Ooh, if she was anyone else she would have been infuriating.

"I can't believe he was a serial killer," I said, staring at the wanted poster.

"Now, you know he isn't technically a serial killer," she said.

"What do you mean? It says so right here: *'burglary, theft, assault, and* murder.'"

"Just because someone's a murderer doesn't mean they're a serial killer," she said. I couldn't believe I was hearing this come out of her mouth. "I mean, a serial killer? Yeah. Scary. They want to kill people and can't seem to help it. So help you god if you come across one of them. But just a plain old murderer? And you said you guys got along fine? Nah. This guy's a criminal. He's not killing people for fun. He's not gonna kill you for no reason. He might, though, if he thinks you're in his way."

"This all makes me feel so much better," I said, sinking lower into my seat.

"I'm just trying to give you some education about kill-ers," she said simply. "Not trying to scare you."

"Look, this is a one-time thing. I'm not 'out on the road.' It was just *one ride*." My voice started to sounded a bit whiney, so I cleared my throat. "I mean, how was I sup-posed to know?"

Hailey paused, considering her response. "Did you get that sinkin' feelin' in your stomach when you saw him?" she finally asked.

I thought about my instinct to run and hide when Lloyd pulled up.

"Well, yeah."

"Did your Mistake-o-Meter give you some sort of alarm?"

"My what?"

"You know," she said. "Your 'Mistake-o-Meter.' Everybody's got one. You gotta pay attention to it while you're on the road."

I thought about it. She was right. I did have a Mistake-o-Meter, and I'd ignored it with Lloyd. I'd even ignored it when Will ruffled my hair after the high dive.

I was starting to feel really claustrophobic in the dark truck cab. Just *thinking* about my Mistake-o-Meter was making it go crazy. Worse, it was telling me that what I was doing was insane. *What am I doing in a truck crossing the country? Who did I think I was that I could go and rescue my mom alone?*

I had made a big mistake. I was just a kid and I could have died. Really died.

I started hyperventilating. I tried my mom's Instant Calm Breath Method but it didn't help. I could tell I was about to start crying—like real, snot-dripping, reckless-abandon, fetal-position sobbing. Luckily, Hailey saved us both from that. She put her small hand on my arm and gave it a little squeeze, and then began talking in her soft voice.

"Look, it's not easy out here. I can tell you first hand. I've been there before."

I wiped my face and sat up so I could hear her better, biting my lip to keep from blubbering.

"Let me tell you about the tools you got, Aaron," she said. "So you won't be so... vulnerable. So first you got the Mistake-o-Meter—it goes up to five." She showed me her hand, her fingers stretched out. "If you feel a one on the meter," she showed me one finger, "you gotta be ready for anything. You register a two? You ready your escape plan. Three? Use that escape plan and don't look back."

"And what if it's at a four or a five?" I asked.

"You should never get yourself into a four or five unless you wake up tied to a railroad track, kid," she said. "If you even *suspect* something's that bad, you get the heck out of there."

"He was so nice, too," I said, resting my face against the cool window. "I don't get it."

"Perfect transition to the other tool you got: mistrust."

"Is that a good thing?" I asked.

"Yeah, when you use it right. And you should be using it a lot out here. You don't trust anyone but yourself. People will try to get you to trust them and you just mistrust them right back. You don't trust anyone until they've *earned* your trust, you see? You can trust your brother or your sister or your friends or your teachers, because maybe they've earned your trust."

Maybe not, I thought, picturing Will.

"But when you're on the road?" Hailey continued. "Uh-uh. Your only friend is yourself. I know it sounds cruel, but that's how you gotta do it."

"So you don't trust me?" I asked.

"Not on your life," she said, but in a sweet way. "I just met you. Sorry, Aaron."

"It's cool," I said.

We drove in silence for a bit and I thought about it. I felt small and powerless, and more in over my head than I had since I left home. Hailey's words about not trusting anyone shouldn't have made me feel better. But somehow they did.

As we rolled on through the night, I couldn't get back to sleep. I pulled out the golden scarab Mom had sent me. I held the little piece of metal in my hand. It sounds silly, I know, but it made me feel calmer. Just having that small connection with my mom.

I sat there and thought about Lloyd—I mean, *Dan the Killer*—out there on the loose. I could call the number on the poster and report him, but the cops would probably want to question me and then hide me somewhere so that he couldn't find me. They'd probably send me off to live in Alaska in the Witness Protection Program. I'd have to change my name and always look over my shoulder and learn to sleep with a gun and—

Actually, it was starting to sound kind of cool, especially following the pool incident.

But they'd never let me go without Dad and the Jerk. I might have been down with the whole witness protection thing if I didn't have to take them along.

Besides, if I called the cops, I'd never get to the circus.

I decided that I'd write a letter after I had Mom home safe with me. Or make a phone call. Was it selfish to wait? What if Lloyd—*Dan*—killed somebody else? Would it be my fault? I figured I didn't have much choice. If I called the police now, my plan was shot.

I settled back in my seat, watching the dark sky out the window. I thought about Eli and how he had almost gotten me killed with his ride choices. He would have to start being more careful about who he talked to online.

WE GOT TO SANTA FE, New Mexico early in the afternoon with plenty of time for me to get to Albuquerque by bus.

If Brenville was in the high desert, this was the *real* desert. I'd never seen anything like it. I'm talking adobe houses, pink mountains, and cactuses. Hailey said it hardly ever rained in New Mexico, but there were a few dark storm clouds on the horizon. The rest of the sky was a brilliant, clear blue. And everything was so wide open and flat, you could see forever. "Land of enchantment," Hailey called it.

She took me to the south end of town, where she said I could get a bus to Albuquerque, no problem.

"I wish I could take you all the way there," she said, "but they track my miles. Stay by that bus stop, right over there. The Albuquerque bus should get here in no time."

"Well, thanks for the ride. And the advice," I said reluctantly as we came to a stop. I really didn't want to get out of the truck. When she leaned in to hug me, I felt this warm glow all over. I awkwardly hugged her back.

"Stay cool, *Aaron*," she said, her hot breath on my neck making me feel even *more* awkward. "And listen to your heart, okay? When things get weird, you book it, right?"

"Right," I said. "Mistake-o-Meter at the ready."

"And don't trust anyone, okay? Not unless they earn it first." She patted me on the shoulder as I gathered my things. I jumped out of the truck with my backpack and suitcase and looked up at her.

"What's your real name?" she asked. I thought for a little while about that. I figured Hailey had earned enough trust for a little truth.

"My name is Spartacus," I said.

"And where are you going?" She didn't bat an eye at my name.

"I'm going to see my mom."

"Well," Hailey said. "Tell her I said howdy."

Then I said the sappiest good-bye ever. I don't know what I was thinking—it just came out. "I won't forget you."

"Likewise, Spartacus."

Hailey reached out and pulled shut the passenger side door. I stepped back as the truck lumbered off down the road. Hailey hit the horn twice, and then she was gone.

It started to sprinkle and I didn't even care.

She liked me. She called me cool.

Smiling, I walked toward the bus stop, Will's black hat keeping the rain off my head. I was only hours away from confronting the circus. Which meant I was about to start the most dangerous part of my journey.

I waited for an hour, but the bus didn't come. The rain kept pouring and there wasn't a speck of shelter that I could see. I walked over to the bus stop post, which I should have done sooner. There was a small tag hanging off of it that read:

> *Due to state budget cuts, the Santa Fe to Albuquerque bus line is no longer in service. We apologize for the inconvenience.*

Oh my god. Could my luck be any worse?

I had never planned on hitchhiking. That was one thing Eli and I agreed was totally out of the question. It was too dangerous. *But then again, look how safe Eli's rides had turned out,* I thought bitterly.

Anyway, it didn't seem like I had much of an option. But even when I decided I needed to hitchhike, I couldn't put my thumb out. My arm was dead at my side. Even the *idea* of putting my thumb out seemed embarrassing and... well, *scary*. I started remembering everything I'd heard about hitchhiking, even though all the stories I knew were about the hitchhiker being crazy, not the driver. Eli told me how his cousin's friend's dad had picked up this guy who—

Suddenly, out of nowhere, a car horn blared right behind me.

I hadn't even put my thumb out.

CHAPTER 9

I TURNED TO FIND A very tan, white-haired lady behind the wheel of a white Lincoln big enough to have its own area code. In the passenger seat sat another old woman with glasses and blue hair pulled back in a bun so tight she looked like she was forced to smile whether she was happy or not. Blue-Hair waved excitedly at me.

"Where you headed, young man?" White-Hair asked, leaning over Blue to speak to me. At least she didn't have a hook. There were always hooks in hitchhiking stories.

"Albuquerque," I answered, putting on my best smile in hopes of covering up the I-just-ran-away-from-home-to-rescue-my-mother look. It must have worked because Blue leaned back and unlocked the door behind her.

"Well, don't just stand there. Hop in before the po-po see you!"

I got in, heaved the door closed, and settled into the velvety backseat just as the light drizzle turned into a heavy shower. It only then struck me that what she had just said was pretty strange. Po-po? Was she talking about the police? I'd heard Will say something like that before.

"Good thing we have the cover of this storm," said White. Blue grunted in agreement and I raised an eyebrow. Without looking, White pulled the boat of a car out onto the highway, causing a smaller car to slam on its brakes to avoid hitting us. Neither Blue nor White seemed to notice.

"You never know when they'll come around the corner and nab you," White muttered while Blue nodded in agreement.

"Who?" I asked, hastily putting on my seat belt.

"What?" asked Blue.

"Who?" I repeated.

"Who *what?*" asked White, looking at me in the rearview mirror.

I shut my mouth, wishing Blue had left her window down because the entire car smelled horribly of vanilla air freshener. There were five yellow trees dangling from the rearview mirror alone. More hung above the back doors. I held out as long as I could, but after a silent minute, I rolled down the window just a crack so I wouldn't suffocate.

"You roll that window back up, young man," White said sharply and, because I didn't know what else to do, I did. I tried to hold my breath.

"Dangerous," said Blue, shaking her head.

"I was asking who would sneak around the corner and nab me?" I asked finally.

"The Pigs! The Fuzz! The Po-Po! The Law! The Constabulary! The ol' Black and White!" White creaked out.

"Police," chimed in Blue.

I wasn't sure what the "constabulary" was, but I thought I was getting the idea. Blue turned around in her seat to peer at me. I could only see her eyes over the headrest, her thick glasses making her dark eyes look at least ten times their normal size.

"Why would the police care about me?" I asked nervously.

"You tell me," said White. "You break out of the clink?"

Blue's eyes just blinked at me.

"What?" I asked. This was getting weird.

"Bust out of the slammer? Skip bail? Fly the coop?"

"Fugitive," Blue whispered and I just stared at her.

The red arrow of my Mistake-o-Meter started to creep upward as the car drifted all over the road, cutting off cars and running red lights, windshield wipers at full speed: *thwakita-thwakita-thwakita.*

"I wasn't in jail," I managed between gasps of vanilla-scented air. I closed my eyes tight as White narrowly avoided hitting a blue van.

"Just as I thought!" beamed White. "On the lam!"

"Look, I don't know what you're talking about," I said, gripping the handle above my door, the air freshener flapping against my arm. I was about to tell them I'd rather *walk* to Albuquerque when White's eyes narrowed in the mirror.

"Are you packing a biscuit?" she asked coldly.

"A *what?*"

That's when we swerved into oncoming traffic to go around a car slowing for an exit.

I truly believed it was my last moment alive.

Somehow, through a commotion of red brake lights, horns, and skidding tires, we avoided unavoidable death.

"*Hippies!*" White cursed, shaking a veiny fist at the traffic in general.

Blue either didn't notice or didn't care that we'd nearly been flattened like a pop can.

I was starting to think that this was more than just a three on my Mistake-o-Meter—it was starting to look like a four or a five. A Flashing Red Bad Idea.

"A *biscuit!* You know, a slug thrower. A six shooter." White was all but shouting, gesturing with her pale, wrinkly hand. "A rod! A gat!"

"Gun," Blue whispered.

Hailey had been right. You can't trust anyone.

"Are you carrying? Strapped up? Packing heat?" White finished.

"No!" I exclaimed. "Of course not!"

I *need to get out of this car, I need to get out of this car,* I chanted to myself, desperately trying to figure out an escape.

Through the windshield, the rain was coming down hard. The road in front of us was just a blur. There was no way these old ladies could see where they were going.

"Ask him his name," White said to Blue. But before she could, White changed her mind. "No, no, never mind. I don't think we should know it."

"My name is Ryan," I said. These crazy bats wouldn't remember what I told them anyway.

"I can't hear you!" said White, putting her fingers in her ears and letting the steering wheel spin on its own. The Lincoln immediately veered to the right.

"Steer!" screeched Blue, grabbing the wheel. She pulled too hard and we went flying toward the shoulder. I thought we were going to go into the ditch but a curb stopped us, the hubcaps singing against the concrete. My heart thudded so hard in my throat I thought I was going to choke.

"Gimme the wheel!" White squawked, wrenching the car back to the left. "You know you can't drive," she admonished Blue before turning back to me. "She lost her license, poor thing."

"Yes," agreed Blue somewhat wistfully.

White looked at me again in the mirror. "So Randy—"

"Ryan."

"Right. Brian. We're supposed to believe you don't have a gun?"

"Wait, wait, wait," I said, holding my hands up. "I'm just a kid. I just need to get to Albuquerque. I'm not a criminal or... whatever it is you think I am. Really." I swallowed loudly.

"Sure," said White, squinting at me. "I think he's in disguise," she whispered to Blue out of the corner of her mouth.

"Really?" Blue mumbled back, still facing me. Once again, I could only see her big bug-eyes.

Reality must have taken the day off.

"Check his bag," White said, and before I knew it, Blue, a creaky old lady nearing a hundred, grabbed my suitcase from my lap as easily as Will snagging my cupcake.

"Give it back!" I leaned forward but my seatbelt locked and tightened across my lap as White slammed on the brakes.

"Chill, Rambo," she said coolly, looking over her shoulder at me.

"Please, please, just look at the road," I pleaded, covering my eyes.

And just when I thought things had spiraled completely out of control, they got worse. I uncovered my eyes to see Blue pull a pistol out of the glove compartment.

"Oh crap, *holy crap!*" My blood turned to ice as Blue fiddled with an honest-to-god, reach-for-the-sky gun.

"Lady, please!" I cried, pushing myself back into the velvet seat. "I mean *geez!*"

Out the window I could see people driving, all completely unaware that I was being held against my will. They shook their fists at us and shouted as we ran them off the road and went hurtling past them. We slowed for a sharp corner and I reached for the door handle, but Blue shook her head at me and White glared at me in the mirror. Her voice turned quiet and sweet, as though she were offering me a cookie.

"Don't make us mad, Rufus," she said. We kept driving. How was I going to get away?

I decided to panic.

My mouth began sputtering anything and everything, and before I knew it, I was telling them I had to get out so I could save my mom and had to give Will his money back and make my dad proud. Telling them things I didn't even know I felt until the words came tumbling out. The only reason my lips stopped flapping was because there wasn't any air left in the car.

That, and Blue slapped me. The big ruby ring she wore cut my cheek and when I reached to touch it, my hand came back with a smear of blood.

"Hush," she said sternly.

"Cool it, Ralph," White added.

Blue then proceeded to go through everything in my suitcase. She showed my rescue plan to White who made a *tsk*-ing noise and then stuffed everything back in, except for the scarab, which I saw fall onto the seat.

"Spy," Blue concluded, chucking my bag back at me.

"*What?*" I squeaked.

"Quiet," she growled in her tiny voice. That's when I noticed that the bag had hit the rearview mirror when Blue flung it back at me.

The mirror had moved and White couldn't see me.

We left the city limits and began picking up speed, blasting down the highway at what had to be a hundred miles an hour. White threaded the car in and out of the lanes of traffic like a needle.

I thought about knocking White over the head with my flashlight, but I couldn't hit someone's grandma, gun or not. I mean, they might have kidnapped me but, well... they were *old*. What can you do when they're *old*? Besides, if I hit her, we'd crash for sure.

"I'm not a spy," I said. I was trying to be calm, but there wasn't a single person in that car who didn't hear my voice shaking.

"What's with the camo paint then?" countered White. "And the disappearing ink? The—" she squinted her eyes. "*Top Secret Escape Plan?*"

"*I'm a runaway!*" I yelled, shocking both ladies and myself. "I have to hide and escape sometimes, don't I?" I couldn't help glaring at the gun bouncing in Blue's hand as the big white Lincoln clipped a smaller car.

"What should we do with him?" White asked Blue. Blue shrugged.

"You can let me out here," I said, leaning forward. "I won't say a single word about—" About what? What was this anyway? "Well, any of this. I promise," I finished.

"You've seen too much," said White.

"Yep," said Blue.

"No, I haven't!"

"You know everything," said White.

"Everything," repeated Blue.

"No, I don't! I don't know *anything!*" It was well beyond the time to panic. Hailey would have been so disappointed.

"You've heard all our plans."

"Plans," echoed Blue.

"What plans? I didn't hear any plans!" My face broke out in a cold sweat, making the cut on my cheek sting. Suddenly, I had an idea.

"Look out, it's the po-po!" I screamed, pointing out the side window.

"Where?" they both shouted at once. White slammed on the brakes and the car started skidding across the wet pavement. I heard the cars around us screeching (and crashing), but I knew what I had to do. I threw myself and my bags out the door.

I was aiming for a cool tuck-and-roll, like something from a James Bond movie. But I probably looked more like a kid accidentally falling out of Grandma's car. I clutched my suitcase to my chest and rolled away from the Lincoln in a rough, sloppy tangle of limbs. The wet blacktop bit into my knuckles and knees and I couldn't stop my head from knocking against pavement.

"No!" I heard White wail. I sat for a moment in disbelief, only brought back to earth by cars honking and swerving around the Lincoln. And around me. Two cars flew by on either side of me, landing with a horrible crash in the ditch. I watched White and Blue struggling in the car. Their tires squealed as they made a sudden right turn.

Right into a cop car.

Holy. Crapola.

I peeled myself off the road and broke into a limping sprint. Holding my backpack and suitcase, I jumped down into the ditch and tried to scramble up the other side. My fingers dug into the wet dirt but the edge was too steep to climb.

"Easy there," boomed a voice above me. I turned around to see a huge silhouette looming above me. I could just make out the police badge on his chest through the pouring rain. I closed my eyes and slumped down into the ditch. I was exhausted. I was done.

CHAPTER 10

I WAS SITTING IN AN air-conditioned office at a police station somewhere in New Mexico, waiting for the policeman to come back and ask me some questions about the old ladies. The last I'd seen of Blue and White, the police had been gently handcuffing them and nudging them into the cop car. White had actually tried to spit in a cop's face, but she was too short.

Insane.

I could tell the police officers didn't know who I was. Maybe it was the dirt on my face (I'd seen my reflection in a window and I barely recognized myself) or the fake name and address I'd given them. Maybe it was the fact that they had their hands full with two little old ladies who'd created the worst traffic pile-up in state history.

For whatever reason, everyone had been really nice to

me so far, but I knew I had to get out of there. I was in the main lobby of the police station, which wasn't very big. There were three desks and a bunch of office equipment, but not much in the way of escape routes. There was a locked door that led to the rest of the building, and a window with bars on it. I guess they were used to keeping suspects in the room. Or at least suspicious-looking kids.

I was alone for now, but somebody was going to come back soon. They'd offer me a damp towel to clean my face, and then they'd see my freckle and—I didn't want to think about it. Not when I was this close. Plus, my bags were at my feet and I knew it was only a matter of time before they asked to search them. It just seemed like something police did.

As I waited, I eyed Mom's gold scarab, sealed in a plastic evidence bag and laying on the desk in front of me. An attached sticky note read:

Recovered at scene. Run past FBI? *Interpol?*
Also, check against known art-theft list.

It was just a silly piece of jewelry, but it was special to me and I wanted it back. I sat on my hands to keep from grabbing it. Not just yet. I'd get it on my way out—if I could find a way out. I looked around the office again. There was no way I could squeeze through the bars in the window. I guess that was pretty much the point. What about the air conditioning vents? I saw one next to the window, but it was only a foot across. How did people always get away through vents in the movies?

I dropped my face into my hands for a moment before standing up. That's when I saw the bulletin board covered in posters of the FBI Most Wanted List above the copy machine. And guess whose face was front and center? Lloyd—Dan—Lloeke's.

Extremely dangerous.

The letters were big enough that I could read them from across the room. I went over and looked at his face again. Honestly, he hadn't looked that terrifying in real life. He stared out of the poster with gleaming eyes and a twisted mouth. He looked so angry, you had to wonder if he'd tried to kill the camera guy right after the picture was taken. I shivered, remembering how close I had been to him.

I wondered if I should tell the cops about Lloyd, but then I realized that if I did, they probably wouldn't let me out of their sight. I pushed the thought away and instead tried to memorize the faces of the other people on the list, just in case Eli sent another one to pick me up. Hailey would probably think that was a smart idea.

The guy in the poster beside Lloyd's was wanted for armed robbery, murder, and extortion. Compared to Lloyd, he looked completely boring and normal. He had neat, short hair and a little polite smile. You would never have thought he was a murderer. Like Hailey said, you couldn't tell with people. Better to mistrust them first just to be on the safe side.

The last paper on the wall was this really fuzzy black-and-white picture that must have been taken with a security camera. It showed a three-story building at night, lit up by a few bright streetlights. I could just barely make out a man's silhouette on the top ledge of the building. He had his hands on his hips and his head turned to the side and facing up, kind of like a pose you'd see a superhero make. Under the picture was written *Georgia*

O'Keeffe Museum Robbery, Santa Fe. It was dated the night before.

Georgia O'Keeffe must have been a painter. There were small, color copies of maybe seven paintings that were missing—bright close-ups of flowers and trees. And one of them had a price scrawled beneath it that was vigorously circled. *$14 mil.*

Mil? As in, *fourteen million?*

Wow.

Crazy. I didn't know people actually robbed museums. I thought stuff like that only happened in the movies. Then I thought about Lloyd. And Blue and White. They weren't exactly the normal, everyday types either.

I went back to looking around the office for a way out but came up with nothing. There was no way out. I sent a silent apology to Mom. I had failed her. The cops were going to know I gave a fake name. I was trapped.

I sat down and felt something poke me through the lining of my jean pocket. It was the note from Lloyd, the one he'd told me to look at later. I read the quote again:

> *Maybe there is no peace in this world for anyone,*
> *but I do know as long as we live, we must be*
> *true to ourselves.*

I looked at my name at the top of the page. *Spartacus.* Funny how Lloyd had tried to make me feel better about my name. And what was the other thing he'd said about the movie? Freedom is worth fighting for—even if you die trying?

I thought about it and decided he had a point. I couldn't give up now. Not after having come this far.

Think, Spartacus, think.

I looked at the window and suddenly I had an idea.

But it was at that moment that the officer entered the room.

"So. You say one of them pulled the gun on you?" Garcia was gripping the stub of a pencil in his hand, taking down my story. His nametag said *Garcia*. No officer, no rank, just Garcia.

"Yeah. The blue-haired one had the gun."

The officer jotted this down. Just then the phone on his desk rang and he picked it up, swiveling around in his chair.

"Garcia here."

I leaned forward, trying to read what he had been writing, but I couldn't make anything out.

"Yes? Yes. Really? I see…" he swiveled his chair back to look at me. "I'll call you back."

"So, Jeff," Garcia said, hanging up his phone. "Where are your parents? We tried the number you gave us and it's been disconnected."

I looked down at my hands. *All right. It's time for the plan.*

That's when I started the waterworks. I know, I know, it's not particularly brave, but it was always a useful skill whenever Will was about to pulverize me. And if I'd figured right, it was going to come in handy here, too.

"Hey," said Garcia, looking at me with concern. "Don't do that. What's wrong?"

"It's just that…" I stopped and heaved a huge sob that made my shoulders shake.

123

"Hey, hey, hey," Garcia said, uncomfortably, patting my shoulder. "Hey! Do you want a soda or something?"

"Yessir," I sniffled, looking up at him with what I hoped were grateful yet watery eyes.

"All right. Just hold on one second." Garcia left the room and I almost felt guilty. He was an all right guy. But that didn't stop me from using his telephone to break the window.

I took off my shirt and tossed it out the window. Then I snatched Mom's scarab off Garcia's desk. For the final part of my plan, I wedged myself into the small space between the huge copy machine and the wall. There was hardly room for a cat, let alone me, but I kept letting out my breath and scrunching my way down even further. Somehow I got myself wedged in there.

Fifteen seconds later, Garcia barged in.

"Jeff!" he shouted through the bars of the window. Then he said a curse word, then, "How the heck did he...?" followed by another curse word. I was beginning to feel lightheaded from lack of air.

Garcia rushed out the door, shouting, "Elwood! *Elwood!*"

"Yep?" came a voice from down the hall.

"Jeff bolted."

"He *what?*"

And that's when Garcia, Elwood, and the person at the front desk—the only officers on duty—should have left the station.

But they didn't.

My vision was going dark around the edges from not breathing and Elwood and Garcia were coming back into the office.

"He couldn't have fit. It's impossible—" Elwood was saying. Just then I fell out from behind the copier.

"What the heck is going on here, Jeff?" Garcia exclaimed, seeing me shirtless on the floor. In two seconds, I was pinned to the ground with my face pressed against the white tile. And then I was handcuffed.

Really. Spartactus Ryan Zander, the kid who'd never been in any kind of trouble (apart from exposing himself to his whole hometown) was officially a criminal. Might as well put my face up there next to Lloyd's and call it a day.

"Well, there goes the case against the two old ladies," Elwood was saying. "No one will believe this witness now."

"Look, Jeff," Garcia said, heaving me to my feet and holding me by my cuffed hands. I hung there ashamed, like a cat held up by the nape of its neck. "I don't know what that was all about, but you've just *drastically* changed the nature of this investigation."

Elwood snagged my suitcase from the recycling bin where I'd tried to hide it under the shredded papers. He followed Garcia and me down the hallway. We passed the lone female officer at the front desk, a whole row of closed doors, a restroom, and then we arrived at a room with a little plastic plaque that read *Prisoner Processing.* Elwood opened the door for us... and inside?

Blue and White.

I felt like I'd eaten a bucket of ice cream, all cold and urpy.

The two women were sitting on a bench and were—get this—*shackled together at the ankles.* There was a metal contraption connecting them at their feet, and each had a hand handcuffed to the end of the bench. They seemed completely helpless, sitting there murmuring to each other like they were discussing quilt patterns.

I shivered as Garcia pulled me into the room.

"Hello, ladies!" said Garcia.

"It's *Randy!*" White hissed to Blue, leaning down and fiddling with her restraint, trying to get herself free.

Free to strangle me, no doubt.

"Impossible," said Blue, shaking her head at me.

"Jeff here is going to keep you ladies company while we handle some business. Then we'll figure out what we're going to do with the three of you."

Garcia sat me down on a bench across from Blue and White. He removed my handcuffs and handed me a shirt to put on, and then zip-tied my wrist to the arm of the bench. At least I wasn't handcuffed any more.

"I'm sorry. I didn't mean to—" I started to plead but Garcia held up his hand.

"You're starting down a dangerous path, kid," he said before dropping his hand to my shoulder. "And if I were to let you go now, you'd stay on it. You'll thank me someday."

I was getting ready to cry. Real tears this time, not the act. But I held it back. Not now. Not in front of these crazy old women.

And with that, Garcia and Elwood left, shutting the heavy door behind them. I heard them say goodbye to the woman at the front desk, and then their voices trailed off down the hall. This was bad. I noticed my bag and suitcase beside the door, just out of reach. Elwood must have set them there.

I brought my free hand up and felt the scab on my cheek where Blue had slapped me with her ring during the car ride. I looked up to see Blue and White staring at me intensely. I flinched, waiting for their wrath.

"You have to get us out of here," White whispered.

She looked desperate. I was so caught off guard, I couldn't believe it. They *didn't* want to kill me?

"I can't go back to prison. I just can't," said White.

"Can't," Blue commiserated, her eyes huge and watery and cartoonish behind her glasses. They both held their spindly, cuffed hands out to me, as though I had the key, as though I were there to save them or something. I caught a whiff of that vanilla-roma tree scent still lingering on them.

"Wait. Wait. I really can't help—" I stammered but White interrupted me.

"You don't know what they do to old women like us in prison, Brandon. Poor Clementine would be shivved at Bingo by nightfall."

"Shanked," Blue corrected her.

"I—I don't have the key," I said. "And I'm tied up, too!"

Not to mention the door that was undoubtedly locked. There was no point in getting untied.

White looked at Blue and then nodded her head. Then, to my complete disgust, Blue took out her top dentures and held them out for me.

"What are those for?" I asked, leaning back.

"Use them for your zip-tie," said White. "One of the pointy teeth has a serrated edge for stuff like this." She turned to Blue and said quietly, "You took the cyanide pill out of them, didn't you?" Blue nodded.

"What? No!" I was so grossed out at the thought that I had to close my eyes. When I opened them, White had taken them from Blue and was drying them on her sweater.

"Look, see, now they're nice and clean."

"Sparkling," Blue encouraged.

I looked from the teeth in White's hand to the plastic tie attaching my wrist to the chair. It was only part of a solution.

Even if I got out of the restraint, I'd still be locked in. But I had to try, didn't I? If I had even the smallest chance, I had to try. Anyway, I was already in so much trouble, what did one more thing matter?

"Let me… just let me try for a second before I use the… the teeth, okay?" Blue smirked and leaned back, watching me with a toothless, amused look as I stretched and pulled and picked at the plastic tie. It did nothing but make my wrist raw.

I didn't have much time.

"Gimme the teeth," I sighed. White smiled and handed them over.

I won't go into detail about the teeth. Let's just say I gagged and leave it at that.

I sawed at the plastic with the sharp incisor and, in a few minutes, I was able to snap the zip-tie off.

"Genius!" I said, rubbing my wrist. I handed the teeth back to Blue.

"Yep," she said, popping them back in without wiping them off or anything. Ugh.

"Right," said White. "Now us."

My stomach sunk. I'd already forgotten that part of the deal.

"Still don't have the keys," I said. I wasn't about to remind them about the mini screwdrivers I had in my suitcase, right by the door.

"Start yelling. When the Capo comes in, you knock her out," White said, eyes shining.

"Capo?" I asked.

"Copper," Blue said.

"When she comes in, you grab her gun," White continued. "Or, wait, you can use the leg of this bench, here."

White began kicking at the leg of the wooden bench with her one free foot.

"Stop!" I said, putting my hand out and on her bony shoulder. "Shh! You want her to hear us? Besides, I can't do that. I'm not hitting any cops."

"What? We scratch your back and you don't scratch ours?" White's eyes flashed at me with a hint of the fire I'd seen earlier that day. "You want hush money to do it or something?" I took a step back, shaking my head.

"I will not club a police officer," I said. "I'm grateful you helped me get free, but—"

"You a coward?"

"Yellow," muttered Blue. "Chicken." She said it in that fake quiet way people say things when they're acting like they don't want you to hear, but really they do.

"You heard her," said White, her face hardening. "You don't have the cojones to spring a goomba?"

"A *what?*" I asked, incredulous. Again. I'd played this role before...

"Wingman! Esé! Comrade!" Blue supplied.

Apparently Blue could now say more than one word at a time.

"You don't care about your friends, is what you're telling us," said White.

"No, it's just that—" I had to figure out how to get out of there, not waste time talking to them. And they were making so much noise. What had they said about attracting the officer with noise?

"Ah, so it *is* the coward thing." White sat back, smirking. It was like something Will would say.

My face went hot—she knew she'd hit a nerve.

"Milquetoast. Pantywaist," taunted Blue.

"Pantywaist?" I repeated and Blue nodded, sneering.

"You couldn't take the heat," White said, that slight, creepy smile on her face. "So you went belly up and turned snitch."

That's when it hit me. I knew how to get out of there—without clubbing anyone.

"You know what?" I said, leaning forward. "I *am* a snitch. I'm the bad guy."

"*You!*"

I didn't expect White to be so fast—her free hand shot out at me like an electric eel, her grip strong and cold on my throat, her thumb pressing into my Adam's apple.

"The heavy!" roared Blue. "The black hat!"

"Get... off... me," I choked, knocking her claw away. I backed away as they wrestled with their handcuffs. They were going crazy, despite being cuffed to the bench.

"I knew it! I knew it!" White sputtered.

"I told them everything," I said loudly. Then I sat back down on my bench, and arranged my arm like I was still tied to the bench.

"Defector! Snitch!" bellowed Blue. "Stoolie!"

"You old hags are going to be in the clink a long time," I said smugly.

At this, they went berserk, jerking at the bench so hard the wood started to splinter. They yelled curse words at the top of their lungs, including some I'd never heard before.

"So help me, Brian, I will use your skull to hold my yarn balls!" White screamed. Yes, she really said that.

"Hey! What's going on?" It was the female officer, opening the door. "Keep it down in here!" She went straight over to Blue and White, not even throwing a glance my way.

Before the door could close, I sprang to my feet, grabbed my bags, and dashed into the hallway. The door slammed shut behind me, interrupting the officer's startled shout.

I heard her fumbling with her keys and took off down the hall toward the side exit of the police station.

"You're gonna pay for this, Brian!" I heard White crowing. "Mark my words!"

Maybe she was right. Maybe I *would* pay for it some day. But at that moment, I was free.

CHAPTER 11

Outside, the rain was still coming down in sheets and tasted clean and crisp. I crouched behind a squad car and gulped air like a nearly drowned man. I felt like hugging the ground. I guess after spending time in the slammer, freedom can make you want to do that.

I was about to just run off across the scrubby desert, when I saw it: My Out.

It was the big white Lincoln. Blue and White's smashed up car was being towed out of the parking lot.

I'd thought it was the last car I'd ever want to see, let alone get *back into,* but there it was. And this time, rather than looking like a giant white hearse, it was like some junkyard beacon of hope.

The tow truck came to a full stop at the parking lot exit, right in front of me. The driver was looking the other way.

I glanced back at the police station. No one had come out yet.

It was now or never.

I sprinted across the wet blacktop like the fugitive I was, and watched the driver as I opened the back door. No reaction. A fog of yellow vanilla-roma poured out of the car. Taking a last breath of clean, freedom-tinged air, I threw myself inside.

I DIDN'T WANT TO MAKE any noise so I didn't close the door, but it was hard to hold onto it as we bumped down the road. Luckily I wasn't going too far—at the first empty intersection, I bailed out and ran, bags clutched to my chest, hunched low like I was getting out of a helicopter. I dove into a shallow ditch beside the road... and the driver continued on as if nothing had happened.

I did it. I really did it. I escaped from jail.

I lay there in the wet ditch even as the rain came down, dizzy, laughing, snorting, kicking my feet, and generally looking like a crazy person. And when I saw the yellow vanilla air-freshener snagged on my suitcase handle, I laughed even harder. I laughed until I could barely breathe. I couldn't tell what was rain and what were tears. I'd finally done something spectacular, and I'd come away with only cuts, bruises, and sore muscles. Okay, so the injuries were adding up, but the point was that I'd made it out *alive*. I'd actually succeeded at something.

I got up and started walking beside the dirt road, away from the police station. And, while I'm not the kind of person to believe in signs and crap like that, suddenly the sun came out. A few minutes later, it was like it had never rained at all; the ground soaked up most of the water and the air was dry and warm. I actually laughed out loud again.

For the first time since leaving home, I felt like I might pull this whole thing off.

But while I was excited about my successful escape, I'd also never been more tired in my life. It was only one in the afternoon and the show was at eight. If I could get to Albuquerque, I'd have time to mentally prepare myself, call the cops, and then maybe get some quick shuteye. I just had to *get* there.

Also, I needed to call Eli.

The road had only a few small houses along it and it looked like a pretty poor area. A few blocks ahead, there was a rundown convenience store. I made a beeline straight for it, toward the phone booth out front. I found a couple quarters in my backpack and shoved them in.

"HE WAS *WHAT?*"

Hearing Eli's squeaky voice of disbelief was almost enough payment for nearly being killed by Lloyd. Almost.

"A killer," I repeated. "They call him 'The Cue.'"

"You've got to be kidding me. I have to look this up."

While Eli's fingers clacked away at his laptop, I read him a few other items from Lloyd's wanted poster. "Wanted for burglary, theft, assault, and murder... armed and dangerous."

"Oh my god," said Eli. I knew he'd pulled up his photo online. "And he even had the—"

"Yep, the tattoo on his right arm."

"Dude, I'm so sorry. Why did you even ride with him? Look at him! He's a monster!"

I closed my eyes and told myself to be patient with Eli.

"Luckily, I'm still alive," I said. "And Hailey, the girl trucker? Much better choice."

"Right! The Geology Fighting Championships."

"But she dropped me off in the wrong place."

"What? She was supposed to take you all the way there."

"You'll never believe it. She dropped me off and—" I was about to tell him everything, about Blue and White and the police station, but then I shook my head. "Never mind. It's a long story. Let's just say I'm somewhere in the middle of nowhere between Santa Fe and Albuquerque."

"Got any details?"

I looked around and saw two faded street signs.

"Looks like I'm on the corner of Foster and Acoma."

"Acoma? Oh, okay, I found you. You're near Algodones."

"Where's that?"

"You've got like thirty miles to go, but you can't walk that."

"You're telling me," I said, looking at the brown landscape. "I'm in an actual *desert*. It's even got cactuses."

"Call me back in five, okay? I'll get you something."

"Remember, it's the last show! I have to get there by eight!"

But Eli had already hung up. I went inside the store and bought a whole quart of water. The guy behind the counter watched me intently while I finished it in one long drink. I knew I must have looked suspicious, but I was so thirsty, I didn't care. Then I ate three hotdogs from the hotdog warmer, while the guy cringed.

"I don't think I've ever seen anyone eat those," he said.

"They're not bad," I said, swallowing the last mustardy bite.

"No, I mean, I don't think anyone's ever put new ones in there."

I gave him a look, but licked my fingers anyway and then smiled. "Very funny."

"I think your cheek is bleeding."

In the restroom, I saw that the scab from Blue's ring-slap had cracked. But that was really the least of it. I mean, if I thought I looked bad after the chicken truck and the library, I was a wreck after Blue and White. No wonder the store clerk had been giving me a weird look. My face was filthy and bruised and bleeding. There was a gaping hole in my shirt and a tear in the left knee of my jeans, which were muddy from laying down in that ditch. It wasn't pretty.

I changed my underwear, washed my face, and then put on a clean shirt and jeans. I felt like a new person and the guy at the counter nodded his head. Much better.

Out front, I called Eli back.

"Okay, I got it. It took some creative web searching, but I got you a ride nearby—crazy, right?"

"That's why you're the best," I said. "Lay it on me."

"So I found a blog posted by some Goth girl in Algodones. She and a group of friends are meeting up at a cemetery nearby and—"

"A cemetery?" I repeated, not liking the sound of it.

"And then they're going to the circus," he finished.

"How do you know this?"

"People put way too much information online. Anyway, just trust me on this. The girl's name is Marianne. But she calls herself Calyxtus."

"Calyxtus?" I said.

"Yeah," said Eli, laughing. "Some Goth thing, I guess. You need to meet them there at dusk."

"When's that?" I asked.

"You know, *dusk*. It's when the sun goes down. Don't be difficult."

I looked at my watch. Plenty of time.

"They don't know you're coming," said Eli. "I couldn't get in touch with them. So you're going to have to find a way to introduce yourself and get them to give you a ride. Maybe just beg them. Or give them money."

"I hope this works," I said, sighing.

"One more interesting little detail," said Eli. "I almost forgot—they hate Bartholomew just as much as you do."

ACCORDING TO ELI, THE CEMETERY was maybe an hour away. I was keeping the highway on my left, but was walking through the brown, scrubby grass, away from the small, peach-colored houses and the roads. I couldn't believe I hadn't bought any food to take with me when I was at the store. Somehow, the hotdogs hadn't made a dent in my hunger; they were like eating dust. And I'd run out of the food from home, except for the can of spaghetti, which was dumb to bring without a can opener. I was so hungry that my stomach felt like it was eating my esophagus. I drank the last of the water in small sips, to conserve it.

What I wouldn't give for one bag of chips. One pork chop. One—

I shook myself awake. I couldn't get delirious. I heard you could go crazy, walking in the desert, imagining oases and pork chops and stuff. So I started whistling hoping it would help me focus, but the only song I could think of was a Rolling Stones song. One that, for some reason, felt like it had been playing on loop in my head since...

Yesterday.

It was the song from Lloyd's tattoo.

Wait. No, *Dan's* tattoo. *Lloyd was a killer named Dan.*

I still didn't want to believe it. And seeing as I was losing my mind in the desert, a murderer really wasn't something I wanted to focus on. But try as I might to get the song out of my head, I soon found myself humming it. Then, I was singing at the top of my lungs.

"Hey, let me to introduce myself, my name's Lloyd, I've got a scary face!" I shouted. I couldn't remember any of the right words, what with my thoughts all jumbled and slow in the heat, but I sang on anyway. "Been riding my bike all year long, stole and killed, I'm a huge nutcase!"

I stopped and pulled out the wanted poster and stared at it. His eyes on either side of the paper fold were like two black buttons. Like two holes.

Like two bullet holes.

A huge nutcase was right—this man was insane! The hairs on the back of my neck stood up and I stuffed the poster back into my pocket. Then I remembered one of the lyrics, a real one:

"What's confusing you is the nature of my game."

But what was it? What was Lloyd's game? And why hadn't he killed me? And what if he'd been following me ever since he dropped me off at the funeral... and he showed up right now?

The heat really was getting to me. I tried to clear my head, but the song just kept repeating and repeating: "Pleased to meetcha! Hope you guess my name!"

It's Spartacus.

It's Casey.

Navin.

Aaron.

Brian.

Dan.

Lloyd.

Then I tripped and fell and scraped my palms.

I WAS ON THE VERGE of getting what Eli warned me about: Desert Delirium. I had to get out of the heat and get some sleep before I passed out and got eaten by wolves or whatever lived in New Mexico. Giant pythons or something. Just a fifteen-minute snooze. Just ten. Just a minute…

I shook myself again. I knew I had more than enough time to get to the cemetery ahead of the Goth kids. I just had to get there and then I could sleep…

That's when I saw a walled green garden ahead, looking strangely out of place in that brown and yellow landscape. I thought, *here it is: insanity. The garden will just keep moving further as I get closer.* But it didn't; it stayed right where it was. I wasn't sure it was real, though, until I touched the rusty gate for myself. It wasn't a garden at all—it was the cemetery. A little stream ran beside it, and a bunch of green trees poked out over the top of the walls, some of them quite big. For a cemetery, it sure looked inviting. Part of that must have been the heat, though.

I needed sleep. As much as I didn't want to sleep in a cemetery, that's where the trees were, and I was going to need some shade.

The cemetery was set up with all the graves in the middle and a ring of trees around the outside. The gravestones were packed pretty tight together. Some of them were really ancient looking, just little broken-looking blocks, and then there were some new ones near the perimeter. There was no place to lie down that wasn't a few feet from a grave. So where was I going to sleep? There was no way I was sleeping on the ground. I didn't want to touch that cemetery grass, made healthy from dead-people fertilizer.

The trees? There was one really large one that looked promising. And I'd slept in a tree before, back when Eli and I used to hang out in his tree house.

I hid my suitcase behind a bush and then hoisted myself up, one branch at a time, until I made it up to a large Y about eight feet off the ground. I threw a leg on either side of the wide branch, and lay my face against the bark, exhausted. It really wasn't too bad. Comfortable, even.

I was lost to the world the moment my eyes shut.

I WAS JUST A LITTLE kid when I first saw Mom fly.

I was coming home from playing with Eli, I think. I remember being in the front yard and seeing this black-and-white figure standing on the roof of our two-story house, leaning forward like one of those women on the fronts of pirate ships. It took me a few seconds to realize it was Mom. I raced to the house, but instead of calling out to her, I ducked behind a rhododendron bush.

What was she doing?

I watched in wonder. She stood there in her black swimsuit, hands on her hips, head tilted toward the sky, her toes curled over the edge of the red roof tiles. Then she turned her eyes down toward the ground. Only her black hair stirred in the breeze.

Mom always did weird things, but I'd never seen her on the roof before. I shifted my weight and a twig crunched underfoot. When I glanced down at the noise, she jumped.

I burst from the bushes but couldn't even muster a yelp, imagining her crumpled on the ground in the backyard.

But instead, there was a weird *sproing* and then she reappeared in the air a second later, sailing over our backyard fence, doing three backward somersaults, and then landing in the front yard with her back to me and her arms raised over her head.

She stood for a moment before turning around, arms still up, and beaming like a lighthouse. She stood that way until she saw me, my eyes wide and my mouth hanging open. The look of joy melted right from her face.

She walked over to me in her bare feet, her eyes searching for any sign that I was alive inside, because on the outside I wasn't moving. Really, I was a little scared. She knelt in front of me and took my hand.

"You can fly," was all I could say.

"Not yet," she said softly. She leaned in closer, her voice just a whisper. "Don't tell anybody, okay? Not William, not Daddy, not Eli. Okay?"

I nodded.

"It's our secret, Spartacus." She searched my blank face to make sure I understood, touching her cool forehead to mine.

THAT AFTERNOON, IN THE CEMETERY in the middle of the desert, I dreamt Mom crashed into a heap in the yard instead of just bouncing harmlessly off the neighbor's trampoline.

I woke with a jolt, confused. I couldn't remember where I was. Eli's backyard during a sleepover? No, wait. New Mexico. In a tree. *Getting ready to rescue my mom.*

All of this weirdness made me think I was still dreaming, so I pinched the flesh of my hand between my thumb and forefinger. The fact that it hurt sent that crackling electricity of adrenaline down my spine. I remembered it all. The kids I was supposed to meet. In a *cemetery*. At dusk. Was it dusk? I couldn't see the sun, and it was definitely starting to get dark. I couldn't have missed them, could I? The very thought made me groan out loud—and then I heard the voices coming from under the tree.

"*Shhh!* You hear that?" It was a girl's voice. Right below me.

"No," said a guy's voice. "Be quiet and concentrate."

"Puck, I really think I heard someone."

"If you did, then we're on the right track," said the guy, who must have been Puck. "Keep still."

There was a short silence and then they started humming—a weird droning noise.

I don't know why I didn't immediately tell them I was there—I knew these were probably the kids Eli had told me about. I mean, how many people hang out in a cemetery at night? But I was pretty creeped out and I had just woken up. That, and Hailey's advice echoed in my mind: mistrust everyone.

I decided to keep quiet and see what they were doing before I popped up and said, "Uh, hey, you know, I just happened to be in the same graveyard as you and wanted to know… are you going to the circus?"

Just thinking about how I was going to ask them for a ride made me blush.

I moved like an ant in honey, raising my head a bit at a time to try and see what was happening below. Finally I did. Three people, all in black, right below me. They faced each other and had candles set up in a circle between them. One guy was bent over on his knees like he was bowing, his face pressed in the grass. Then he sat up and looked straight up at me. Uh-oh, he'd heard me! Then I took in a sharp breath—his face was painted white, like *moon*-white, with black stuff around his eyes and lines across his lips.

No, not like the moon. Like a skeleton.

But he wasn't looking at me. He must have just been looking at the sky.

He was maybe sixteen or so, but it was hard to tell with all his makeup. He lit a knotted bundle of weeds on fire and waved the smoke around his head before passing it to the girl next to him and putting his face to the ground again. The others did the same. The spicy-smelling smoke rose up to me and I choked back a cough with my fist.

What were they doing?

"You ever wonder what it would be like to be buried alive?" said the non-skeleton-faced guy, Puck.

"*Shh!*" went the girl. Was this Calyxtus? It had to be.

They continued humming. I shifted in the tree, trying to see more than the tops of their heads, but my backpack made a loud rustling sound.

Their humming stopped and I flattened myself against the branch, cringing.

Nice one again, Spart.

"You *had* to have heard that," said Puck.

"It's happening," said Calyxtus.

"Do you think that was him clawing at the coffin?"

A light went on in my head: they were having a *séance*. Talking to the dead. I knew all about séances because Will had a fake one for our dead gerbil, Blueberry Pie. He'd actually dug her up and then, while we were chanting, he lowered her into our séance circle using a fishing line. It ended up being really gross—and kind of sad—rather than scary.

"It was above us, you creep. The coffin is under us. Anyway, stop being so morbid," said Calyxtus.

"It's not morbid," Puck said. "In fact, it's totally a scientific question."

"This isn't the right time," she said. "Do you want to see Mr. Prizrak or not?"

"I *do*," whined Puck.

"Then shut up."

I noticed that the skeleton-faced guy hadn't said anything at all. He was pretty creepy.

Puck said, "Try the incantation one more time."

The girl began to speak, "Zacharias Prizrak, it is on this momentous evening we beseech you to join the living. We have waited for the hour of dusk to ask you to rise on this magical evening, this most *auspicious* evening. First, the moon is in the seventh house, just as it was the night of your murder."

"Murder," Puck repeated.

Skeleton Face rang his bell. I shivered.

"Second, as Jupiter has aligned with Mars in this, the month of June, the barrier between the world of the living and the world of the spirits has reached its weakest point. The living are but shadows lost. Only in death is peace restored to mankind."

The bell rang again.

"Third, and finally, your killers have returned tonight, as if to mock your death," Calyxtus intoned.

"We shall help you seek revenge," both Calyxtus and Puck said together.

"We shall help you seek revenge," continued Calyxtus alone, "on your killers, the despicable and evil Bartholomew and his circus."

Bartholomew? Killers?

There was a weird tightening in my chest, kind of like how I'd imagine a heart attack would feel. I gasped for air and a full-body spasm sent me falling out of the tree.

CHAPTER 12

THE PHRASE "GETTING THE WIND knocked out of you" sounds a bit too mild to describe what happens to your body when you fall eight feet out of a tree. Not only that, but it glosses over the fact that not only is all the air going *out* of your lungs, none of it is going back *in*. And that means no air for gasping in pain, no air for shouting curse words, and, worst of all, no air for explaining that you're not the summoned ghost of Zacharias Prizrak.

When I hit the ground, Calyxtus started screaming bloody murder. They all scattered away from me.

"He fell from the sky!" she yelled.

After a few seconds, though, they returned. Calyxtus leaned her pale face over me. Her hair was red—so red that in the slant of remaining daylight, it looked like it was on fire.

"Crossing over must have been so painful! Look at him." She put her many-ringed hand out and touched my face while I just writhed there, gaping like a caught fish.

"Oh my god! He's so scratched up," said a voice I recognized as Puck's. A narrow white face with big curly brown hair appeared in my field of vision, looking concerned. Puck wore a weird, formal-looking cape, like a vampire in an old movie. "I guess that makes sense, because he had to break through all sorts of dimensions to get here."

"Ughhh," was all I could manage.

"He's so young," said the girl. "Is it really him?"

Skeleton Face came to loom over me. The other two looked up at him while he stared at me. I imagined him stomping me with his large leather boot. Instead, he just shook his head in a definitive *no* before walking away.

"He's just some kid!" said Calyxtus, jumping to her feet. She blew out the candles and threw them along with the blankets in a basket before chasing after Skeleton Face. "He's not a spirit, Puck! Duh!"

"He might be," said Puck, looking wounded. "He could be Prizrak in his younger form. I've heard of that."

"I'm not—" I stammered, trying again. "I want to—" The air wasn't coming yet. I wondered if I'd punctured a lung, if I was going to suffocate. Puck stood looking down at me a moment longer, looking doubtful.

"Yeah, this sucks," was all he said before following the others.

"Uggghhh," I gasped again. I had to ask them about the circus. I had to get to the circus! It was so late—they were my only hope. Somehow, I picked myself up and ran after them. Skeleton Face was sitting in the driver's seat of a black, roofless Bronco while the other two packed up their séance stuff in the back. I limped over to them, but they barely looked at me when I cleared my throat.

"Uh, hey," I finally said. "I know this is weird, but I was wondering if—"

"Get out of here, kid," said Calyxtus. She put her hands on her hips. She was in some sort of weird Victorian dress, black velvet with a string of safety pins crisscrossing the front. She must have been wearing twenty necklaces. "We've got work to do. Don't come gawk at us, *got it?*" She glared at me with icy blue eyes before shouldering a backpack. Puck stood to the side, looking bored.

"I wasn't *gawking*," I said weakly. "I was sleeping and I woke up and you were there."

"You were sleeping in a graveyard tree?" asked Puck, suddenly interested. Calyxtus didn't look impressed.

"And fell out. So sad," was all she said before stomping toward the front of the truck.

"What were you doing sleeping in the tree?" asked Puck. He looked more relaxed after she left.

"I needed a place to sleep, so I slept." I had to get Puck on my side, so I lied. "Cemeteries are so, uh, you know... peaceful. I usually sleep in them when I can. And the tree was really, uh, comfortable."

"I like the way you think," he said. "Well, we're headed out. Going to this circus. Sorry we woke you." He went to the front of the truck and when Skeleton Face started the engine, loud death metal music started blaring. I watched as Puck squeezed past Calyxtus to get into the back seat.

What was I doing? I was going to let them leave?

I ran to the open window on the driver's side and, even though Skeleton Face just looked at me with that silent stare of his, I said it. Sure, it was in a rush, and the words just poured out, but I said it.

"Could I come with you guys? I promise I'll stay out of your way. I've only got a couple bags." Skeleton Face's eyes narrowed, so I went on. "You don't know what it would mean for me to get a ride. I need to get to the circus. It's a matter of life and death!"

"Death?" Calyxtus asked, her face perking up. Skeleton Face, still not speaking, stared me down.

After what seemed like an eternity, he nodded.

WE WERE DRIVING ACROSS THE darkening desert in the roofless truck, me and Puck in the backseat, Skeleton Face and Calyxtus in the front. Puck's black cape flew behind his seat in the wind.

"I feel like Rob Zombie really gets me, you know?" Puck was saying loudly over the rushing air and the blaring synthesizers. "They don't make music like this any more."

Even though I really didn't think the music was that great, I didn't remember ever feeling so cool… and then Calyxtus turned around in her seat. "What are you, kid? Like fifteen?"

I nodded in time with the beat and she took it for a yes. Instantly, I felt even cooler.

"I really thought tonight would be the night," Puck said.

The séance! I'd almost forgotten about the whole Bartholomew-killed-a-guy story! Getting the wind knocked out of me had pushed it right out of my head.

Skeleton Face stopped at a stop sign and he and Calyxtus started kissing. I tried to look away and pretend I wasn't seeing them mash their faces together. Puck looked depressed.

"Zacharias Pizz-hat, right?" I asked.

"Prizrak!" corrected Calyxtus, pulling away for a second

"Did you say the circus killed him?" I asked.

"Oh yeah," Puck said. "It's a well-known fact."

"What happened?" I asked.

Puck looked excited to be telling the story. "See, Zacharias was a famous magician in Bartholomew's Circus. He could disappear into anything—a box, a refrigerator, a small safe. He'd just bend himself up, lock himself in—and *poof!* He was gone!"

"Dark magic," Calyxtus added. She was looking at me in the sun visor's mirror, reapplying her lipstick after the big smooch. "That's how he did it."

"But before that, he was just a P.E. teacher here in Algodones."

"No he wasn't, you nitwit," said Calyxtus.

"I'm telling the story I heard, okay?" Puck glared at her.

"Anyway," Calyxtus took over for him, "he was one of the greatest magicians in the world. Like the real deal. None of this fake camera-trick, rigged cards kind of thing. Real spirit-realm stuff. But nobody really knew about him because he was only allowed to perform with Bartholomew."

"And they wouldn't let him leave," said Puck. "Bartholomew never lets *anyone* leave. It's like the mafia—once you're in, you're in for life. The only way to leave that place is in a body bag."

I swallowed hard. I'd read a lot of rumors on the Internet about Bart, but this one was new to me. I'd never thought about him killing people before—what if my mom was afraid to leave because she knew how dangerous he was?

"How'd Prizrak get killed?" I asked.

"One night they were performing in Chicago, and Prizrak climbed into a small trunk onstage and did his disappearing act as usual. The audience cheered, expecting him to come back, but the show went on. Everybody forgot about him. The circus up and left and went to another town. Three days later, they found his body in an empty bank vault."

"He was dead?" I asked, confused.

"Yeah."

"How'd he end up in the bank vault?"

"You tell me," Puck said, his eyes glinting. "A magic trick gone wrong? A setup?"

"Bartholomew couldn't control Zacharias's dark magic," said Calyxtus, turning back to face us. "It was too strong—and Bartholomew was afraid of him. So, during the show, Bartholomew used his *own* black magic to trap Zacharias's soul in the trunk, which had an ancient Egyptian mirror that Bartholomew had bought from Romanian gypsies. Bartholomew channeled Zacharias's material vessel, his body, into the spirit realm and then into that bank vault. At least that's what they say."

"He got sent into that airtight bank vault on the Friday before a three-day weekend," said Puck.

My head hurt trying to follow the way that they talked.

"He died of suffocation in there."

I swallowed hard, thinking about all of the things I knew about Bartholomew. Kidnapping, black magic, performers killed in accidents, animal abuse, and now this—whatever it was. Murder? Maybe. I didn't really believe all the stuff about the magic. But it was still a crazy story. There had to be some truth in it if these guys believed it so much.

WE GOT INTO ALBUQUERQUE JUST before 7:30 PM. When we stopped at a convenience store a few minutes from the circus, I tried to remain calm. Really, I was itching to get moving.

I stayed in the car with Puck and Calyxtus while Skeleton Face (who still hadn't spoken and didn't seem to have a name) went in to buy snacks and boxed wine. He was either twenty-one or he had a fake ID. Calyxtus said we had to stay in the car or it would blow the whole deal (but she promised he would bring me some food for my poor empty stomach).

Puck and Calyxtus were saying something about auras and past lives when it hit me.

It was about to happen.

Time to get myself together.

My plan was to go into the circus with just the empty suitcase, so I took everything from my pockets and suitcase that I didn't need and stashed it in my backpack.

"What are you doing?" Calyxtus finally asked, seeing me stuffing my backpack. I could barely zip it.

"Uh, getting ready," I said. I couldn't tell them what I was doing, even if we did all hate the circus. She watched me with skepticism as I changed into my suit shirt and tie from the first day, and, even though it was warm, pulled on my dark blue hoodie. I added Will's black baseball hat and then slipped his pocketknife into my right pocket and the small screwdriver and ball of string into my left. I was putting Eli's dad's stethoscope around my neck when I saw the phone booth in front of the store. Right. The most important part of my plan: call the cops to let them know I'd be there.

I interrupted Puck and Calyxtus just as they began to discuss the correct etiquette for a public spirit-summoning.

"I have to make a phone call, okay? Please don't leave without me."

"We won't," said Calyxtus as I got out of the car.

Inside the booth, I dialed the 800 number that I knew by heart and went through the FBI's recorded phone menu without even listening. I knew it that well.

"Federal Bureau of Investigation, Oregon," came the voice. "Missing Persons Division."

I took a deep breath and then, with my sleeve over the mouthpiece, I said it.

"The missing child, Spartacus Ryan Zander, will be at Bartholomew's World-Renowned Circus of the Incredible tonight. In Albuquerque, New Mexico."

"Who is this?"

"That's not important."

"How do you have this information?"

I hadn't thought that far into the conversation, so I hung up, heart pounding. It was officially happening!

And that's when I saw her through the window, in the convenience store. She was in line in front of Skeleton Face.

It was Mom.

CHAPTER 13

SINCE MY MOM LEFT, I kept having this dream where I'd see her in weird places. I'd dream that I was walking home after school, and she'd be walking down the other side of the street. Or I'd dream I was in class and she'd stroll by out in the hall. Or in places I'd never been before. She would always be going about her own business, and never even notice me.

When dreams suddenly happen in real life, though—that's when things get really weird, like you're not sure if you're in the real world or in the dream world.

BY THE TIME I'D RUN to the Bronco, pulled the suitcase out, and launched myself back out on the sidewalk, Mom was already out the glass doors and walking away, her tall red boots clacking on the cement. Except for the circus-type boots, she was in street clothes, which was weird because the circus should have been starting any minute. I practically bowled her over, suitcase in tow.

She turned, shock showing on her face as I grabbed her hand.

"Mom, I know it's a surprise to see me," I said, racing through my rehearsed speech. I pulled her by the arm toward the side of the building as I spoke. "There's no time to explain. You have to get in the suitcase now. I'll get you out of here."

"What are you talking about? Let go of me!" Mom pulled herself free and gave me a look like she didn't know me. "And you're nuts if you think I'd fit in your stupid suitcase."

I couldn't believe this was happening. I mean, I knew it was possible, what with the whole Stockholm syndrome thing, but still!

"I'm here for *you,* Mom," I said, slowly now, in what I hoped was a calm voice. I'd heard them talk this way to mental patients on TV. "Just get in the suitcase." I took her hand again, but this time she shook it off more violently.

"*Let go of me!*" she hissed. "Why do you keep calling me that?"

Now *I* was shocked. I stared at her, and she glared back at me with the yellow streetlight playing across her face. I realized something was wrong. I mean, *this was my mother.* It was.

But that wasn't her nose.

And there was a mole on her chin. Mom didn't have a mole. But the rest... the rest was... *it was Mom.* But it wasn't...

Just then a man's voice came from the other side of the parking lot.

"Hurry up!"

"Coming!" Mom yelled back, walking away from me.

I hesitated for just a moment before chasing after her. At that point I was only fifty percent sure it was Mom, but I couldn't just let her go.

At the other end of the dimly lit parking lot, Mom joined a large man in a suit. Neither of them were even looking back at me as they walked toward—gulp—a black van! It looked just like the one in my imagination, the one Eli had described the day after Mom disappeared. Could it be that this really *was* Mom, but that the circus had disguised her for some reason?

I had to do something. I couldn't let them get away again. When the man stopped to get his keys, I swung my suitcase up blindly and hit him in the head.

I don't think he even flinched.

When he turned, unscathed and unconcerned, I saw that he wasn't a man. I mean, he was, or at least he had been at some point. But somewhere down the line he'd turned into a shark.

Yeah, I'm talking about an honest-to-god *sharkman*.

No hair, no eyebrows, and eyeballs that were completely black. He had flaps of skin on his neck that looked like gills. He even had a dorsal fin that poked through a slit in his jacket. *How does a man have a fin?*

And I'd just hit him in the head with a suitcase.

"And you did that because…?" the sharkman asked me, speaking carefully. That's when I noticed that he had way too many teeth, teeth that were filed down to points. All my organs felt like they were shrinking at the same time.

His blank, black eyes narrowed, but he didn't take a step toward me. Instead, he turned to the mom lookalike.

"Come on, Charlene," he said. "Let's get this show on the road. We're late." Mom looked at me like I was a bug to be stomped. I mean, Charlene did. Then she bent down to whisper in my ear.

"I'm not who you think I am and you'd better back off with your little suitcase trick before you try it on the wrong woman. You do this again and Bartholomew will pop your head off like a dandelion. Got it?"

I nodded carefully, my head feeling only barely attached to my body. Then, the sharkman and my mom—I mean my not-mom—got into their black van and drove off into the night.

I DRAGGED MYSELF BACK TOWARD the convenience store parking lot, feeling like my whole body was a dead weight. Not-Mom and Sharkman were probably headed to the circus now, meaning I had *more* people to watch out for.

Ugghh.

I felt sick and shaky just thinking about it—and thinking about that guy's teeth. And his gills. Then, I remembered that Bartholomew kept a plastic surgeon on staff. Besides making Bartholomew look young, maybe he made men look like sharks. And was that why that lady looked like Mom?

Skeleton Face stood in front of the Bronco, waiting. I picked up my pace and clambered behind the folded front seat, flinching when he slammed it down after me. Calyxtus and Puck just stared as I put my suitcase at my feet.

"So, you sleep in cemeteries *and* you knock huge freaks over the head with suitcases?" Puck asked finally. I blushed. I didn't know they'd been watching me.

"You're one crazy piece of work," said Puck. Calyxtus gave a low whistle of agreement.

"This, um, this isn't just a normal day for me." Boy, was it not.

"That guy was what, a vampire?" Calyxtus said.

"No, I think he was a shark," I said. "He had a fin."

"Circus folk," said Puck. He looked off in the distance, narrowing his eyes. "They cross everyone."

Skeleton Face got back on the road. The traffic was thick. Up ahead about a mile, searchlights crisscrossed each other in the sky. Bartholomew's searchlights.

We were close.

As we slowed to a crawl in the line of traffic leading up to the circus, I was startled by a low, gravelly voice.

"You said getting to the circus was a matter of life and death."

It was Skeleton Face. *Skeleton Face was actually talking. To me.* His white eyes met mine in the rearview mirror for a split second before going back to concentrating on the brake lights ahead of us. Puck and Calyxtus sat there with their mouths open, exchanging a look.

"Steve hasn't said a word in three weeks," Puck whispered to me. *Steve?*

"Life… and death," Steve repeated, making each word sound like he was weighing them in his hands. "What did you mean by that?"

I didn't answer right away. I weighed words, too: the lies I could tell. The truths. Maybe I should tell them everything. I mean, they hated Bartholomew almost as much as I did. But then I remembered what Hailey had said: you don't trust people until they've earned it. I liked these guys and all, but what if they couldn't keep a secret? What if they blew my plan?

"Whose death?" Steve said. "Yours or...?"

"My family's," I answered, not meaning to say even that. It just slipped out, but when it did I knew it was the truth. That's what I'd meant when I first said "life or death," even if I didn't realize it at the time. If I didn't get Mom back, I would blame Dad, I would blame Will, and I'd blame myself. And Will and Dad would never trust me again. No matter what happened, if I didn't get Mom back, things would never be the same in the Zander house. Ever.

Steve swung into a makeshift parking lot in someone's yard. The big, jovial guy taking our parking money saw Steve's made-up face and the weird clothes in the car and grinned.

"Well, I see the circus *has* come to town!" the man laughed, handing Steve his change. When no one laughed, he tried again: "Send in the clowns!"

It wasn't the awkward silence alone that stripped the smile from the guy's face but also the force of the four sets of glaring eyeballs. He was outnumbered.

"Uh, take the last spot there, by the fence," he muttered, looking sheepish.

Apparently the stink-eye is a million times more effective when you're in a group.

I could really use a posse at home, I realized. *Comrades.* Another Blue and White word.

We marched single-file down the side of the highway, headed toward the fairgrounds. Just before we reached the black-barred fence, Skeleton Face—I mean Steve—stopped so abruptly that Calyxtus walked right into the back of him. The crowd passed around us like we were stones in a creek, looking at us warily (I think it was Puck's cape, more than anything).

"This is where we need to leave you," Steve said. "We can't have outsiders witness the séance."

"Oh, hey, no problem," I said, honestly grateful to be losing them so I could concentrate. "Thanks again for the ride, though. It really helped."

"We're happy to help any kindergoth," said Puck.

"Let's not get carried away," said Calyxtus, turning to him with an irritated flip of her hair. "He's no kindergoth."

"He could be. Or maybe he's a baby bat. But in a good way. Look at him! Sleeps in cemeteries, wears a tie? And look at that sunken, pale face…"

I have a sunken, pale face? The road must have been getting to me. Still, I had no clue what they were talking about. I needed to get out of there. Mom was maybe a hundred yards away, and I was just standing here.

"He might just be weird," argued Calyxtus.

"You're always so snotty!" Puck shot back.

"I'll remind you both we have a spirit to summon," Steve said seriously, like an angry parent. "Now *quit it!* Both of you."

I shifted from one foot to the other and then remembered something I had to do.

"Hey, before you go, would you guys mind blocking me for a second?" I asked and they let me arrange them next to the large green dumpster that was by the fence. "Puck, could you hold your cape out?"

"It's a cloak," Puck sniffed, but he did it anyway. While the three of them stood there, I ducked behind them and pushed my backpack as far under the dumpster as I could, hopefully where no one would see it. I scrambled out to find Puck raising his arms in his cape even higher than I showed him, like a giant bat. And he was hissing.

"What are you *doing?*" I exclaimed.

"If they're going to stare, I might as well give them something to stare at," he answered, grinning at a little boy who looked truly afraid. Calyxtus looked annoyed, her black lip curled. I sensed another argument and headed it off.

"So are you guys going in?" I asked.

"No," said Calyxtus. "We're going to find a quiet place out here where we can commune with the spirits."

"Oh, okay. Thanks again," I said. "I have to get inside before... well, before it's too late." I hoped that sounded ominous enough for them.

"What are you going to do?"

"The less you know the better," I said. "It goes too deep." Steve nodded at this, as if it all made complete sense to him.

"Give them hell," said Puck. "For all of us."

I nodded. "Thanks. And good luck to you guys with the whole Zacharias Prizehat thing."

"Prizrak," muttered Calyxtus.

"May your fortune be in life—and not death," said Steve. I didn't know what that meant, but it didn't sound very encouraging. I gave them a half-wave before stepping into the river of people headed to the circus.

CHAPTER 14

CHURCH-ORGAN-Y CIRCUS MUSIC MIXED WITH the voices of the crowd in a loud, crazy whoosh. Everyone was stamping their feet, trying to get past the narrow gate before the show started. I had to get in before the crowd shrunk down. They were my camouflage.

I muttered *excuse me*'s while elbowing my way through, knocking into people's legs with the suitcase. Some guy called out "Hey!" as I pushed past and accidently stomped on his foot, but I ignored him and kept battling the horde.

As soon as I got through the front gate with Mom's suitcase, I was paranoid that everyone knew who I was, even in the dim light. My telltale freckled lip felt like a spotlight, like a homing beacon, sending out the message, *"The runaway is here!"* I also had Sharkman and Not-Mom to worry about. Any moment, someone might recognize me and drag me to meet Bartholomew. I got really worried when I saw two uniformed guards standing on either side of the entrance, but they didn't seem to notice me.

Up ahead were the ticket takers, funneling people through a few lines. I let myself be pushed forward with the crowd. I could either pay to get in, or try to sneak around back. I'd have to play it by ear.

I was almost to the edge of the hubbub when, through a break in the crowd, I saw the tent: red canvas with lights glowing through a tear in the roof. I wondered why they weren't using the fancy-looking red and blue striped dome tent from the photos on the website. It wasn't too impressive actually. More of Bartholomew's lies—the pictures on his website were probably from a much better circus.

I was almost to the tent's entrance when I saw, about a foot to my right, a NO TRESPASSING sign, and the darkness beyond. That's where I needed to be—on the side of the tent that was away from the lights and the people.

I glanced over my shoulder, making sure the guards weren't looking in my direction, and then zipped around the right side of the tent. Whether anyone in the line saw me, I don't know—but no one said a word.

As soon as I left the main area, I was plunged into darkness, with only the passing spotlight occasionally reflecting down from the night sky.

I pulled up my dark hood, just in case anyone was back there with a flashlight. I waited for my eyes to adjust and then picked my way around the tent stakes and ropes, rehearsing my story in my head, the if-I-get-caught story: *I didn't have any money to see the circus, I thought I could just peek in a little. I'm really, really sorry, and it will never happen again.* It wasn't great, but I was going to stick to it.

Or run, whichever was easier.

I was prepared to see a whole swarm of trucks behind the circus tent—the trucks that carried the performers, animals, and equipment—but so far there was nothing.

I pulled my stethoscope out from under my sweatshirt and put the earpieces in. The stethoscope made me feel even more like James Bond than the suit. I crept along, running the round chestpiece along the canvas, listening for the right spot to go in. I didn't really know what the right spot would sound like, but I was pretty certain I'd know it when I found it.

The noises were clearer through the stethoscope. I could actually hear kids whining for popcorn and cotton candy and parents telling them to wait until intermission. I continued around the back of the tent, listening and searching for a way in, inching toward the voices ever so carefully, my steps silent. I pushed the chestpiece further along, off the main tent and onto a rectangular tent that jutted from it. Right there, at the corner where the round tent met the rectangular tent, I could hear two voices directly on the other side of the canvas. I held my breath, knowing I was just inches from them. They were whispering.

"It's the one on the right that's out. It just blew."

"Didn't I tell you to re-check them all beforehand?"

"Did you hear what I said? I said it just blew out. What was I going to do beforehand? See into the future?"

Cursing followed and I grinned, moving ahead. I'd made it past all the tourists and the commoners—I'd found the workers in the staging area.

Bartholomew was probably in the ring announcing, and there was no reason for security guards to be in back with the performers. No one would notice me once I was inside and backstage because everyone would be too busy. At least that's what I hoped.

I kept poking along, listening for a safe, silent spot. I heard things being dragged around and assembled, people giving directions, but nothing helpful. I didn't hear my mom or anyone talking about her. Finally, though, along the back wall of the rectangular tent, things were quiet. No voices, nothing being moved.

This is the spot. I took off the stethoscope and pulled out Will's pocketknife. Kneeling on the ground, I put the knifepoint to the canvas. This was it.

This. Was. It.

My heart was pounding and my hands were shaking. I was moments from trespassing, from destroying property. *Moments from seeing my mom.*

Come on, Spartacus, I ordered myself. *Do it.*

Somehow the name made me feel a bit braver.

I took a deep breath and plunged the knife in.

I peered under the flap I'd made in the tent and saw that I had cut my way into what looked like the performers' bathroom. It was a small, dark space with a metal trough for a urinal, a portable sink, and a makeshift door made out of a hanging curtain. *Perfect.* I wriggled in through the hole I'd cut, pulling the suitcase behind me.

I walked over and peeked behind the curtain door, half expecting Mom to be standing right there. But the canvas corridor was empty, no one in sight.

I didn't want anyone stumbling in on me while I got ready. I looked at the curtain. There was a rope hanging from it that I tied to the bottom of the tent, effectively "locking" it. Then I shoved the suitcase under the small metal washstand.

Now for the tough part. I had to walk among the circus folk—and it was only a matter of time before someone saw me and asked what I was doing there. The further I could get before that happened, the smoother the plan was going to go. To buy myself more time, I had to blend in.

Looking in the bathroom mirror, I was expecting to look kind of mature, like someone who could possibly be working a summer job at the circus... but the kid staring back at me looked all of ten years old. Dirty, pale, scared. I pulled my sweatshirt off and stuffed it next to my suitcase. Underneath I had my white shirt and tie, almost the same outfit I'd worn to the funeral. I straightened the tie and flattened my hair with water from the sink. I tried to wipe a smear of dirt from my forehead and discovered it was a bruise—maybe from the car accident? Then I tried some different facial expressions, trying to capture the maturity I felt—my best was a half-scowl that kinda made me look like Will. I decided it was good enough.

The tent hallway was strung with dim, red light bulbs. It was still empty, which seemed a little weird to me. I would have thought there would be at least a few people bustling around.

Taking a deep breath, I strode, purposeful and scowling, out from behind the curtain and toward a bundle of black and red stilts leaning against the canvas. I hefted two heavy sets onto my shoulder, hoping to look like I worked there.

The corridor led past a series of curtained "rooms." I made my way carefully, sneaking a look into each one. The first was an empty dressing room with a couple of makeup desks with those mirrors with lights all around them. The second was full of costumes: feather boas, all kinds of hats, huge pants, masks. In the third room, a lady stood in front of a mirror, facing away from me. She had a pirate ship tattooed on her back and was pinning peacock feathers into her long black hair. I peeked into the next room, where there was a small old man sitting in a child-sized lawn chair and smoking a cigar. I mean he wasn't just small, he was a bona fide little person, as small as a kindergartener. Fighting the urge to stop and stare, I kept moving.

Then I heard a booming voice from the direction of the main tent. It was the announcer or the ringmaster—maybe it was even Bartholomew himself. The voice asked the audience to turn off their phones, then said that they wouldn't be able to leave during the performance.

That's when I reached the last curtain.

I crossed my fingers, desperately hoping to find Mom on the other side.

I opened the curtain an inch—and almost screamed when I saw a headless woman propped up in a chair. I put my hand over my mouth and it took a few seconds for me to realize it was a dummy. It was just very, very realistic.

The rest of the room was filled with really cool things. There was a shrunken head on a plant stand, a birdcage stuffed with cooing white doves, a bunch of chainsaws, and what looked like an umbrella stand full of swords.

I stepped back into the hallway. Well, that was all the rooms. All that was left were the main backstage area and the ring where the show was taking place. Bart's circus wasn't that big. Where were the lions or the tigers or other animals? I decided that they probably wouldn't store the animals in the tent; they'd keep them somewhere safe, like in trucks.

But where were their big trucks? You'd need trucks to keep animals and equipment in, wouldn't you? You'd think they would have been out back, but I hadn't seen any.

Then I heard the audience, their shushing flowing through the tent walls like the sound of the ocean. What followed was a long expectant silence.

It was starting.

For a split second, I imagined what it would be like to be on the other side in that moment right after the lights go out but before the show begins, watching the circus like a regular kid with Will and Mom and Dad. I was about to get all boo-hoo-ey when I heard some people talking nearby and I remembered my mission. I started walking back the way I'd come, toward the backstage area. I was startled when a girl about my age, with black hair and dressed in black sequins, rounded the corner.

"Remmy?" she called in a loud whisper. I flattened myself against the curtains to make room for her to pass. She headed to the back of the tent, back toward where I'd seen the little man. She didn't so much as glance at me. "Remmy!"

Still safe, I moved on. The hallway opened up into an almost pitch-black common area. I could see a few faces lit up by flashlights here and there, and a large, red-curtained entrance to the main ring. A small group of performers was lined up in front of it, hopping and stretching, like runners getting ready for a race. There were only fifteen or so performers total. No animals in sight. Not one hundred people, like some sites said. Bartholomew's Circus was pretty unimpressive.

Beyond the red curtain, a strobe light began to flash, sending darting shadows into the small room. I scanned the faces in the audience for my mom, and for Sharkman and Not-Mom. I still held the stilts high on my shoulder so that they blocked my face. In the darkness and crazy strobe light shadows, it was almost impossible to recognize anyone. It didn't help that nearly everyone was wearing makeup or a mask.

My eyes landed on a female mime in an old-fashioned tuxedo. Too small, too young. Then there was the woman closest to me, wearing a black leather swimsuit, with a giant, ten-foot snake draped around her shoulders. The snake could probably swallow a Labrador and still have room for dessert. The lady was letting the snake smell her face with its darting tongue. Interesting, but not my mom.

Suddenly it made sense why I hadn't seen Mom yet. Obviously, she was already out there onstage with everyone else. Up in the catwalks or under the stage, waiting to explode out of something. I relaxed a bit, knowing my chance would come, even if it meant waiting for her to return at intermission or at the end.

When the introduction music started on the other side of the curtain, everyone tensed, including me.

"Ladies and gentleman!" came the announcer's voice from onstage. My grip tightened on the stilts.

"We are charmed to entertain you on this very curious evening! The fine performers you are about to see have prepared a veritable feast for your five senses! There will be OUTSTANDING things here, in this very ring, UNUSUAL things that you may not understand—TERRIFYING things you'll wish you didn't understand—and ASTONISHING things you may never wish to see again. But I assure you, ladies and gentlemen, that you have arrived, out of sheer serendipity, at a SPECTACULAR event you'll never forget. We're sorry Bartholomew couldn't make it, but we know you're going to have more fun with us as we bring you—The World-Renowned Sideshow of Curiosities and Mayhem!"

As the performers rushed out through the curtains, my mouth hung open and I struggled to understand what I'd just heard.

Sideshow of Curiosities and Mayhem? I repeated to myself. Wait. Had they changed their name?

I saw the audience through a gap in the curtain. Their faces flashed orange, reflecting flames on the stage.

A *sideshow...? What's a sideshow...?* And what had the guy said about Bartholomew?

I started to hyperventilate as the snare drums began rat-a-tatting wildly. Now I understood why there were hardly any performers or workers. And no animals. No big trucks.

They'd left. They'd cancelled their show. This wasn't Bartholomew. This was a sideshow, whatever *that* was.

Stupid tears pooled up in my eyes so I could barely see. I stood there like a moron, still holding the stupid stilts.

Then the drums faded and everything went silent, like I had just dived underwater. The room was spinning—it felt like the performers were circling around me. A woman in a red tutu bumped into me as she rushed past, but it all felt so far away. I fell over much easier than I should have, dropping the stilts and mumbling "sorry, sorry," the whole way down to the ground.

CHAPTER 15

THEY TOLD ME LATER IT was a nervous breakdown, but I knew it couldn't have been *that* bad.

I knew all about nervous breakdowns. Dad had one once at Will's statewide triathlon when Will's bike wheel came off. It was right at the start of the race, too, when the racers had just taken off and the crowd was cheering. Will's bike made a big snapping sound and Will went down hard while his wheel went rolling away.

Then Dad kind of made a snapping sound, too. He just lost it, flinging his hat to the ground and shouting, "RE-RIDE! RE-RIDE! RE-RIDE!" Some other fathers came and took him away and I had to pretend I didn't know him. He'd always taken Will's bike riding a little too seriously.

Yeah, there was no way I'd been *that* bad.

But apparently the circus people were worried the audience

would hear me. As they led me out a back door in the tent, I was yelling (according to them) the whole way, *"You deserve this, Poop Lip! You really, really do! You stupid idiot!"*

Which is pretty ridiculous. I might have been a little upset, what with coming a thousand miles to save Mom, and finding out she'd just left town, and being a criminal and a runaway and, basically, a complete failure. Sure, I was upset. But would I really go out of my mind and forget what I was doing and start shouting? Did I really think I deserved to fail like that?

I guess the answer in my mind was yes. Yes, I did.

THE NEXT THING I KNEW, I was waking up sitting on the bumper of a tractor-trailer.

And I don't mean waking up like you do in the morning. It was more like I just gradually faded back into my body—which was already in the process of doing stuff without me. I was sitting up in the back of the trailer with my legs hanging off the edge. Cupped in my hands was a mason jar filled with something cool. I smelled it. Lemonade. How long had I been there, drinking lemonade? Where was I?

It was dark and we were outside, not too far from the circus tent. The occasional burst of music and cheers from the show interrupted the quiet. Wait, *we?*

I did a double take. A small boy sat beside me, smoking a cigar. I could see the orange of the tip burn as he inhaled.

"Life's just like that sometimes, you know?" he was saying at a fast clip. I felt like maybe we'd been talking for a while, but I had no idea what we were talking *about.*

The child waved his cigar in the air. Scratch that. It was a man, a very small man, waving his cigar in the air. I remembered seeing him in the dressing room earlier. Right.

"You see that opening, that light," he continued, "and know life is about to change. You think you made the right choice and then *bam!* just like that, you're having a nervous breakdown backstage at the wrong circus. Or, in his case, stuck, staring up at the fangs of death."

I nodded politely and then looked to where he was gesturing with his cigar.

A few feet from the trailer, a flashlight was set up on a tripod, shining down on a hula-hoop laid out flat on the ground. In the center of the hula-hoop, half-emerged from a crack in the asphalt, was a rat. A large, gray, squeaking rat, its front paws scrabbling at the ground, its back-end squeezed—and stuck—in the crack in the pavement. A few inches away from the rat, a dirty, white cat sat very still, its eyes wide with interest.

I felt like I had just woken up into a dream.

"Life imitates the circus and the circus imitates life," the old man said. And that's exactly what was in front of us: a small, bizarre, miniature circus. The hula-hoop was the circus ring. The cat was the ringmaster. The rat was... just a rat, I guess. Add in the music coming from the real circus and it was almost funny... in a sick way.

"What will happen to it?" I asked. Just watching it made my stomach squirm, like it was me trapped there.

"If we leave it? I'd say it has three ways out." He spoke around his cigar and counted on his hand. "One, a heart attack. Two, starvation—but that would take some time and doesn't seem too likely with Lousy sitting right there watching, does it? And Lousy himself is the third option."

I watched with wide eyes as Lousy the cat hunkered down on his belly to watch the rat. He didn't seem ready to do anything anytime soon. He looked quite content just watching. At least for now.

"You're not just going to leave it in there, are you?" I asked.

"Why shouldn't I?" he said. "It's life. We all make choices, without knowing what the result will be. We all end up in the wrong place at the wrong time..." The child-sized old man looked up at me knowingly from under his wild gray eyebrows. "What responsibility do *I* have to help it out?"

"'With great power comes great responsibility,'" I said, the quote just coming into my mind. "I guess because we know we have the power to help, we should at least try."

The old man nodded, pursed his lips, and looked impressed.

"Very wise, very wise, yes," he said. "That was Winston Churchill, right?"

"Uh, no," I said. "Actually it's from Spiderman."

"Mmmm," he said, looking back at the struggling rat. "Well, it's wise, nonetheless. What say you we get him out?" He reached back into the trailer and pulled out what looked like a giant pair of pliers with a spring in the middle and a wide, flat spatula thing on the tip.

"Here." He handed the weird tool to me before hopping down and plodding over to the hula-hoop. He nudged the cat out of the way. "Get, Lousy!"

I got off the truck and knelt with him next to the rat. It had gone motionless, but I could see its whiskers twitching and I swear I could hear its little heart tapping away at the speed of sound.

"So, you want me to just... grab him?" I asked.

"No, no, no," he said. He indicated the tool I was holding. "These are spreaders. Put them in the crack next to him, as close as you can, and then squeeze the handles." He put his hand on the cat and held him lightly by the scruff of the neck.

I put the spreaders in the crack and squeezed, like he'd said. In a few seconds the ground moved just enough, and the rat darted away into the darkness. The cat tried to chase it, but the little man held him for a good count.

"Give him a fighting chance, eh, Lousy?" he said. Then he let him go. Lousy took a few steps in the direction of the rat before changing his mind and rolling in the dirt instead.

"What are these for?" I asked, holding the spreaders up.

"For when the lion doesn't let you go," he said. He took them from me and used them like a cane to push himself to his feet.

"Name's Remmy," he said, putting out his hand. I shook it.

"Spartacus," I said, without thinking. I don't know why I said it. I'd never introduced myself as Spartacus before. I cringed a little bit, wondering if I'd really screwed up big time. If he decided to mention me to Bartholomew, I'd be in big trouble.

"Spartacus? Oh, *really* now," Remmy said, giving me a double-take. "Now *that's* a circus name. I'd say you're ready."

WHILE REMMY WENT INTO THE tent to get us some food, I sat there wondering what to do. I could just head home. My running away would be a lesson to Dad and Will, a message that I wasn't going to put up with their crap anymore. I imagined walking in the door, putting my bags down non-chalantly, while they sat open-mouthed in the living room. I'd wave hello, get a soda from the fridge, and when I'd come back, they'd still be sitting there, staring. Dad would finally say, "Where have you been?" and I'd just say "Out" before going up to my room.

The thought made me smile.

But, on the other hand, I could also imagine being sent to boarding school—which really wouldn't have been too bad considering my current status as the Brenville boy who had bared all. But it was more likely I'd be grounded and trapped in the house with Will and Dad. Forever. That thought didn't make me smile.

Remmy came out, holding two bowls of hot chili. We sat in lawn chairs—him in a small one, me in a regular-sized one—and ate. It was hard not to gulp it down. After I finished my bowl, he went to get me more. I had three bowls.

The sounds of the show continued to drift out from inside the tent. Cheers, yells, organ music. I felt more peace-ful than I had since I started my journey. I guess once the worst has happened, it's easier to relax.

As we ate, Remmy talked, and I learned.

Remmy's sideshow, The World-Renowned Sideshow of Curiosities and Mayhem, was the sideshow for Bartholomew's Circus. Remmy explained that the sideshow is actually supposed to perform *with* the circus.

"But on the side, get it?" he asked. "Sideshow?"

Remmy's team usually traveled with a lot of different circuses and carnivals and even did a few state fairs, but things had been slow, so they had signed a three-year con-tract working only with Bartholomew.

"We've always been our own company," said Remmy. "Sure, we travel with them and it saves on cost, and maybe it pays better than being on our own, but they don't respect us." He spat on the ground. "But then, I don't respect *him*. No ringmaster worth his salt would cancel at the last second and have the sideshow fill in. And on the last night of his run when everybody's expecting the best show? No sir."

"So you guys perform if he doesn't show up?"

"Yep—but then we're not the *sideshow* any more. Then we're just *The Show*," said Remmy, fanning out his fingers dramatically. "And it's a shame, a dirty shame, to treat customers like that. These people, they didn't come to see us. Now, I'm not saying we're not giving them a show. You ever seen our show?"

I shook my head.

"Oh, you should. I mean, we do it all. We got the knife throwing and the sword eating, The Human Blockhead, Spidora, and The Two-faced Man, and all the fire breathing stunts—but you'll see it all tomorrow."

Why would he think I'd be seeing the show tomorrow?

"But these people?" he continued, ignoring my confusion and gesturing at the tent. "They don't come for that. They want the trapeze, the lions, the elephants. They want Athena, the Human Cannonball. The big stuff."

My eyes widened at this. This man actually knew my mom! I couldn't say anything about it, though. Not yet anyway. Got to keep up the *mistrust*. Right, Hailey? Even if Remmy did seem really swell. *Swell?* Did I actually call someone swell?

Remmy was still going on about Bartholomew, looking miffed. "You just don't cancel like that. And he's done this kind of thing twice in the last year. Who does that?"

"I don't know," I said politely.

"I've been in the sideshow sixty-three years now, and I never seen no one do it like this. Bartholomew's got a good circus, I admit. But he runs it all backwards. Not professional in the slightest. Like he doesn't even care about what people think. It's not just the cancelling. It's everything. They don't tell us anything until the last second. They give us our cut of the profits late. To get any info out of them is like pulling teeth."

Remmy paused for a moment, catching his breath. He spooned some chili into his mouth, and then said thoughtfully, "Bartholomew seems like a real gentleman when you first meet him, too. But then you get to know him and… I'm just disgusted with the boy if you want to know the truth. I think he's a no-good fink."

"Why did they cancel?" I asked.

Remmy eyed me like he wasn't sure how much he should tell me. "Well, this time they said their lead girl had given everyone Pink Eye. Doesn't that just beat all? *Pink Eye shouldn't stop a circus.* No sir, no circus with any sense of civic duty, anyway." He spat on the ground again. Then he looked at me with a knowing grin.

"You looked confused earlier when I said that you'd see our show tomorrow," he said. "You thought I didn't notice. Maybe most people wouldn't. You don't get to be a show-man like I am without being able to read people and keep some patter up and then come back to it."

"I *was* wondering what you meant by that," I stammered.

"Well, I assumed you'd be with us tomorrow, and not leaving our fine company, because I know that you're trying to get a job with Bartholomew."

I paused, confused. Then I nodded with a grin. I had to go with this. It was a good cover, now that I thought of it…

"How did you know?" I managed to ask.

Remmy winked at me and pulled a flask out of his jacket—a flask of something that smelled really strong, like something from a medicine cabinet. Lousy appeared out of nowhere, rubbing against his chair.

"Kids showing up at the circus is old hat," he said. "Bunch of kids want to get a job with Bartholomew's. But kids accidently showing up at our little old sideshow when they think they're at Bartholomew's? That, my friend, is *new* hat."

He took a drink from his flask and then poured a little bit in the lid and set it on the ground. The cat drank it up like it was cream. Then, as if he was reading my mind faster than I could connect the dots and see the whole picture, Remmy invited me to travel with the sideshow to Bartholomew's next show in Las Vegas—just two days away.

"And we'll give you some help for your tryouts. You can't breathe fire yet, can you? Yeah, that'd be a good one for you to learn. Don't look so agog, boy, it's not flattering."

I *was* agog. I don't think I'd ever been agog before, but I was then. Breathe fire? I was going to learn how to *breathe fire?*

"Why would you help me?" I just about squeaked.

"Well, there was this man named Winston Churchill—a man who was very much like Spiderman," he said. "And this man said, 'the price of greatness is responsibility.' And since the Sideshow of Curiosities and Mayhem is great—and since Churchill is the only church I've ever attended—I feel it's my responsibility to help you out.

"Besides, I like your moxie. I think you deserve a chance," he added. "I may not think too highly of Bartholomew's Circus, but I can understand why you'd want to join up."

"Thank you," I said, reaching out and shaking his small hand so hard that he had to pull it away. Just thinking about getting to Bartholomew's gave me adrenaline again. Adrenaline and hope.

But I had to find out how safe I was, how much I should mistrust old Remmy.

"Do you guys know Bartholomew's people pretty well?" I asked, hoping it sounded like I was just trying to schmooze for the job.

"Kid, do you know what your butt crack looks like without a mirror?"

"Uh," I thought. "I don't know. I mean, it probably looks just like any butt crack. So, yes?"

"Well, you've got a good point there," said Remmy. "But what I meant was no, not really. I mean, in some ways we know them pretty well. We work with them a lot and know their performers and their acts. But Bartholomew runs a pretty tight ship. He doesn't let us in the tent when the circus is going on. And none of his people get too friendly with us."

This was all good news for me and The Plan. If the sideshow and Bartholomew's people weren't too close, that meant I could stay better hidden from the circus.

"But," Remmy said, his face going serious. "You have to know what you're getting into. I want you to really think about this tonight, before you do anything."

He leaned forward in his seat and I did too.

"Bartholomew's may be a circus, but it sure ain't no picnic. That circus has some mean folks in it. Like the kind of folks you wouldn't want to turn your back on unless you were wearing chainmail under your jacket, if you get what I'm saying."

I wasn't sure I did, but I got his general point.

"I don't want to talk too bad against Bartholomew's, because there's a lot of good folks, too, but I think you should know."

I wasn't sure what expression I should put on for Remmy: shocked by the news or determined to join the circus despite Remmy's warnings. Inside, of course, the news didn't surprise me. I already knew Bartholomew was evil.

I don't know what Remmy read in my face, but he leaned back in his chair.

"Just think about it, okay?"

I nodded, and he seemed content with that.

It turned out Remmy didn't actually perform in the side-show—he was what was known as the "outside talker."

"The outside talker," Remmy said, "is the guy who stands outside the circus or fair or whatever, and talks to people outside to try to get them to come in. And I was one of the best. You should have seen me when I was at the top of my game and we had a Single-O set up on the midway," he said. "I can get any mark to pay any amount to see something."

He told me a Single-O was one of those things you see at the fair where there is just one thing inside, maybe a scary animal or a lady covered with gorilla-hair or a fake head in a jar. Sometimes the animals are taxidermied, like the alligator-man I'd seen once in Washington—a mummified alligator with a human head.

"We have a pretty great Single-O with Matilda, if I do say so myself. She's a genuine killer from Madagascar!"

"Matilda," I repeated, thinking about the spreaders from earlier. "What is she? A lion? A bear?" Or maybe he was he talking about a person.

"A killer. That's all you need to know. Here's a clue—if she looks at you and decides it's your turn to go, she'll point a finger at you. Then it's just a matter of time before you're dead."

"Why would anyone want to see that?" I asked.

"So you believe it?"

"No, not really," I scoffed. But I hoped he wouldn't make me see her. It. Whatever it was.

"You have to see her. You'll be beating yourself up the rest of your life if you don't."

I saw that he was trying to sell me on Matilda like I was one of the people at the fair.

"Just tell me, not like I'm a, uh, what did you call them?"

"Marks? The suckers?"

"Yeah, like I'm not a mark—is it real?"

"Do your parents know where you are?" Remmy shot back. I sat back in my seat and looked away, embarrassed. I didn't answer.

"See? There are some things you can't tell people," he said. "Even if you like them."

I looked back at him and he gave me a small apologetic smile before lighting up another cigar.

He told me how he'd been with the sideshow since the 1950s. He and another performer, a younger guy named Robin Marx, had bought the sideshow a few years back. Robin was the front man inside, running the whole operation, keeping the performers comfortable and the patrons happy.

"You won't find a much better bunch than my gang," said Remmy, nodding his head. "But then, you'll be meeting them all soon. What say we get you set up for the night?"

WHILE REMMY WAS SETTING UP a small bedroll for me in one of the dressing rooms, I fetched my suitcase and headed toward the fairgrounds entrance.

The show was still going on, so the parking lot was packed, but there was no one around. I wondered if my Goth friends might still be around somewhere, trying to wake the dead. They'd probably figured out it was the wrong circus, though.

I pulled my backpack from its hiding spot under the dumpster, and started walking back, lost in thought. Why had Bartholomew split town? I thought maybe it was because his goons had spotted me in the convenience store parking lot, but Remmy said they'd cancelled that morning... *before* they had seen me. Did Bartholomew get scared for some reason? Something had to have happened. Well, then again, Remmy said Bartholomew had done that kind of thing before.

Speaking of not showing up, apparently the FBI hadn't thought a missing kid was any more important than a kidnapped mom. Either that or they had done a really bad job looking around. I guess I was lucky because if they *had* shown up, I would be on my way home by now.

I hurried back to where I'd been sitting with Remmy. He was hanging out by the back of the tent.

"Hey, the circus is wrapping up. You ready to meet some sideshow folks?" he was saying as I walked up. I half-lied to him, saying I was falling asleep standing up. As much as I wanted to meet Remmy's friends—and as much as I *really* needed to sleep—I had to take some time to think about things.

"Hey! Sleep when you can, that's my motto. Well, one of them, anyway."

As he led me through the tent, I tried to think of some small talk, like maybe telling him how long I'd been on the road. But I couldn't even remember how long it had been. It felt like weeks, months even. I did the calculations and discovered it had only been two days.

"My parents know I'm here," I piped up, really just as a way to break the silence. "Just in case you were wondering about that."

"Don't make stuff up, kid." He didn't look at me when he said it, he just kept on walking. But he didn't sound angry, either. "I'm small but I wasn't born yesterday. Besides, no one is going to ask any questions around here, so just keep your cool, all right?"

We passed by several performers in the hall, including a girl with dark, wild hair dressed in a suit with lightning decals. It was the same girl from before, the one who was about my age. She stared at me as we passed, but Remmy kept moving ahead. He was pretty fast for being so small and old. When we reached my "room," he pulled back the thin curtain. There was a small oriental rug rolled out on the asphalt with a stack of folded quilts on top of it. There was a puffy pillow on one end. At first I was like, *is that it?* But then, after another moment, it looked so cozy and comfortable, I was actually kind of touched.

"It's not much, but it'll have to do," he said. "It'll be nicer in Vegas. Breakfast will be at seven sharp. Get a good night's sleep. You're going to need it."

And with that, I was alone again. I pulled the curtain shut behind me and set my stuff down. I had a little bit of light from the string of red lights running along the top of the tent.

Remmy had put a small stool next to the bedding like a nightstand. On it was a drinking glass half-full of something amber-colored... what was it? I took a whiff and smelled that horrible medicinal smell from earlier, from Remmy's flask. It was so strong that I felt dizzy just smelling the fumes.

Uh, I think I'll save that for later.

I sat down on the quilts, emptied everything out of my backpack and pockets, postcards and all, and went to work.

It was time, as Eli would say, to "review the evidence."

In my little makeshift room behind the sideshow, I separated the postcards into two rows: code and no code. When I was done sorting, I had two equally long rows. Then I arranged each row by date.

I'd done this tons of times before, always thinking something would jump out at me, some obvious connection. That's what happens in the movies. But, as always, I just sat there staring, coming up with nothing.

It was a cold night and the tip of my nose felt like an ice cube. I just wanted to snuggle down into the bed and think about everything tomorrow.

Snap out of it, Ryan! Focus!

I turned the postcards over and re-read the notes Mom had written.

Eli and I had always focused on the ones with secret messages. They were all from horrible-sounding places like Crashup Mountain, Arizona and Farewell, Arkansas. The names just got worse and worse over time:

Eek, AK
Accident, MD
Bummerville, CA

Crashup Mountain, AZ
Hell For Certain, KY
Breakneck, CT
Deadman Reach, AK
Why, AZ
Nothing, AZ
Imalone, WI
Little Hope, PA
Last Chance, CO
Defeated, TN
Farewell, AR
Poopout Hill, CA

I sighed and was about to go through the other cards again, searching for any anagrams I'd missed, when I noticed something weird: on September 9th, Mom had sent a postcard *without* a secret message from Nuevo León, México—I remembered it came in a small box along with the scarab—and then *the very next day* she sent one *with* a code from Eek, Alaska. There was no way the circus could travel that fast.

I studied the cards from the weirdly named towns. And then, there it was! The movie-esque realization.

And I about had a conniption.

Did you know that there are things called postmarks that the post office stamps on mail to tell you where they were mailed from and when? You probably did. Well, would you believe I didn't know that? I figured that if you saw a post-card from Nothing, AZ, you could assume it came from Nothing, AZ. And when you saw that your mom had written September 12th at the top of her message, you could assume that it had been written on September 12th.

Pretty stupid, huh?

What I'd just discovered was that all of the coded postcards, all of the ones from crazy little towns across the country, had a little circular stamp on them that said *Pole Station, Antarctica, 1956, 8 AM.*

In my defense, the postmarks were very small and light. Also, Eli hadn't noticed, and he'd studied the cards even more than I had. But we'd always been so focused on the messages, we never bothered to study the cards themselves.

Mom must have sent the coded postcards to someone in Antarctica, who then sent them to me. You know, in case Bartholomew had someone checking her mail. But why would she bother putting them in code at all, then? Why not just tell me what was going on? An extra precaution? That didn't explain why the postmarks said 1956, though. I couldn't explain that one, (although I got a weird vision of my mom going back in time to mail them).

Lloyd's wanted poster, which was spread out next to the postcards, caught my attention. Lloyd's grinning, madman face. The face that was so different than I remembered it being in person.

I tried to focus back on the postcards, but I was tired and my mind kept drifting to all the crazy things that had happened over the last few days. I couldn't stop thinking about Lloyd and my brush with death, which led me to thinking about Hailey, which led me to thinking about Blue and White, which led me to thinking about the police station and the two nice cops, and then onto the story of Zacharias Prizrak and his dying inside a bank vault.

Criminals. Crime. That was the connection here. But was it important?

Crime.
Murder.
Kidnapping.
Robbery.

Robbery. Puck and Calyxtus said that Bartholomew used his magic powers to trap Zacharias Prizrak in a locked bank vault. Even if he really did have magical powers, why would he send someone into a bank vault?

Unless he was trying to rob it.

Robbery. What had I seen about a robbery recently? Oh, right, the security camera picture of the museum robber from the police station. The Georgia O'Keeffe Museum. The picture showed a man standing on the high ledge. I'd had this weird feeling of déjà vu when I saw it. There's no way it was important—I wouldn't have even seen if I hadn't taken that ride with Blue and White.

An image of Mom from all those years ago, standing silhouetted on top of our house, just before she jumped—that's why the picture had caught my attention. And why it was still so much lodged in my thoughts.

The pose of that figure on top of the Georgia O'Keeffe Museum was *exactly the same pose that my mom would take when she was about to do something crazy.* Something dangerous. Like jumping off a building. It was exactly the same pose she'd had right before she jumped off our roof. Hands on her hips, face turned slightly outward, looking toward the sky. If I hadn't assumed the person in the picture was a man, I would have noticed it immediately.

I quickly went digging in my bag and pulled out the picture my mom had sent me from the circus, the one of her standing in front of that big, white, cartoonish cannon. Her pose here was exactly the same. The same as my memories. The same as that figure in the security photo.

It couldn't be a coincidence. It just couldn't. Why would Bart cancel the circus on his last night in town? Unless he was worried because something went wrong?

Like maybe Mom getting caught on camera while trying to rob a museum.

Who better than my mom to rob places? She knew how to climb, she knew how to jump, she knew how to contort herself. She was an evil villain's dream come true!

I got chills up and down my spine. Actual chills, not the adrenaline charged chills I'd felt when I was riding with Lloyd or before jumping off the high dive for the first time. No, these were real supernatural, premonition-type chills, like the kind you get sometimes in bed late at night when you think you see something moving in the closet. The kind of chills that only happen when you're pretty sure something very, very bad is coming.

I tried to calm down. I closed my eyes and breathed hard. Was it possible I was overreacting? Maybe I was seeing things that weren't there. Maybe it was all a coincidence. Maybe I needed some sleep. I could hear my inner-Will saying, "Yeah, that makes a lot of sense" in that sarcastic voice of his.

But then another thought struck me and I pulled out the gold scarab that Mom had sent me. It was still in the plastic police evidence bag with the note: *Recovered at scene. Run past* FBI? *Interpol? Also, check against known art-theft list.* Maybe the cops had another reason for thinking it was stolen, besides the fact that it was in Blue and White's car.

All of these questions were making my eyes and brain and heart hurt.

With this new idea in my head, I turned back to the post-cards to look for more clues. It was just at that moment that the red lights above me went dark. I guess there wasn't much of a choice about bedtime around here. I groped my way over to the pile of quilts and lay down.

In the dark, as the sideshow settled around me, an idea crept into my head. And even though I was very tired and maybe not thinking straight, I was pretty sure it was a good idea. As I slowly slipped away into much-needed sleep, I tried to hold onto it.

It was very, very important.

CHAPTER 16

I DON'T KNOW HOW I slept, or even *if* I slept. All I knew was suddenly there was sunlight and a weird lapping sound. I opened my eyes to see a dirty white cat drinking from a glass next to my head.

Lousy. Remmy. The Sideshow of Curiosities and Mayhem.

Call Eli.

When I jumped up, I startled Lousy, who knocked the whiskey glass off the chair. I don't know how I was fast enough, but I caught it before it hit the ground.

I was sore. Even sleeping on the pile of quilts, I felt like I'd slept right on the hard ground. I checked my watch—a quarter after six. I had forty-five minutes to find a phone, call Eli, solve a mystery, and get back in time for my free ride to Vegas.

I packed everything into my backpack except for the code-less cards, which I slipped in my pocket. I'd grab my bag and suitcase when I got back.

Outside, a few workers were taking stakes out of the tent. No Remmy in sight. I considered asking one of the workers for a cell phone, but then figured my conversation with Eli would take too long and be too awkward. I remembered seeing payphones just outside the fairgrounds, and took off in that direction.

"OKAY, VEGAS," ELI WAS SAYING over the phone.

This was after I argued with a groggy camp counselor for a good two minutes before convincing her that it was very, very important that I talk to him.

Eli had seen the announcement that Bartholomew's had cancelled and had already been hard at work.

"I got you a ride all figured out. There's this Mormon choir bus—"

"No, no, no, I'm good for that. I got the ride all taken care of."

"You do?" He sounded a little disappointed.

"The sideshow is going to give me a ride on their bus."

"Now *that's* what I'm talking about!"

"I need something else though. Listen carefully. Search for 'Monterrey, Nuevo León, Mexico.'"

"What about it?"

I looked down at the first "normal" postcard from Mom. "Check the news from September. Robberies. Art gallery robberies, bank robberies, something like that."

"Why am I doing this?" he asked. I ignored the question

and waited. "The MARCO—the Museum of Contemporary Art of Monterrey. How'd you know? They lost an entire collection by one artist. He was a gold sculptor. They said that—"

"Does it say anything about a scarab?" I interrupted.

"No... no, no scarab... wait. Yes!" he exclaimed. "Wait, you don't think that—"

"Now search Philadelphia, for October."

"Geez, bossy much?" he asked, but I heard him typing and clicking. "Crap—again! The Academy of Natural Sciences lost their—I don't know how to say this—their *Had-ro-saurus fo-bla-something*. A giant dinosaur skeleton. It just went missing one night. Where are you getting this stuff?"

I leaned back against the glass in the booth, my hand to my forehead. *It was happening. It was all really happening.*

"Hello? Ryan? What's this for?"

"They aren't just stealing people," I said.

"Devil in a hang glider!" Eli cursed. "*What are you talking about?*"

"I think I figured it all out—Bartholomew is using his kidnapped circus people to rob places. It's all in the postcards. I mean, it's not *in* them. It's where they're from..." I looked at my watch. Crap. It was already 6:45!

"Look, just a few more, to make sure. Here's the next: Lebanon, Ohio. November."

A pause. Then, "Warren County History Center. Some antique crap and—oh, get this, antique postcards."

I flipped back to the postcard from Lebanon—it looked modern.

I moved on. "Springfield, Illinois. December."

"Antique books and some fine china from the Abraham Lincoln Presidential Library."

"Abe Lincoln's *china?*" I repeated. "Like plates and stuff?"

"Looks that way."

Going on like this, we discovered that Bartholomew had knocked off at least five museums in the past ten months. I only had ten postcards, but I knew they performed somewhere different every few days, so maybe all this was only the tip of the iceberg.

"This sure explains why they don't put the circus dates on their website, huh?" I said with a smirk.

"No kidding. I can't believe they made your mom steal that streetcar from the Minnesota Streetcar Museum," Eli said, his voice full of awe. "I mean, how did she even *do* it?"

"It doesn't mean it's her," I snapped. I wasn't about to explain to Eli that I thought it might be Charlene. Not now. Not until I knew more. Anyway, I had to get off the phone.

"Well, if she is doing it—and I'm not saying she is," Eli added quickly. "But if she is—it could be that Stockholm thing. You know it even happened to Amelia Earhart?"

"I have to go," I said. "The next time I talk to you I'll have my mom with me. I hope."

"Just let me know if you need anything. I'm here for you, friend."

"Sure," I said. I was about to hang up when I thought of one last thing.

"Hey, Eli—thanks."

"You're welcome. Good luck, Ryan."

"Thanks. See ya."

I booked it the last few blocks back to the fairgrounds, thinking about what it all could mean. There was no way this was a coincidence. I thought back to the Prizrak bank vault story. I should have asked Eli to check on that, too. I made a mental note to look it up later.

I came up to the fairgrounds gate and glanced at my watch. 7 AM on the dot. I was just in time. I was starving and looking forward to that breakfast Remmy had promised me. I was imagining all sorts of warm things like hash browns and eggs and pancakes. I thought I could almost smell the food. I wondered what it would be like, eating all together, the crazy sideshow folks and me.

That's when I got close enough to see that the sideshow tent was gone. And not just the tent. Everything was gone.

There were no trucks. Nobody around.

No Remmy.

I'd only been gone, what, forty-five minutes? How could they have packed up so fast? I looked at my watch and it said 7:04. They wouldn't just leave me, would they? Remmy had practically *promised*.

I sat down hard on the sidewalk as my heart broke in my chest. And when I realized my backpack and suitcase were also gone, it broke a second time. My heart was in fourths.

Don't cry, I willed myself. How much worse off was I really than if I'd never met Remmy? Sure, I didn't have my stuff. I didn't have the suitcase. But I could figure out another plan. A better one. I could get through this. I still had Eli on my side. I still had Will's money in my pocket.

Go back to the payphone and call Eli. My inner voice was actually being helpful, for once. I took a deep breath. I felt calmer.

All right.

I'd gone maybe twenty feet down the sidewalk when I heard the squeak of old brakes coming up behind me. I turned and saw the sideshow bus, with Remmy's grinning face sticking out the door.

"I told you 7 AM sharp, didn't I?" he called.

CHAPTER 17

THE MOMENT I STEPPED INTO the bus, everyone inside greeted me with an enthusiastic, "Hello, Spartacus!" which I answered with an awkward smile and a wave. There were about twenty people, and I recognized some of them from backstage the night before.

"Where have you been?" asked Remmy. "We've been looking for you. Hurry up and take a seat." Remmy slid into the driver's seat and I realized with a start that he was actually driving the bus. I wondered how he could see the road, let alone reach the pedals, but I didn't want to stare.

The bus was set up all crazy, like you'd expect a circus bus to be. Someone had changed it so that people could live in it—there were oriental rugs on the floors and across the ceiling, and some of the windows had these plastic static clings that made them look like they were stained glass. Then there were the three sets of narrow bunk beds in the back, stacked three tall. They were more like shelves, really, but the tops ones had posters tacked up above them, like you'd see in a kid's bedroom. Some had curtains hanging down that made them look really cozy.

There were so few people that most of them had their own seats. I saw my backpack and the suitcase in the seat right behind Remmy, so I sat there.

"I thought you'd left and changed your mind because of our talk last night." Remmy pulled the bus away from the fairgrounds. "But I should have known a kid like you wouldn't be scared away that easy."

He gestured back toward the guy across the aisle from me.

"Spartacus, meet my business partner, Robin Marx. We own the show together."

Robin Marx was a big, sturdy man with a thick handlebar mustache and a black bowler hat. "Pleasure to make your acquaintance, Mr. Spartacus," he said. He had a dramatic, booming voice, and I thought I recognized it as the announcer's voice from the show last night. His mustache was mesmerizing. It was so big and thick it looked cartoonish and bounced when he spoke. "So you think you're ready for Bartholomew's?"

For a moment I thought he was talking about my rescue plan and had no idea what to say. Then I remembered they thought I was trying to join the circus.

"I hope so," I said. "I mean, I think so."

"Bartholomew's is a pretty big show for a First of May to start in."

"A what?" I asked, thinking I'd heard him wrong.

"That's what we call a novice," he said. "A beginner. A First of May. You have some tricks ready? Some daredevilry?"

"Uh, well—" I searched my brain. "I can throw knives." I wasn't great at it, but it was the one thing Mom had taught me how to do.

"That's always a showstopper," said Robin. "What else?"

That wasn't enough? I brainstormed, thinking of what was the best lie I could tell.

"I can also," I said slowly, "get out of traps. Like small suitcases and being tied up and stuff."

"Oh, we've got a regular escape artist here!" Remmy turned over and beamed at me. "We could use one of them, couldn't we, Robin?"

"Hey, stop, Remmy. There's Zeda," Robin said. He was leaning over his seat and pointing up ahead.

The bus lurched to a stop. Zeda stood on the corner, waving at us. She was a pretty girl, with black hair tied back in a ponytail. I realized she was the younger performer I'd passed twice last night.

The bus stopped just for a second, long enough for her to jump on. She had a couple of big white paper bags in her hands.

"Breakfast is here!" Zeda announced to everyone, holding the bags up high as the bus pulled forward. The people cheered in the same way they had for me.

She turned to me and I realized I'd been staring. I tried to make it look like I was only looking at the Rainbow Bright tattoo on her arm.

"Hey, I remember you," she said. I didn't say what I first thought to say, which was, "I remember you, too." Because I did. Of course I remembered her. She was... well, she was beautiful. Beautiful in a completely different way than Erika Dixon was with her carefully styled hair and shiny pink lip gloss. Different than Hailey with her trucker clothes and goofy smile. This girl had dark, exotic eyes, and her hair was crazy and tangled, but still looked somehow like a beautiful planned-out work of art.

Get a grip, Spart.

"You're the one who went crazy last night, right?" Zeda said, smiling.

I winced and blushed at the same time. *That* was why she remembered me. Of course. This was Erika Dixon and the Brenville Pool all over again. Nothing had changed.

"Yep," I said, forcing a smile. "That was me."

"You want to help me pass these burritos out?"

"Sure," I said with a lot more enthusiasm than made sense, and then I stood up too fast. She noticed both, but just smiled at me and handed me one of the bags.

I remembered why girls my own age made me so nervous. They always were so much more confident than I was. Plus they acted like they knew it. Oh, yeah, and they were all taller than me. Zeda was no exception on all counts.

"That's my daughter," said Robin sternly, but his eyes twinkled. "Don't get any ideas."

"*Lame*, Dad," she said, but giggled. I forced a small, dry laugh and then followed behind her, helping her hand out the breakfast burritos.

"Have you met Spartacus?" Zeda asked almost every single person. It felt really uncomfortable being introduced as Spartacus, like she was making fun of my name. I definitely was not used to that. I reminded myself that they were circus people and that their names were probably as weird as mine was. I nodded at everyone and responded vaguely to their "So, you want to join Bartholomew's, eh?" questions.

It was funny seeing all the same people from the night before without their masks and snakes and clown faces. In the daylight, there was nothing all that freaky about any of them. I mean, there were still tattoos and piercings and the woman whose makeup made her look like Cruella Deville, but no one was doing anything crazy like hammering a nail up their nose (the Human Blockhead routine Remmy had told me about) or staring into space.

Everyone looked, well, *normal.*

WHEN I RETURNED TO MY seat, I was glad that Zeda stayed in the back so she wouldn't see me devour my burrito in a few seconds like a ravenous animal.

"They really know how to do the green chili here, don't they?" asked Robin. I looked up from the crumpled paper in my hands to see Robin still had half his burrito left.

"I've been on the road a bit," I said sheepishly. "Haven't had much hot food."

"It's okay," he said good-naturedly. "I'm going to lick the wrapper when I get done with mine, too."

I put my backpack and suitcase on the floor and stretched out in my seat.

"Do you know how long it is to Las Vegas?" I asked Robin.

"At least nine hours or so," he said. "It's gonna be a grueler." He settled back into his seat, pulling out a fat book and turning to the first page.

I sat back and watched the New Mexico scenery flying by in a sandy, brown blur.

I was headed to Las Vegas. To Bartholomew's. To my mom.

And this time, I just might have a little help.

The bus fell into a quiet, relaxed groove, with hardly anybody talking. My mind returned to the robberies and how everything fit together. It seemed pretty clear that Bartholomew was robbing places wherever the circus went. Eli had seen the evidence, too. I hadn't imagined that part of it.

I was trying to decide what it all meant. *Does it change anything?* I wondered. No, not really. My mom still needed my help. I still had to get her out of there. I guess what had changed was that I wasn't breaking into just any old evil circus any more. Now I was trying to free Mom from inside a tent of professional criminals.

I was going to have to make a better plan.

Remmy had said that the sideshow knew Bartholomew's Circus pretty well. Maybe I could get them to give me some more information without blowing my cover.

"Remmy?" I said out of the blue, kind of startling myself. Remmy looked back at me in the rearview mirror.

"What you need?"

"Uh, what's the… what's the layout of Bartholomew's tent like? Is it kind of similar to yours?"

Remmy looked at me suspiciously.

"What do you want to know that for?"

Keep cool. Don't make it too obvious.

"Just curious," I said, shrugging off the question. "I thought if I could learn about how his tent is set up, I could figure out the best way to audition."

Decent cover.

"Well, if you want some tips, we can give you a little training right now."

Training? On the bus? I must have looked a little skeptical.

"Trust me," said Remmy. "Go into the back and find Nero. The skinny guy with the sideburns. Ask him to teach you something."

Okay. What could it hurt? And maybe I could press this Nero guy for more details about Bart's circus.

I got up from my seat and walked down the aisle. Most people were sleeping. I saw Zeda in one of the bunk beds in the back, her tattooed arm hanging out.

Seated near the middle of the bus was a guy with dark sideburns shaped like lightning bolts. He was dressed all in black, including these black leather bracelets with shiny metal spikes. He was staring out the window as I approached, absentmindedly flipping a knife around his fingers the way Will spun pencils.

"Hey. Are you Nero?" I asked in a soft voice, trying not to wake anyone.

"Yeah," he said, looking up kind of dazed from the window. He smiled when he saw me. "Spartacus, right?"

"Right. Cool sideburns," I said, touching my face where his lightning bolts were. It was the first time I wished I could actually grow facial hair.

"Thanks," he said. "They're kinda my thing."

I nodded, then said, "Remmy said you might be able to teach me something for Bartholomew's?"

"Mmm, right," he nodded, thinking. "Let me get some stuff together and I'll meet you up at your seat. That way we won't wake up everyone back here."

In a few minutes, Nero switched seats with Robin so he was right across from me. He had a small tackle box and a book with him.

"What do you do in the sideshow?" I asked.

"Well, my big thing is swallowing stuff—razor blades, swords, umbrellas—"

"*Umbrellas?*" I asked skeptically.

"Yeah. It's just like swallowing a sword. They're not open or anything. Right now I'm working on the world record for most swords swallowed at the same time. The record is seven, so, you know, I'm working on nine. Just to make sure no one breaks it for a while." He laughed.

"What's the trick?" I asked.

"The trick is that there *is* no trick," he said. "You're actually swallowing a sword."

"You're going to teach me to swallow swords?" I said, eyes wide. "*On the bus?*" I was terrified and thrilled. But mostly just terrified.

Zeda, who had obviously been listening to this all the way in the back, snickered and Nero grinned.

"It might take you six months to work your way up to a small *dagger,*" he snorted. "Besides, that's the kind of cool stuff you'd get to do in the sideshow. But you're a Bartholomew-man, right?"

I nodded reluctantly.

"Right. No sword swallowing under the big top. Strictly the big time there. But I can teach you something that will come in handy in any circus."

I was excited. What was I going to learn? Trapeze stuff? Lion taming? Magic? I knew we were on the bus but maybe he was going to give me some starting-out theory.

Nero opened the tackle box, exposing tubes of paint, palettes, and little sponges.

"I'm talking," said Nero, "about face painting."

Face painting?

My eyes immediately glazed over.

"I promise you," he said. "It's not just painting horsies and rainbows."

A little more than an hour later, Nero had taught me how to paint myself in two different clown styles. I wasn't too impressed. Then I washed it off and he showed me how to put different shades of green and brown on my face to make camouflage, like you'd see hunters wear.

"You can even put stuff under the paint, to make a big nose, or a wart or something," he explained.

He showed me how to paint my face to look like a lion, with a big, yawning mouth and sharp fangs.

"You're getting good at this," said Nero. "You're a pretty decent artist."

This *was* getting kind of cool, but I still felt like I was wasting my time. I needed to gather some kind of information while I was on the bus. Who knew how long I'd have after we got to Vegas?

"Have you ever seen the guy with Bartholomew's who looks kinda fishy—I mean, like an actual fish?"

"His name's Finn," he said, his lip curling in disgust. "Yeah, I know him."

"I saw him—um, I saw pictures of him online," I stammered. "Is that just paint or..."

"It's real," he said grimly. "Well, kind of. I think he started out with the gills—maybe an accident at birth or something, but then he got the fin implanted. Then he filed down his teeth and started wearing those contacts that cover his whole eye."

"The black ones. Right," I said, remembering his face. I shivered in the hot bus.

"I don't know why Bartholomew even has him in the show," said Nero. "He's not very talented—but I guess it gives the circus the scare factor that Bartholomew's looking for. Personally, I think it really creeps out the kids."

"What's Sharkman—I mean, Finn—what's he like?"

Nero didn't answer right away, but then he looked at me, deadly serious. "He's bad news. I'd stay out of his way. He's not going to be your friend."

"Do you think that... well, I mean, I heard that Bartholomew has a plastic surgeon who travels with him?"

Nero furrowed his brow, looking confused. But I rushed on, "I mean, do you think they ever make... well, make performers look like other people? Maybe so a trick looks better?"

I was thinking about Not-Mom.

"No, I never heard anything like that," Nero said. "But then, there's a lot of strange stuff that goes on with them."

"Like what kind of stuff?"

I thought that Nero started to look kind of uncomfortable.

"Well, a lot of them are really cool. I don't want to say they're all bad. But, if I were you, I just wouldn't ask too many questions. They don't like that."

Of course then I had a million more questions. About Bartholomew. About my mom. But at that moment we slowed and pulled into a rest stop.

"Thanks for showing me all that," I said to Nero. When I went for the towel to wipe off my face paint, Nero stopped me.

"You're with a sideshow," he said. "Leave it."

NOTHING REALLY PREPARES YOU TO watch sideshow people do their *thing*. And I'm not talking about lightning bolt sideburns and face paint. I'm talking about seeing something impossible with your very own eyes. Like Nero said, there is really no trick to swallowing a sword. It's not a prop, like a retracting sword or something. It actually is just sticking a sharp blade down into your guts. Well, *around* your guts.

While we were stretching our legs at the rest stop, Nero took a sword out from a storage space under the bus. It had a gold hilt covered with jewels and was almost as long as his arm.

"So, the sword goes into the mouth, then down the throat," Nero explained. He mimed the movement of the sword outside his body.

"Next, it passes the voice box, goes down the esophagus, and then between the lungs. Then you kind of nudge the heart to the side—"

I coughed.

"Nudge? Your *heart?*" I asked, my insides squirming.

"Yeah. Then you relax the lower esophagus, and you put the blade through the diaphragm, then past the liver, and down to touch the very bottom of the stomach."

"Where your *food* is?"

"Well, yeah. Unless you do it wrong and puncture an organ on the way there—then you're dead."

By then, we had small audience of two families and a lady with a Chihuahua on a leash. The four kids were looking from Nero to me in awe, like they thought I was part of the show.

"Isn't that dangerous?" asked the dog lady, looking concerned.

"Definitely," he said. He took out an apple and held it one hand. With the other hand he held the sword up and let it rest lightly on the apple. Without any effort from Nero, the weight of the sword pushed the blade all the way through the apple.

The dog lady looked even more distressed. Nero pulled a cloth out of his pocket and wiped down the blade.

"Do people ever die doing this?" asked an old guy.

"Not if they do it right," Nero said.

And then, without hesitating, he did it. *He swallowed the sword.* To the hilt.

All of us held our breath.

When he pulled it out again—and there wasn't a lung skewered on the end or anything—I stopped trying to look cool and applauded with everyone else as Nero took a bow.

"Oh, wow!" I said, my eyes bugging out as I shook my head. "That was awesome!"

I caught Zeda watching me with a half-smirk from across the parking lot. I stopped hooting and clapping like a regular carnival mark and tried to look cool. At least I still had my face painted so she hadn't seen me blush.

"All aboard!" Remmy called from the bus. "Five minutes!"

I ran to use the bathroom one more time, and washed the paint off my face while I was at it.

I was the last one back on the bus. Everyone was ready to go, and Remmy closed the bus door behind me with a thwack as I stepped on. Just as I sat down in the front seat, I was suddenly lifted up in the air.

"*Hey!*" I yelped.

It was Nero and Robin. *What the—?*

Nero held my arms at my sides while Robin started wrapping a heavy rope around me. I struggled against them, but they were too strong and too fast.

"What are you doing?" I yelled at the top of my lungs.

"What's it look like we're doing?" grunted Nero. "We're tying you up."

Everyone on the bus was standing up in their seats, laughing as I was spun around in the narrow aisle. Even Remmy, as he drove, was laughing hysterically.

My heart thumped as I realized that I'd been tricked. I had trusted them, even after Hailey had warned me not to trust anyone. They knew who I was. They were all in on it. They'd been working for Bartholomew all along.

CHAPTER 18

"YOU WON'T GET AWAY WITH this," I growled. This just made everyone laugh harder. Which made me so angry, I started fighting back even more. I kicked Robin in the shin and he cursed. He wound the rope even tighter around my legs.

"Gosh, boy, you're a fighter, aren't you?" Robin hooted. He turned to Nero. "Did you hear that? *'You won't get away with this?'*"

"Classic," answered Nero.

I stood there, glowering at them. I was about to spit in Nero's grinning face, the way they always do in movies (or, the way White had done), when they both took a step back.

"Now escape," said Nero.

"You're funny," I said, glaring at him. "People will be looking for me."

"No, no, no," said Nero, shaking his head, his face stretched in a smile. "Seriously. Escape."

"What?"

"Yeah," said Robin. But not like a villain. Like my gym teacher encouraging me to do a pull-up. "We wanted to see your amazing rope escape skills."

I wished my hands weren't tied up so I could have used them to cover my red, red face. That's right, I'd told them I could do stuff like that. What had I been thinking? I turned to face the front of the bus so I didn't have to look at anyone (especially Zeda) while I struggled with the rope.

"Sorry about kicking you," I said to Robin in a quiet voice.

"My fault entirely," he said sincerely, his hand on his chest. "We shouldn't have jumped you like that. Seemed funny at the time."

"Uh, I'm a little bit out of practice."

"Take your shoes off for a start," Nero said.

I slipped off my shoes and well... just kind of wriggled around, trying to look like I knew what I was doing. I was able to get my feet out of the ropes, but it was slow going.

"Try laying on the floor," Robin suggested. "That way you can use the floor to move the ropes for you."

With some work, I was able to get on my knees, then to the floor. It was a little easier. As I struggled, everyone else kind of went on with what they were doing, not paying attention to me.

It took me about fifteen minutes to finally get free. I stood up exhausted and soaked with sweat. There was polite clapping from the passengers and I took a slight bow before falling over in my seat. Robin gave me a bottled water while Nero wound up the rope.

"Tough, huh?" asked Robin. I nodded, gulping the water. "Ready for the second round?"

I laughed and drank some more water.

"No, I'm serious," he said. "Stand up."

I gave him a look. "Do I have to?"

"Well, you got out. So you technically did it. But sorry to say, it wasn't impressive. It's not going to bowl anybody over, except maybe your little sister—" (I bristled) "—and there's no way Bartholomew would keep on watching you after the first four minutes. Come on, try again—but this time, we'll give you some tips."

I took a deep breath and stood back up.

Turns out that the most important part of escaping ropes is what you do while you're being tied up. Robin and Nero taught me to puff out my chest, hold my arms a bit away from my body and flex my muscles to make myself bigger while the ropes were being wrapped around me. That meant I'd have more slack to work with. And, if you did it really well, like Houdini did, no one would even know you were even doing it.

The second time, with their instructions, I was out in five minutes. The next time I was out in three, the next in two.

The applause from the bus that last time was genuine and loud. "Ready for the big time!" called someone from the back. I caught Zeda's eye as she gave me an appreciating look. I bowed deeply and then collapsed in my seat, suddenly exhausted and peaceful. Then I slept.

WE ARRIVED IN LAS VEGAS around four in the afternoon. Bartholomew's trucks weren't there yet, so I felt pretty safe hanging out in the open, helping everyone set up. I helped hold stakes and pull ropes while they put up the sideshow tent and then I helped carry boxes inside.

A large, square container covered with gray canvas was sitting in the shade of the sideshow's lone truck. I was about to peek under the canvas cover when a voice spoke up from behind me.

"I wouldn't do that."

I turned to see Zeda stepping down from the running board of the truck. She'd been putting on dark lipstick in the side-mirror.

"Why? What's under there?" I asked, feeling myself getting nervous again.

"*Who's* under there," she corrected me. She grinned at me when I took a step back from the box. Then she pulled a stick of gum out of her skirt pocket and popped it in her mouth before offering me a piece.

"Um, okay, *who's* under there?"

"Matilda," she said crossing over to something that resembled a wooden cutout shaped like a person.

Matilda. I'd forgotten about her. The box was the right size for an animal. A lion? A tiger? I took another involuntary step away from the cage.

"Come on, Spartacus, you're braver than *that*," she said, laughing.

"Actually, I think I'm a coward," I confessed. It felt good to finally say it.

"I don't believe it," she said.

"I am. If you don't show me what's under the canvas, I won't be able to sleep tonight."

Zeda gave me half a smile. "Daytime is not a good time to see her. Here, help me carry this thing."

We moved away from Matilda's cage to carry the wooden dummy (for knife throwing, Zeda explained) across the parking lot.

"So what is she?" I asked. "Is she a lion? A tiger of some sort?"

Zeda laughed, amused.

"Matilda is an aye-aye." She said it like *eye-eye*. "She's an endangered lemur from Madagascar."

"A lemur? Like, what, a monkey? A deadly monkey?"

"Sorta like that, yeah," she said with a sly look.

"What's her death trick, then?"

"It's not a trick." She blew her bangs out of her eyes. "It's all myth—and it's why she's so endangered. Some people in Madagascar think aye-ayes are some sort of death omen, so they kill them. They have this really long finger and the myth is that if it points at you, the only way you can stay alive is by killing it. It's ridiculous. But, of course, Remmy, who is completely old-school, sees nothing wrong with promoting a stupid superstition to make some money."

"You're pretty angry about this," I said, not knowing what to say.

"Of course I am!" she said, looking at me with fiery eyes. "How can I feel good exploiting the very reason she's endangered?"

Zeda's face was flushed. I'd never heard anyone speak with so much feeling for a monkey before.

"So when can I see her?" I asked.

"I'll introduce you tonight, when she's awake. You'll see why I love her so much."

We walked in silence a bit more before she spoke up again.

"That's such a cool name. 'Spartacus.' Is it real?"

"Unfortunately," I said.

"Are you kidding?" she said. "It's awesome."

"Well, not if you don't live in a sideshow," I said and then felt bad, like maybe I'd insulted her. I changed the subject quickly. "That's a cool tattoo."

"It isn't real, you know," she said. "You can't get a tattoo until you're eighteen without a parent's consent."

"Yeah, that sucks," I said, acting like I already knew that. "Well, it looks real, anyway. What is it? Permanent marker?"

"Yeah," she said, helping me set the wooden board down. "I've retraced it every day for over a year now to prove to Dad that I wouldn't regret having it as a tattoo. He's still saying no."

I thought about all the stupid stuff I'd get tattooed on me that I'd probably regret after a few months. I bet Lloyd even regretted his tattoo—especially because it made him easier to identify.

"I'll give you one, too, if you'd like," she said, nonchalantly.

"That'd be cool."

"I'll think up a good one for you in the next day or so, one that suits your personality. Then you could retrace it until you're ready to get it done for real."

"Cool," I said. And I meant it, except I knew I didn't have the next day or so to hang out with Zeda or the sideshow. Bartholomew was going to arrive that night or early the next morning. And then what? How was I going to go back to being incognito after the circus arrived? And what if one of the sideshow people told Bartholomew's people I was there, waiting to try out?

Why did you give them your real name, butt face? Will's voice had returned to make me feel stupid… and it was working. I was lost in thought when Zeda spoke up.

"Hey, Spartacus?" she said. "Want to learn something cool?"

LETTING A GIRL I HARDLY knew talk me into breathing fire might be one of the stupidest things I'd ever done.

"I'm going to do it a few times, and you're going to watch," she said, gathering up a box that said *Zeda Marx* on it. "And then I'll teach you."

"You're going to teach me to breathe fire?" I asked, my voice cracking halfway through the question.

"Shh!" she hissed, putting her hand to her lips. "I'm not supposed to show you. Dad said it was too dangerous for a novice, but I think you'd be great. Unless, of course, you don't want to," she added, her dark eyes daring me to say no.

"No, sounds good," I managed. She told me to fill a bucket of water from the spigot and meet her around the side of one of the buildings where nobody would see us.

It turns out that, like sword swallowing, there is no trick to fire breathing. There's lighter fluid, a torch, and a flame, and then—*bam!*—there's fire flying from your lips!

I'd had crushes on girls before. There were a couple girls besides Erika Dixon in Brenville that I'd liked at some point. Of course, I'd never really talked to them or told other guys I liked them, or even admitted it to myself, because when you start liking girls, you have to be ready for rejection. I already had enough of that in my life.

But after seeing Zeda do her fire breathing act, I knew there would never be another girl for me. Zeda was *it*.

"And you do this in the show?" I asked, watching her put the torch out with a wet towel.

"Yeah, that's my thing," she said. "I do a whole fire routine you can see tomorrow."

I shook my head in amazement. "Aren't you, like, my age?"

"I'm an old soul," she said, preparing her tools again. "I met a fortune teller at a show once who told me I'd been breathing fire for thousands of years."

"And you believed that?" I asked. I'd meant it as a real question, like I was really curious if she believed it, but I think she thought I was judging her.

"I mean, I'm not saying I *for sure* believe it," she said huffily. "But I think anything's possible."

I shrugged, not wanting to upset her.

"Are you ready?" she asked.

"I don't know." And I didn't. If Robin didn't think I was ready for this, should I really trust his daughter to say I was? My Mistake-o-Meter was flashing a blazing red three. But when I looked at her holding the torches out to me, her pretty face looking at me expectantly, I couldn't say no.

Some things are just out of our control.

For the record, I did it right the first three times.

It was the fourth time, when I tried to show off, that the wind changed and blew the flames back in my face.

"Oh, no!" Zeda shrieked. With zero hesitation, she grabbed the water bucket and tossed it on me. One moment I was breathing fire, acting cocky—and the next I was soaked to the bone, torch still smoking, and looking at her in amazement. I didn't really understand what had happened.

"Oh, Spartacus, I'm so sorry," she said, giving me a hug, even though I was drenched. She looked like she was about to cry.

"What, uh, what happened?" I asked, dazed, hugging her. I patted her on the back because she was patting mine.

"The wind shifted and…" She pulled away and touched my face, inspecting, looking for something. "Nothing. There's… nothing?"

She looked confused.

"What?" I asked, thinking I'd missed something.

"Well—honestly, your hair should be singed and your eyebrows should probably be burnt off, but…" She stepped back, looking at me like I was a strange specimen. "You're a fire-breathing miracle."

I WENT AND CHANGED INTO my holey jeans and my last black t-shirt. Then I joined Zeda and the others on some picnic tables, where we all ate pizza.

I sat there, trying to think of what my next move was going to be. Honestly, though, I wasn't thinking too hard. I mean, how often do you get to hang out with a sideshow and a cool, fire-breathing girl? And they were *all* cool. Nero entertained us with more of his tricks, and the woman with the huge snake came out and did a belly dancing routine. Zeda told me about what it was like for her living on the road.

So I was a bit distracted from my mission. But I had the vague idea that I could just make myself scarce when Bartholomew's people started showing up. Maybe I could tell Remmy and Robin to keep my presence a secret, because I wanted to surprise Bartholomew when I was ready.

Zeda had come up with an idea for my tattoo a lot sooner than she'd thought she would. She told me not to look while she drew on my bicep with permanent markers. It felt really good, sitting there while she held my arm and lightly brushed the markers along my skin. I was kinda hoping it would take a really long time for her to finish.

"Now she's got *you* wanting a tattoo?" Robin asked, walking up.

"I don't know yet," I said.

"You'll want one when you see how cool this is going to be," Zeda said. Robin laughed and pulled a mirror from his pocket and applied some wax to his mustache. I couldn't decide which was cooler—Nero's lightning bolt sideburns or Robin's handlebar mustache.

"Do you go to school?" I asked Zeda, watching Remmy feed pepperoni to Lousy.

"I do it online. I'm going to graduate early, though. I'm already taking classes through one of those online universities."

I turned to look at her in surprise and she turned my face away.

"Don't look yet!" she laughed.

I was working on my fourth slice of pizza when a big truck rolled up towards us. It was a normal-looking brown delivery truck, except it didn't have a company name or anything on it. And it was driving pretty fast. Everyone in our camp went quiet, watching it get nearer. I had an instinct to run, thinking it might be Bartholomew. Then the truck stopped short, maybe ten feet from us.

"Not again," Robin said. He put on his bowler hat and stood up.

Remmy stood up on the bench, squinting at the truck before cursing, like he knew who it was.

"Walk with me, Robin," he said, his lips not moving. "Keep me from tearing the messenger's fool head off."

I DIDN'T KNOW IT, BUT over the past three days, I'd been mastering the ability to handle disappointment. It was the little letdowns—like Lloyd being a murderer and the museum theft stuff—that helped get me ready. Oh, and the circus not being in Albuquerque—that sure was a big blow.

The old me, the *not*-Spartacus me, might have started crying or something.

The old me would have screamed and shouted and stomped and knocked something over. Who was I kidding? The old me would have just given up and gone home.

Well.

The new me didn't do any of those things when the next letdown came, when Bartholomew. Cancelled. Again.

What was the point? It was just toughening me up for future letdowns, right?

I LISTENED TO REMMY AND Robin talk to the truck driver, my nails biting into the wood of the bench. The bench was my cool and I was hanging onto it for dear life. I didn't dare think about what my new plan was going to be. That would have sent me over the edge.

Remmy's constant stream of curse words made it kind of hard to gather the exact details of the conversation, but the basic gist was this: Bartholomew had changed his plans (again) and booked a two-day gig in Portland, Oregon.

Starting tomorrow.

Yep. Oregon. Not too far from where I'd started this whole journey.

So I sat very still, hoping to either: a) avoid another nervous breakdown, or b) at least get around the corner and away from Zeda before shouting, *"You deserve this, Poop Lip! You really, really do!"* once again.

"Unbelievable," Robin was saying as they walked back to the tables. Everyone in the sideshow was watching them carefully, except Zeda. She was still drawing, pressing the pen so hard on my arm that it hurt. She was, however, the first one to speak up.

"So, I suppose they want us to perform tonight and then go to them?"

"Of course they do," Remmy fumed. He spat on the ground.

"This is just so stupid," Zeda muttered under her breath. Only I heard her.

"Well," said Robin, stepping in. He took off his hat and examined its brim. "In lieu of going, Remmy and I could send a message back with the delivery guy... that is, if it's all right with all of you."

Everyone blinked at one another for a moment before Nero stood up.

"I think we should be done with Bartholomew," he said. "I wouldn't care if he *doubled* our pay."

"Me neither!" said the snake lady, standing up.

"Well, if that's how you all feel... let's put it to a vote. Yea or nay?"

There were so many "yeas" that I swore there were fifty people and not just the twenty. Remmy grinned at Robin.

"Then that's it," Robin said. "We're free."

"Tell Bartholomew to find himself a new sideshow!" Remmy shouted to the truck driver, who didn't look like he cared all that much. Everyone at the tables cheered. (Well, except me. I was still willing myself to stay sane.)

"Yeah! We're our own show again. Who needs them?" Zeda jumped up from her chair and hugged Nero, her dad, Remmy, and then—*me*.

"You're better off with us, anyway," Zeda said, giving me a half-smile—or was it a *shy* smile? No. There was no way *I* had made a girl shy. She was still looking at me, grinning, when the driver yelled out:

"What about that animal? You gonna help me load it up or what?"

"Bartholomew is paying you, isn't he?" Remmy bellowed. "You got two arms—use 'em!"

Zeda turned to me with tears brimming in her eyes. Not happy tears.

"He's going to take Matilda back," she whispered.

"What? I thought she was yours?" I said.

"No," Zeda said. "She belongs to Bartholomew. But we've always taken care of her. Bartholomew doesn't know how to take care of her. They kept her in this tiny cage and she was all dirty and, oh, she can't go back!" The tears spilled over the rims of her dark eyes and rolled down her cheeks. It almost made me forget all about my problems. Almost.

Zeda was just about to stomp off, but I grabbed her arm and whispered, "I need to talk to you."

I TOOK HER AWAY FROM the group, where no one could overhear us.

"What's the plan?" she asked, looking hopeful. Even that teeny smile was like a hundred heavy-duty flashlights and I wanted to melt.

No time for melting, Spartacus.

"I need to get on that truck," I said.

"Oh, I thought this was about Matilda," she said, her face falling. "But you don't need to get into Bartholomew's. We'll teach you so much more than—"

"I don't want to join the circus," I blurted out. "My mom is with Bartholomew's Circus and she's there against her will. I'm trying to get her out."

"Your *mom?*" She took a step back. "Who's your mom?"

"Athena," I said. "The—"

"The Human Cannonball!" she gasped, covering her mouth. "Right! Oh my god, you look just like her! She's amazing!" Zeda's face darkened suddenly. "Wait. You're saying she was kidnapped or something?"

"Yeah," I said. "I know it sounds crazy. But trust me. She told me herself."

"I believe you," she said. "It doesn't sound as crazy to me as you'd think. I know Bartholomew is a bad guy. I was going to tell you about him later. I thought we had more time. But you can't think you can just waltz in there and get her back."

"I know it's not going to be easy," I said.

"Not easy?" she said incredulously. "You got that right. Bartholomew's a weird dude. Those people are always doing odd things. And they're violent. One time, Finn almost put Nero in the hospital just because he was looking around backstage. My dad thinks they're involved in some kind of crime ring but he can't prove it."

I considered telling her about the museum robberies. But I wondered if that might put her in danger. Instead I just said, "I know it's going to be hard. Just last night I ran into this double Bartholomew made of my mom—"

"No way—*the doubles!*" she exclaimed, actually hitting me in the shoulder with her excitement. "I read about that but didn't think it was real! Have you ever seen a website called IHateBartholomew'sCircus.com?"

"Yeah," I said.

"I'm telling you, that circus is dangerous. It doesn't surprise me about your mom being kidnapped *or* having a double. There's rumors that once people work for him they never work anywhere else. You're in it for life."

"Like Prizrak," I said in a whisper, remembering what Puck had said.

"You know about him?" Zeda said.

"Yeah, the magician. In the bank vault."

"No, no," said Zeda. "Prizrak was some kind of genius animal trainer, like a lion whisperer or something. It was about five years ago, in Chicago. They found him dead in some rich guy's mansion, in his private safe. He was trying to make friends with some guard dogs, but it didn't work. They tore him to shreds."

I swallowed hard.

"Everyone knew Bartholomew must have been involved, but nobody could prove it."

I wondered which parts of this story were true. Zeda's version sounded a lot more realistic than the Goth kids' story had.

Bartholomew's truck driver went walking by us at that moment, rolling Matilda's canvas-covered cage behind him. We fell silent, watching him.

"Oh, no," Zeda said, her eyes filling with tears again. "Matilda."

I had to stop those tears from rolling down her face again. I just had to.

"Zeda," I said, "if you help me get in that truck, I promise I'll bring Matilda back to you."

"You'd do that for me?" Zeda asked, her mouth open in shock. Inside I was thinking, *Uh-oh. What did I just do?*

"Yes," I found myself saying in a strong voice that didn't sound at all like my own. "I won't let her be another one of Bartholomew's..." I searched for a word. "Slaves."

"You're really a hero," she said, and my face got all hot.

She started giving me tips for handling Matilda, but it wasn't until she started saying stuff like "just keep her under your sweatshirt" that I fully understood what I'd promised. When would I have time to take Matilda back to Zeda? And how would I keep track of a monkey when I was doing everything else? But looking at Zeda looking at me... I didn't even try to take it back. I remembered once Dad told me that girls were trouble, and now I was beginning to think I knew what he meant.

"All right. I'll help you get on the truck if you promise me one more thing," she said.

Uh-oh.

"Promise to be careful."

"I promise."

And then she kissed me.

I WAS IN A DAZE while I got my backpack and the suitcase. I hadn't wiped off my lips, I was just letting her kiss evaporate into the desert air.

I felt like a poet when I realized that's what I was doing.

Concentrate, Poop Lip. Don't be any more of a twit. It was Will's voice again, and for once I was grateful.

I watched from around the corner of the tent while Zeda got Nero and her dad to help load Matilda's cage into the back of the truck. Then Zeda pretended to cry.

"Please make sure they take care of her," Zeda sobbed, collapsing into the stunned driver. "She's not strong enough for the circus life."

"Hey," said the driver, looking around him for some help. Robin and Nero stepped off the truck and looked at Zeda with confusion but, whether they bought her act or not, they were still headed away from the truck. Zeda took the driver's arm and dragged him over to Remmy at the tables—*away* from the truck. The coast was clear.

It was my chance.

I tore across the grass to the truck and jumped in. The narrow opening between the cage and the wall was barely wide enough for my suitcase, but I wedged it in there and crammed myself in after it.

All they had to do was close the back door and I'd be as good as in Portland.

"But she's endangered!" I heard Zeda cry out. I wasn't sure if she was acting then or not. I heard something skitter under the canvas and I flinched. Matilda! I still had no clue what she looked like.

Come on, Zeda, you can stop acting now. Let him shut the truck and get me on the road!

Then I heard Zeda's voice, close to the truck, saying, "No, no. I'll get the back door. I need to tell her good-bye."

I peeked out. I could see Zeda standing at the truck's back door, silhouetted against the fading night sky. She slid a small box across the truck floor toward me.

"*Good luck, Spartacus*," she whispered, right before slamming the door shut, leaving me in the pitch-black darkness.

CHAPTER 19

I DON'T KNOW HOW I fell asleep wedged in behind the cage, but I must have, because I dreamt I was a kid again, riding in the back of our red wagon. It was one turn, one jolt after another, beams of light bouncing through the cracks in the door. A dip in the road bounced my head against the wall and I woke up, thinking Will had just pulled my wagon off into a ditch.

I stood in the dark of the truck, rubbing the sore spot above my ear where I'd also banged my head against the cage. I didn't have a clue how long I'd been asleep, but when I thought about the distance between Nevada and Oregon, I knew I had a lot longer to go. I pushed a button on my watch and saw it was almost ten at night. We'd been on the road for about two hours.

I groped around in my backpack and found my flashlight. The back of the truck was empty except for the cage and the small box Zeda had pushed in at the last minute. I grabbed the box and sat down on the cold metal floor. Inside were a bunch of granola bars, a can of nuts, a bottle of water, a face-painting kit, a book about breathing fire (*Doug the Dragon's Official Guide to Fire Breathing [Without Loss of Life]*), and a compact torch with a small bottle of paraffin (for fire breathing). Finally, there was a small key, a canister of fruit, and a plastic container filled with—*ew, grubs!* Each was labeled, *Matilda.* I'd almost forgotten—I wasn't alone.

The cage waited for me at the other end of the truck, nylon ropes securing it in place. I hadn't noticed before, but the air had that thick, farm-like smell of animal. I guessed it was time to meet Matilda.

I propped the flashlight up on my backpack so it was aimed at the cage and then went to work on moving the canvas aside without untying the ropes—I wanted the cage to look exactly like the driver had left it. I lifted the canvas off of one side, but the light from the flashlight didn't reach the back of the cage.

"Hey, Matilda," I whispered, getting closer. "It's okay, girl. I've got some fruit." I took a banana out of the box, and held it between the bars.

"Here, Matilda. Looky what I have here…"

When you think about monkeys, you usually think of those cute monkeys with the long arms, or maybe, if you don't know the difference, you might think about a chimp or a gorilla.

Never, in your strangest dreams, would you expect Matilda.

I'm ashamed to say it, but I actually let out a terrified "AYIEEE!" when she came into the light. Matilda was not a chimp or a cuddly monkey. Matilda was this black and gray gremlin-like thing the size of a large cat. She had the pale, whitish face of a blunt-nosed possum, the tail of a squirrel, the ears of a bat, and sparse fur like—I don't know, like a cheap stuffed animal. But her eyes! *My god,* her giant eyes were glowing yellow.

"Matilda?" I squeaked. She didn't seem at all alarmed by me—or my scream. She probably got that all the time. In fact, she padded over on four legs before pulling herself up so she stood even with me. She reached through the bars with a long, slender arm—and I saw it. The finger of death. It was longer than all the rest, as thin as a twig...

And she pointed it right at me.

"She'll point a finger at you and then it's just a matter of time before you're dead," Remmy had said. I looked at Matilda, who was still pointing at me and twitching her huge ears and her possum nose. Then I realized the truth of what Remmy had said. It was a fact: I would die eventually. But hopefully not for a while.

Besides, she wasn't pointing at me. She was pointing at the banana.

IT TOOK ME A WHILE to go from just tossing the fruit to Matilda to actually handing it to her. I knew I had to get used to her—I was going to have to carry her out of the truck. *"Under your sweatshirt,"* Zeda had said. I shivered. At least she seemed tame enough.

"You're going to be fine, right Matilda?" I shined the flashlight in her cage and watched her amble back toward the corner, where there was a small log. She tapped at it with her long finger, like she was looking for something. Then she just sat there, looking kind of pathetic. I could understand why Zeda felt so bad for her.

I took out the book on fire breathing and read sitting next to the cage. I read it through twice before checking my watch. Nearly midnight. I had no clue when we'd get to Portland, but I figured I had time to get some sleep.

I put the canvas back the way it had been in case the driver looked in while I was sleeping. Then I ate a granola bar and drank some water. I hate to say it, but I relieved myself in the corner of the truck near the door. I didn't have much of a choice. At least it seemed to trickle out the back door.

I set the box off to the side and wedged myself back behind the cage. I wish I knew how long the drive would take, but all I could figure was that it took nine hours to get from Albuquerque to Las Vegas, and Portland had to be at least twice as far.

I MUST HAVE SLEPT FOR eight hours straight before I woke up with a jolt. We weren't moving, but there was no way we were there yet, either. The driver was talking right outside the back of the truck. I could only hear half the conversation so I assumed he was on his phone. "Keith? Yeah, it's me. Just crossed into Oregon. This drive is killing me. Yeah... I'm busting my balls to get there on time. This is such a waste of my time. They should have just bought the stupid animal a plane ticket."

There was a pause. Then,

"How big is it? It's, well, it's huge... Looks like a tall goat."

Like a goat? I frowned.

"*Oh*, the cage. Let me go measure it."

My blood ran cold. He was going to find me. I felt completely exposed, even from my spot behind the cage. I pressed myself further into the corner as the door trundled up, letting the morning light shine in.

"Yeah, yeah, I'm getting out my tape measure. *Geez*, it smells back here."

I held my breath, waiting for the sound of him climbing in the back, but it didn't come. I did hear the measuring tape hitting the ground outside.

"Yeah, I'd say it's… five feet by… four feet… by four feet."

What? Was he just making it up? I didn't dare look—and apparently, he didn't either. At Matilda, that is. He was scared of Matilda so he was just making it up!

"You got that? Good… Well, *yeah*, she was pointing her stupid hoof at me the whole time, but I don't give a crap. So, I'll be about five more hours… Yeah, this should be a cinch compared to last time. Silverware's a lot easier to haul than paintings, that's for sure."

Paintings!

"Well, Bart's gotta do some of his own legwork. It was too close last time… yeah, well that's a bunch of bull—" The slam of the trailer door cut off the rest.

"You sure pointed your hoof at *him*, Matilda," I whispered. I heard her tapping on the log as an answer. And I would have bet anything that they talking about the Georgia O'Keeffe paintings that were stolen in Santa Fe. If I didn't have enough proof already, this sure sealed the deal. I wasn't imagining it all. But what was that about silverware?

The truck came to life and started moving again.

I leaned back on my backpack, and, try as I might to think about the robberies, I began thinking about the sideshow.

Okay, I thought about Zeda.

She actually kissed me.

That's when I remembered the tattoo she'd been drawing—I hadn't even had a chance to look at it! I got out the flashlight, shined it on my arm, and grinned. She'd drawn a lion, shouldering his way through flames, with *Spartacus* written on a waving banner beneath it. I sighed just looking at it. It really was cool.

After I'd stared at the tattoo long enough, I started to get my stuff together. I emptied out my backpack and separated the things I'd need from the stuff I could get rid of. I couldn't believe I'd packed so much useless—and heavy—junk. Will's scout handbook, for example. Sure, it explained how to make knots and capture squirrels and store water, but had I actually thought I was going to need that?

Sure, just steal my stuff, Poopy. It was Will's voice, threatening me. *I'll get even sooner or later.*

Maybe I *did* need to learn something from the book. Like, how to barricade a bedroom door.

As I thumbed through it, a piece of heavy paper came loose and fell into my lap.

It was a blank postcard.

I shook Will's book and five more postcards slipped out. They were all from different places, places with weird names. Dynamite, Washington; Stop, Arkansas; Asylum, Pennsylvania; Covert, New York; Murder Bay, D.C.; Hazard, Nebraska.

No. It wasn't possible.

I flipped the cards over, scanning them quickly. They all had the mysterious Antarctica postmarks on them. On the back of one card, dated ahead for mid-July, a message was scrawled in sloppy handwriting:

Hello, Spartacus!
Well! Everything is going great out here on the road. Had a grate crowd on the forth of July—so many people, it was crazy! Tell your brother hello and give your dad a hug, ok?

Love,
Mom

This was a really simple code—easy peasy. All you had to do was read the bolded letters: ***Where are you?***

I glanced through a few more postcards. They all had similar messages.

There was only one explanation for this. Will was the one who was sending me the postcards—the ones I thought Mom was sending to ask for help.

Un.

Freaking.

Believable.

The words "seething rage" don't begin to describe what I felt. Even "seething, white-hot rage" doesn't cut it. I was so angry I was *seeing through time.*

Mom hadn't been kidnapped at all, and Will was... well, there was no better way to put it: Will was the most hateful, rotten, vile ass hat to ever roam the earth.

It was probably a good thing I was trapped in the back of that truck, because if I'd had any sort of room to move or stuff to throw, I would have started destroying things—like my fists, trying to punch a building over.

"'*Where are you?*'" I spat out, repeating Will's secret postcard message. *Oh, Will, just you wait. I'll be there soon enough.*

In my mind, I was already home and in Will's room destroying every single trophy in the World of Fartcraft with a sledgehammer. I was shredding the sports posters that plastered his walls. I was beating Will to a pulp with my bare hands. See a common theme here? Destruction. I wasn't Poop Lip any more. I wasn't Ryan. I wasn't even Spartacus. I was The Destroyer.

Yeah, "seething rage" doesn't quite cover all that.

I stomped around in the back of the truck, making up new curse words and fantasizing about which of Will's prized possessions I'd break first.

When I added it all up, the day-to-day crap, the swimming pool trick, and now *this?* I mean, what was *wrong* with him? I seriously wondered if I could get him put away, like how Dad had threatened to do to Mom if she didn't behave normally. Committed. Taken to an asylum.

"Can you do that with fifteen-year-olds?" I mused in Matilda's direction. She didn't answer.

I took a deep breath. Then another. Trying to clear my head. Trying to think...

Breathe. Instant Calm Breath Method... Forget about Will for a minute, Spart. Just think about what this means for the plan.

I ALREADY EXPLAINED HOW MY mom was always doing weird things. There was the jumping off the roof, of course. And the time I found her karate-chopping boards in half in the garage, and the time she practiced kickboxing with a mannequin she got from the mall.

It wasn't until after she showed me her audition video, about a year before she disappeared, that she really began opening up to me. One day I came home to find her throwing knives at a dartboard in the backyard. She was going to stop, but I convinced her to keep going, that I really wanted to learn. We spent the next few hours throwing the knives; she showed me how to hold them so I wouldn't hurt myself, how to feel the weight of the knife, how to fling it with just the right amount of spin. Then Will and Dad got home and we had to stop, which was how a lot of our time together ended after that.

I wasn't that good at the knife throwing that day, but I practiced on my own and got a lot better. I wanted to surprise her, to show her I had a crazy side, too. I got a couple library books on it and read about it online. I practiced secretly with our steak knives against the side of our shed out back.

But Mom could be weird sometimes. Not weird like throwing knives weird; that was okay with me. But weird like—well, let me explain.

After a few months, I finally felt ready and called her outside to see. She watched as I put up a picture of a National Geographic shark on the back of the shed. I stood ten feet away and I did my Instant Calm Breath Method to ready myself for the throw. I pulled back the knife, aimed, and let it fly.

It stuck in the picture, right in the shark's forehead.

Mom was impressed, I could tell. But I should have known better—I'd definitely chosen the wrong time to show her. She was irritated, in the middle of one of her tired, easily frustrated, I-just-want-to-be-alone moods—exactly the opposite of her training mode, when she was learning everything there was to know about something-or-other.

So I shouldn't have been too disappointed when she wasn't more excited. Instead, she said it was really cold and that she wanted to go back inside to lie down.

But I couldn't let her just go back in. I needed to ask her something. I felt like I'd *earned* the right to ask her this—maybe that's why I'd been working on the knife throwing all along.

The question I asked was, "What happens if you get into the circus?"

She went quiet for a moment. As she thought, I realized how tired she looked, like when she got her bad headaches and didn't want to leave her bedroom.

"Well, it's not easy to get in," she said slowly. "It's a long shot for me to make it. I don't think I'm ready yet."

She hadn't gotten the point, so I asked, "But will we get to see you?"'

Her eyes went bright for a moment, like she was really there with me and not thinking about her bed. "Of course you'd get to see me, Spartacus," she said. Her voice was soft but clear. "You'd see me a lot. And I'd come and see you. We'd still be together. I promise."

She even put her hand on my shoulder and squeezed it before turning to go back inside.

But that's what she said: "I promise." I remember it clearly. And she had never broken a promise.

What I'm trying to say is this: My mom was weird. That's pretty clear by now, I guess. Maybe it was because of the car accident. Maybe it was a midlife crisis. Maybe she'd always been that way. Who knows? But whatever she was, she wasn't a liar. Something must have been really wrong for her to break her promise.

So that's why I had to keep going, no matter what. Even if Mom hadn't been asking for my help. Even if the post-cards weren't true. Even if there had been no destroyed house, even if Eli had never seen the Black Van, and even if there was no Not-Mom. Even if Bartholomew hadn't been involved in robbing museums. I knew, beyond a shadow of a doubt, that Mom would have visited me and Will if she could.

So what did this new postcard prank change?

Absolutely nothing.

I still had to make sure my mom was okay.

When I was calm again, I lifted the canvas on the cage and fed Matilda some grubs (all I can say is *ewwww*). After she finished eating, she lay down against the bars with her body warm against my thigh. I sat there and petted her sur-prisingly soft fur, trying to clear my mind. As mad as I was, I couldn't afford to spend all my energy plotting against Will. I needed to focus on what was coming up, what I was about to face in Portland. Bartholomew was today. Will could wait until tomorrow.

So there in the dark, I tried my best to sit still and medi-tate like a monk. As I concentrated, my plan began evolv-ing, improving. When the final idea came, though, it gave me a rush of chills. I was almost too scared to even think about it, but as I tentatively turned the thought over and over again in my mind… I realized it was fairly airtight. That, and it meshed perfectly with my reckless mood.

It was good. This new plan just might work.

By four in the afternoon, it was time to get ready—and I was more than ready to get out of that hot, stinking truck.

We could be getting there anytime. When I got out of the truck in Portland, I'd have to hit the ground running. Literally.

First thing I had to do was use some of Nero's face paint to cover the freckle on my lip. It wasn't the greatest disguise ever, but, short of completely covering my face, there was nothing else I could do. Next, I finished gathering together the things I was going to keep with me. I decided to leave the suitcase behind, worried that it would slow me down. I had another way to get Mom out. But I couldn't put Matilda in it, either. It would just make me look even more suspicious. It was a Catch-22. So, I stuffed it all in the side pockets of my backpack, leaving the main part empty so there would be a nice, big-ish place for Matilda.

I could practically hear Will scoffing, *Just gonna carry a wild monkey in your backpack. Brilliant plan, Poopy.*

It was seeming like a worse idea with every moment. First of all, Matilda was an endangered species. How many aye-ayes did Zeda say were even left? Like, a thousand? What if I squished her in the bag or something?

But with her patchy fur and her large, yellow eyes—well, there was no way I could just carry her around in public.

"I bet you have a great personality, though," I said. Matilda blinked shyly, the flashlight's beam making her delicate, crinkly black ears glow pinkish. As I watched, she reached out with her long finger and touched the door latch, her whiskers quivering.

Think about Zeda. You're doing this for Zeda.

Before I lost my nerve, I fished Zeda's key out of my pocket and flung open the cage door. Matilda didn't hesitate either—she scrambled right up my pant leg and into my arms.

I cringed as she sniffed my face with her damp, pug nose. "You're—you're just like a cat, aren't you?" I said, trying to make myself feel better.

After that, Matilda and I sat in the dark, the backpack open in front of us. I ate the last two granola bars and gave some water to Matilda, who slurped it straight from the bottle.

That's when the truck started to slow down. I put an annoyed Matilda in the backpack and got ready.

CHAPTER 20

THE LOOK ON THE DRIVER'S face was priceless when I burst out from the truck, screaming 'Yahhhh!' I took off like a madman through a parking lot filled with sunshine-yellow trucks. On each of them, in red, curvy letters, was printed: *Bartholomew's World-Renowned Circus of the Incredible.*

I didn't slow down until I'd reached a walkway next to a river and was sure I wasn't being chased by the driver. I was so proud of myself that I shouted again.

"Yesss!"

I'd made it! I felt pretty puffed-up and arrogant as I walked through a busy city park, wearing the backpack with Matilda inside. That is, until I saw a poster with my face on it, stuck to a lamppost. Then another one, hanging in the front window of a store.

Not good.

I couldn't stop the reflex to slap my forehead. *I'm still a missing kid.* I snatched Will's baseball hat out of the bag and jammed it down on my head. At least I'd hidden my freckle. Then I dashed past the two posters, thinking if I could get far enough away from them, nobody would recognize me.

I don't know how that thought had slipped my mind—I'd only been worried about Bartholomew. All my nervousness came flooding back. How was I going be in public if everyone was on the lookout for me? How could I possibly rescue Mom?

As I crept along, though, I noticed that there were kids *everywhere*. I slowed, looking to my left, to my right. Kids with parents, kids alone, kids with big groups of friends.

How about that?

In Portland, I realized I was completely inconspicuous. It blew my mind. In every small town I'd been over the last few days, I'd felt like I would get caught at any moment. But in a big city, there were so many kids wandering around, nobody would even look twice at me!

I let out a shaky breath, before glancing back at the missing poster behind me. Seeing it taped in the window, a weird twinge of guilt passed over me. I couldn't help thinking how I'd probably messed up Dad's whole week—and yes, even *worried* him—but I pushed that feeling away. If everything played out according to plan, all would be forgiven in just a few hours. Mom would be home and Bartholomew's secret would be exposed, for everyone to see.

The circus was set up right at the edge of the park, with the tent backed up against the river. I easily blended in with all the joggers and families out walking.

It's funny—I knew I would catch up to the circus at some point, but I didn't imagine how it would feel, seeing that sprawling circus tent—blue and red, just like the picture from Bartholomew's website. I almost didn't believe it, expecting another Big Let Down. But there was no question: this was *it*. The tent was monstrous in comparison to the sideshow tent. I couldn't stay very close, though—by now, the guy from the truck must have told everyone about the screaming kid jumping out at him, not to mention the missing animal.

As if reading my mind, Matilda started scritching around inside the backpack. I reached back and patted the side of it to say hello, hoping she wasn't getting too rattled around in there. My mind was racing. Would Bartholomew's people connect me with Matilda's disappearance? Maybe, if Bartholomew was expecting me based on my run-in with Not-Mom and Sharkman in Albuquerque...

Don't think about it, I told myself. You can't change what Bartholomew might or might not know. Not now.

But I still didn't have a good grasp on what I was going to do with Matilda once I was inside the circus—not to mention during the rescue.

And why did you promise this again?

Well, I knew why. Zeda. Now I had to deal with it. Sure, Matilda was a small hiccup in The Plan—a tiny, balding wildcard. But the rest? I had the rest figured out.

THE PARK WAS IN DOWNTOWN Portland, running along the river that ran right through the city. I thought I remembered there being a big library not too far away. We'd been to Portland as a family a few times before. Last year, Dad, Mom, Will, and I all came up for a carnival in this same park. It'd been Mom's idea—she liked to get out of Brenville whenever she could. The carnival hadn't been anything big like Bartholomew's, just a few rides and live music and lots of fair food. Mom and I shared an elephant ear and I threw up on The Zipper.

It was the last time we all took a trip together and, as I went down the street, I realized we hadn't left Brenville *once* since Mom had disappeared.

I sighed. Dad must have been pretty depressed with Mom gone. He hadn't really done much of anything since she left—we didn't even get a Christmas tree.

I asked a few people for directions to the library and I was in luck. The library, a huge brick and stone building with arched entryways and marble stairs, was only a few blocks away.

Once inside, I found a computer that someone hadn't logged off of and sat down, propping the backpack gingerly at my feet. Matilda was still calm as a clam in there, moving around a little bit, but not making any noise. I hoped she'd stay that way. I didn't want this library trip to end the way the last one had.

I checked my email and saw that Eli wasn't online. There were two emails from him, though. I opened the newest one first from that morning.

A small wave of panic came over me when I read it.

Funkspiel: They got to me. They only know about Las Vegas. Don't contact me—I can't blab what I don't know. Sorry and good luck.
—Peter.Parker

I resisted the urge to email him back. Eli was right. If he didn't know where I was, he couldn't spill the beans. But poor Eli! I felt terrible. His parents weren't the type to punish with grounding or no TV or something. They might... well, I didn't even want to think about what they might do. It was pretty much the worst thing he'd ever done. But I couldn't dwell on it there in the library. Cruel as it felt to not have a moment of silence or *something*, I told myself James Bond wouldn't abandon the mission—Eli was what Dad would call collateral damage. Eli would be okay—but I'd have to be extra nice to him when I got back.

At least they didn't know I was in Portland.

Except...

Except if Eli told them I was following the circus, it wouldn't be too hard to track me down. Even though the circus website didn't have the Portland performance listed, it would just take a quick Internet search to bring it up, the way Eli had.

That's when it hit me: it was tonight or never.

My heart pounded as I opened the second message from Eli.

Funkspiel: Probable cause to abort mission. Open forwarded email.
—Peter.Parker

I scrolled down and found an email from Will attached. It was from yesterday.

Dear Eli,

I know your at camp but I'm sure you know Ryan went missing on Friday nite. I know you don't think much of me, but I need to ask you if your helping Ryan. If your in touch with him, please let him know that I wrote all the postcards from mom, saying she was kidnaped. I didn't know I'd gone to far until he was gone. Please tell him I'm sorry and ask him to come home.

-Will

The first thing that came to mind was, "Wow, he must feel terrible."

The second was, "Good."

I hadn't run away to make Will sorry, but maybe an *eensy* bit of me hoped he would be—and that was even before I found out about the postcards. Then an evil smile spread across my face, wide and bright. Man, he was going to be in so much trouble when Dad found out. *That* was something to look forward to.

Next I did a search for "Portland Oregon Bartholomew's Circus" and found a news blurb about it right away. The show started at 8 PM. That was just over an hour away. Next, I typed in "Portland Oregon silverware museum." The first result: The Portland Art Museum. I clicked on it. Oldest art museum in the area, blah, blah, blah... and... *Ah-ha!*

Bingo.

Just a month ago, they'd received a gift from an anonymous donor—an extensive collection of European silverware from the 1500s.

"One of the few collections of its kind." Sounded like a pretty boring thing to steal—not nearly as impressive as the streetcar or the dinosaur bones. But it did sound like it would be worth a lot of money. Not only that, the museum was only a few blocks away—within easy reach of the circus.

This is it, I thought. I'd found Bartholomew's target.

I scrolled through the pictures of the silverware collection, feeling weird—guilty, even—for looking, knowing it was about to be stolen. It wasn't hard to imagine Mom repelling down from the roof and swinging through one of the windows.

I shook my head.

Mom wouldn't be there; she'd be with *me*. Bartholomew wouldn't be there either—he'd be in the back of a squad car or at the police station. I played with the idea of calling the museum to warn them, but then they'd call the cops and the cops would alert Bartholomew and Bartholomew would take off again just like he had in Albuquerque and Vegas.

And then I'd be right where I started.

Anyway, it was time for the next part of The Plan. The dangerous part.

I GRABBED MY BACKPACK AND hurried over to the payphone I'd spotted on my way into the library. I pulled a slip of paper out of my pocket, pumped a couple quarters in the slot, took a deep breath, and dialed the number on it.

"Be brave," I told myself, even though my hand had already started sweating.

It rang twice, and then—came the answer...

"Lloyd here."

I opened my mouth and nothing came out. Just hearing his voice made my heart race and my hands go clammy.

Remember. He's not a serial *killer—just a* regular *killer.*

Somehow Hailey's words of wisdom didn't relax me.

He spoke again, "Hello?"

Say something!

"Hey, Lloyd! It's... it's Ry—it's, uh, it's Spartacus," I finally forced out. I couldn't even remember which name Eli had given him.

"Spartacus!" he roared. "How are you?"

"Okay. Well, uh," I stammered before saying all in a rush, "I remembered you said you lived in Portland. Well, uh, my mom's show—I mean, Bartholomew's Circus is in town tonight and I—"

"No way!" he whooped into the phone. "You didn't tell me that before."

"Well, yeah," I said, picking at a taxi advertisement sticker on the wall. I didn't know what to say. "They change their plans a lot. It's hard to tell where they're going next."

Half lie, half truth.

"That's good news," Lloyd said. "You seemed kinda down before. I hope everything's okay."

I nodded into the phone. "Oh, yeah, everything's fine. I wanted to—well, I wanted to see if, well," I trailed off. This was worse than asking a girl out. Not that I'd ever actually done that... "Would you want to go? I mean, you said you really liked the circus."

All true, so it was easy to say. So far so good.

"Well, absolutely! Did you want to meet up for dinner beforehand?" he asked.

"Uh, no! No, this is kind of a last minute invite. It actually starts pretty soon—at 8 PM. I'll just meet you in front, huh?"

I put my hand up to my face. My voice was almost shaking as we confirmed the details—we were going to meet at the ticket booth at 7:45.

OKAY, SO YOU PROBABLY WANT to know why I invited Lloyd the Killer to the circus. The way I saw it, I couldn't just sneak Mom out like I'd originally planned. I'd left behind the suitcase and Bartholomew's was too big, too organized for that kind of child's play, anyway. Plus, they might know I was coming. What I needed was chaos. What I needed was... a diversion—a big, bald, scary diversion.

That's where Lloyd came in.

Apparently, kidnapped mothers and runaway kids weren't enough to get the cops' attention, but maybe an FBI's most wanted murderer *was*. The plan went like this: I sit with Lloyd for the first half of the show, slip away to call the cops at intermission, sneak backstage, find Mom, and tell her everything. A bunch of police officers show up, maybe even SWAT team—Lloyd was an incredibly dangerous fugitive, after all—just in time for the end of the show. The cops close in on Lloyd, Bartholomew thinks they're coming for him, and chaos breaks loose. With cops all over the place, Mom sees her opportunity to get away from Bartholomew, and she and I escape to safety. Once Mom's out of harm's way, we tell the cops about Bartholomew—the stolen artwork, the keeping people against their will, and whatever else he'd been up to. The cops arrest Bartholomew, and throw him into the back of a squad car right beside Lloyd.

Simple, really.

Okay, so maybe it wasn't *ideal*. Everything had to go just right—and I had to explain the monkey in my backpack to the wanted felon I was about to betray. So, yeah, I wouldn't say that the plan was *flawless*. I'd said such things before and been very wrong. But, even though I was terrified by all the dangerous wheels I'd be setting in motion, it was the best plan I could come up with.

Before leaving the library, I ducked into an empty bathroom—luckily it was private, with its own room and door.

I opened the backpack and let Matilda out to stretch her scrawny legs, knowing it was her last snack break for a good hour or so—but she just yawned and then winked sleepily at me from the bottom of the bag.

"Come on, lazy bones," I said, nudging her. "It's a rest stop." I even tried coaxing her with a piece of watermelon, but she only sniffed it and then closed her eyes again.

"Suit yourself," I said, giving her a light pat.

Next, I changed into my dark suit and tie. When Eli and I had planned this out, he'd thought I'd blend in better backstage if I was dressed nice. I'd initially thought it was stupid, but I'd seen it work when I snuck into the sideshow.

Next, I put my pocketknife and screwdriver set in one jacket pocket, and the small torch and bottle of paraffin in the other. Finally, I touched up my freckle with beige face paint. It was funny how much that freckle made me who I was—without it, I didn't look like me at all. I could have been anybody.

As I buttoned my cuffs, smoothed my hair, and straightened my tie in the mirror, I felt very James Bond. Very...
Secret Agent Man.

I scowled at myself in the mirror.

*Not bad, Spartacus. A few more bruises and cuts and
you'll look like an action hero.*

I checked inside the bag, where Matilda was snoozing.
She was even making a little nose whistle, and she didn't
seem to notice me zipping the bag closed on her.

"It'll just be a few hours," I whispered. "I promise." I
just hoped she'd stay calm once we were inside the circus. If
she started making noises or moving around too much, she
could blow my whole plan.

CHAPTER 21

I GOT TO THE CIRCUS an hour before I had to meet Lloyd. I wanted a chance to case the joint. I had to know how the circus was laid out and plot all the major escape routes.

There was a lot more activity than before and the circus was spilling out into the park. There were kids milling around everywhere, trying to get a look beyond the waist-high fence that kept them back. I didn't want to stand out but I was older than all of them, and taller by a foot. And I was also wearing a suit. So I hung back a bit, scheming.

Men and women in yellow shirts bustled around inside the fence, pulling wires tight on the tents and hammering down tent stakes. Just inside the fence were a few booths with food, souvenirs, and face painting.

I wondered if all the circus workers were in on the robberies, or just a few chosen henchmen. I studied them for a bit, but no one looked particularly sinister. I walked the length of the tent, hoping to get a glimpse of the side that faced the river. I'd just reached the far end of the low fence when I saw them: Bartholomew's giant buses, just rolling in.

"No way," I said, under my breath. I mean, I knew Bartholomew was an upscale circus, but *tour buses?*

They looked like something rock and roll stars would travel in, painted with giant, vibrant murals of tumblers, trapeze artists, magicians, tightrope walkers, contortionists, lions, tigers, elephants—all in shades of bright green, red, and orange, and all larger than life.

As the buses pulled in beside the tent, a flood of cheering kids surrounded me, chattering excitedly and pointing. I stood there, heads above them all and scowling, knowing how Bart paid for those buses. Dirty money. And if what Puck and Zeda said was true, those performers were stuck in the circus for life. There were probably bars behind those painted windows.

I snorted and shook my head, laughing at the horrible joke of it all. Three girls, a little bit younger than I was, were watching the circus beside me, and one turned to look at me.

"It's all a big joke," I blurted out to them. She and her little friends giggled, and I looked back at the buses, my face burning red. They didn't care if the circus was evil or not—they just wanted to be entertained. It wasn't their fault.

That's when the last bus pulled in. I knew it was hers, without even reading the side of it. But there it was, in scrolling red letters: *The Amazing Athena.*

The mural was of her face, her black hair changing into rolling hills, shadows of camels and elephants walking along her locks. They'd painted her to look like a super-hero, in deep blues and reds and a crown of stars. When the bus turned I saw the other side where she was painted standing up, with lions at her feet, a whip in one hand and a hoop of flames in the other.

"Holy moly," I said under my breath. But there was the teeniest grin on my face. Even though Bartholomew's was a front for a crime ring, even though my mom and all her fellow performers were trapped there against their will, Mom was still the star of the circus. She'd be able to leave Bartholomew's and find a better circus. She had all the potential in the world—if she could only get free.

We're almost there, Mom.

I heard the girls beside me whispering. I turned to see them staring at me. Wide-eyed.

"Um, your backpack is moving," said one of them.

Matilda!

And it was. I could feel the monkey digging into the canvas like she was trying to escape.

"Oh," was all I said before turning on my heel and speeding back toward the park.

"Hang in there, Matilda," I said, reaching back and patting the side of the bag. The pressure of my hand seemed to calm her and I slowed down.

The parking lot was starting to fill up with families. I checked my watch. I had thirty more minutes until I had to meet Lloyd. I felt that familiar panic rising in my chest.

Breathe, Spartacus.

Lloyd wasn't going to kill me. Not in front of a circus.

As I watched the ticket line form, my fear shifted from Lloyd to Bart. I started to feel really—well, *conspicuous.* The suit was starting to seem like a bad idea. It might help me blend in when I got backstage, but it wasn't helping me out front. Could I really get inside the circus without Bartholomew's people recognizing me?

If only I had a mask...

That's when I got the idea.

It wasn't hard to find a port-o-potty. Taking a deep breath, I went inside. When I opened the backpack, Matilda darted out and clung to my waist, suddenly looking a lot more alert—and nervous—than she had before.

"Easy, Matilda," I said, handing over a banana and then petting her, which seemed to calm her—but she didn't climb down. So, with Matilda hanging on me, I put the toilet seat down and got out my face painting kit. Using the plastic mirror on the port-o-potty door, I painted my entire face with flames. It wasn't perfect, but it was good enough. I stepped back and admired my work in the mirror.

Very clever, kid.

And it was. Not only would I blend in a bit more with all of the rest of the kids (suit aside, of course), but no one would recognize me as Ryan the Runaway, or Spartacus, Son of Athena. I hardly recognized myself in the scratched-up mirror.

"Pleased to meet you," I said stoically to my reflection before laughing. I thought of Lloyd's tattoo. *Hope you guess my name.* Fitting line, for Lloyd.

And for me, too. *Ryan. Spartacus. Poop Lip.*

Guess my name.

I continued thinking about Lloyd as I put Matilda (who was not as easygoing this time) back in the bag. What was that movie quote he had told me again? Someone asks Spartacus if he is afraid to die... and he says... something like *"not any more than I was afraid of being born"*... right?

Sure, freeing some circus folk wasn't exactly the same as leading a slave revolt or anything, but I was still afraid. As I straightened up, I checked my face paint in the mirror one last time.

"How about it, Spartacus? Are you afraid to die?" I asked myself. And suddenly, saying the name out loud, I felt it. I mean, I really felt that name *meant* something. I looked myself in the eye, trying to decide how it felt to be Spartacus. Was I still scared? Yes.

"But no more than I was to be born," I breathed. And I meant it.

I think.

WHEN I STEPPED OUT OF the horrible, hot port-o-potty, it was 7:43. *Here we go.*

The edge of the park was crawling with families and children, and the ticket line was now snaking all the way down the street. Babies were crying and kids were playing in the grass. A clown on stilts stood by the road, holding an upside down sign that said *Circus Tonight!* Some kids threw dandelions at him.

I knew I'd made a good choice with the face paint—the lady with the face painting booth had covered almost every face under ten years old with some sort of animal or scene. My flames were by far the coolest face paint, which helped make up for the fact that I was several inches taller than all of the other kids.

I hadn't ventured very far into the crowd when I felt Matilda moving again. Like before, only more frantic.

Uh-oh.

Suddenly, my hope that Matilda would stay calm during the show seemed incredibly stupid. I mean, the success of my entire plan depended on the mood of a monkey. If she gave me away, I was toast. As if to illustrate my point, she chose that very moment to release a series of short, unhappy screeches. And people definitely noticed. Two little kids stared, mouths open. A lady, lugging a whining toddler, perked up her ear to listen to the noise.

Crap. Crap. Crap.

I ducked behind a funnel-cake stand, away from the people. Despite the crowds, our little spot was out of sight and was the safest place I was going to find. Retreating as far behind the booth as I could, I shrugged off the backpack, hoping Matilda was just bored and not... well, angry. I got out an apple slice, hoping it would calm her down.

"Hey, Monkey, what's happening—"

I never got to the last part of that question.

I'd unzipped the pack the tiniest fraction of an inch when she burst out like, well, like she'd been shot out of a cannon. In two seconds, she'd raced up my arm, leapt off my head, and scrambled up the funnel-cake stand.

Oh, man. I smacked my forehead. She was so quick I never saw it coming! I watched as she settled on a tent support beam about twenty feet above me. She'd been so slow and calm before! I never even thought about what to do if she tried to escape. Why hadn't Zeda warned me? *Just carry her in your sweatshirt!* Great idea.

"Matilda!" I hissed, but she didn't even blink. How was I going to get Matilda back to Zeda now? I was crazy to have made that promise. I'd probably doomed Matilda to her death, being loose in this park in the city.

"Matilda!" I spoke louder. Still no reaction. She just sat looking down at me, calm as can be. I held out the apple, hoping she'd be tempted, but nothing.

The thought of calling Zeda, and how her voice would crack when I told her what happened... well, the thought actually hurt.

"*Matilda!*" I finally shouted. Nothing. But it didn't matter. I was already late to meet Lloyd—I was out of time.

"I'm so sorry, Matilda," I whispered. "I'll come back. I promise. I won't leave you for too long." I thought I saw her tail twitch, but that was all. I put the apple on the grass and wondered if she would stay where she was or if she would accidently scramble out into traffic before I could come back? I had no idea. I sighed heavily.

Coming out from behind the booth, I made a mental note where I was. *After the circus. Maybe she'll still be here after the circus...*

I was still looking up into the shadows of the tent when I heard it.

"Spartacus!" a voice boomed over the squawking children.

I turned to see who was calling my name, even though I knew who it had to be. There he was, looking twice as big as I'd remembered.

Striding directly toward me.

It was Lloyd.

"Whatcha looking at up there? A squirrel?" he asked.

"Oh, hi," I said, surprised again just by the sheer size of him. I turned away from the funnel-cake stand, hoping he wouldn't keep looking up there. "Uh, yeah, big squirrel up there."

"Huh. Well! It's good to see you again!" he said, giving me a hearty pat on my back. "Great face paint. And that suit again. Very dapper."

"Er, thanks." He must have mistaken the look of terror on my face for simple surprise, because he kept grinning.

"Mom, this is the boy I was telling you about. Spartacus, this is my mother, Beverly." He was gesturing to an elderly woman standing beside him and my throat tightened.

His mother? Why did he bring his mother?

"Nice to meet you," said the small, elegant woman, offering me a bejeweled hand. I shook it, trying to hide my shock behind a nervous smile.

"We were about to head to a movie when you called," Lloyd explained.

I nodded, but it didn't answer my larger question: *Could I still use him as a diversion in front of his mother? Have him arrested in front of his pink-cheeked, smiley, elderly mother?*

Without hesitation, I knew the answer. Yes. Yes I could.

I was a horrible person.

"So…" I said, trying to smile a real smile. "How's everything? How was Boise?"

"Good, yes. The lecture went well. But, more importantly, how are *you?* I mean, after the funeral and all?" He seemed so genuine—not at all what you'd expect from a murderous fugitive. I wondered if his mom knew he was a killer?

"Doing good," I answered shakily. We got in line and Lloyd looked around us in a searching way. Was he looking for cops?

"You here with your dad and that bully older brother you told me about?"

"Nah, they couldn't make it," I shook my head as we walked over to join the line. "I mean, they're coming late," I added. I didn't want him to think I was here by myself. "We had some... some family stuff, you know, come up."

"Nothing bad, I hope," Beverly said.

"No, no, nothing bad," I said.

Lloyd squinted. "You alright, Spart? You're a little jumpy."

"Sure," I said. "I'm just nervous about seeing my mom perform." We'd reached the ticket booth and as I reached for my wallet, Lloyd pushed in ahead of me.

"Hey, don't worry, I got it," he said, handing money over my shoulder to the ticket seller, who had tattoos of spiders on her face. I don't know if I imagined it, but it seemed like she was staring at me as she pushed us our tickets.

"Enjoy the show, folks," she said blankly. I tried not to look her in the eye, afraid she'd been told to be on the lookout for me.

"Thanks," I said to Lloyd.

"No problem," he said, gesturing for his mom and me to go in ahead of him. He really didn't seem like a murderer, I thought for the umpteenth time. He was just so... *nice.* Not that that's any reason to trust someone. But still.

"Lloyd tells me he gave you a ride on his bike from Sisters to Boise, is that right?" Beverly asked. We were walking up a long, curving dark hallway that led around the outside ring of the tent, red glowing markers on the floor pointing the way. "Is that where you're from?"

"Yeah," I said absentmindedly, trying to concentrate on how the tent was laid out. There were more concession stands all along the front area—popcorn, corndogs, nachos.

"I love Sisters," she was saying. "Lloyd took me there once for the rodeo—it was such a treat!"

"You go to the rodeo often?" Lloyd was asking.

"What? Oh, sure. The whole family does," I said. I didn't know what I was talking about. We followed the curved enclosure for a little way before finding our entrance. At the top of a short flight of metal stairs, we met the big top.

It was like stepping into a kaleidoscope: bright red, indigo, and grass-green curtains draped the walls while hidden, pulsating lights made all the colors swirl together before my eyes. A strange, pink fog rolled across the stage in waves, drifting into the front rows. A light up in the rafters made stars circle above us.

Even though there was live music swelling and the audience was bubbling with chatter, it all felt so silent in my head that I held my breath. I had arrived. I was really there.

"This is impressive," Lloyd said.

He didn't have to tell me.

Bartholomew had turned the inside of the tent into an exotic place. Most circuses I'd seen in movies had a middle area surrounded on all sides by the audience. Bartholomew's was set up differently, though, with the three rings near the back of the tent, and audience seats in a half-circle, facing the rings. That meant there was a whole backstage area we couldn't see—which is exactly where I needed to go when intermission arrived.

The tent must have had room for a thousand people, at least. Maybe two thousand. I realized I'd been expecting some bleachers on the grass, more like the sideshow had been set up.

Checking our ticket stubs, an attendant in a red sports coat led us to seats that were only five rows or so back from the stage. We were so close we'd probably be able to smell the animals.

So close that Bartholomew might be able to recognize me. Great. I wished I had my hat with me. I hadn't worn it because I thought it wouldn't go with the suit and would draw attention to me.

Says the guy in the suit and the fire face paint, Will would have snorted.

All around us, families filed in. Parents were laughing and pointing out interesting things while clowns wandered through the audience, riling up kids with balloon animals and tripping over people's feet. Lloyd flagged down a vendor and he bought some cotton candy for us. The fluffy pink goodness turned to grainy sugar on my tongue. I had to admit that, despite everything that was about happen, eating cotton candy made me feel a little better. It was all I could do to not inhale it.

"Nice seats," said Lloyd and his mother nodded in agreement. "You always get good seats like this?"

"Nope. This is a first." I tried to smile, but was having trouble. I was worried. What if the lady gave us these seats on purpose? So Bartholomew could keep an eye on me?

"Spartacus? Are you sure you're okay?" Lloyd asked.

"Hmm?" I said, but I panicked, thinking maybe he'd been talking and I'd missed something he'd said. Was that suspicion or concern in his eyes? He was still looking at me, waiting for an answer.

"Yeah. I guess I'm just really anxious to see my mom," I said, remembering how easy it was to lie by telling the truth.

"What does she do again?" asked Beverly.

"She's the Human Cannonball," said Lloyd. "The Amazing Athena."

"We saw her trailer outside!" she exclaimed, nudging Lloyd. "I bet you never get tired of seeing her perform."

"Actually," I admitted. "This will be the first time."

"You've never seen her perform?" she exclaimed.

"She hasn't been in the circus that long—just since the end of last summer, so this will be the first time." *And hopefully the last.*

I put some more cotton candy in my mouth so I wouldn't have to say anything.

Lloyd smiled gently at me. "That's gotta be rough, never seeing your mom," he said sympathetically. I nodded, feeling a twinge of guilt at Lloyd's words. He was a killer, sure—but he was also, in a way, my friend. And I was going to get him arrested by a SWAT team right in front of his own mother. Could I betray the guy who'd encouraged me to stand up for myself and told me it was okay to embrace my ridiculous name?

The lights began to dim. There was no turning back.

CHAPTER 22

"LADIES AND GENTLEMEN, BOYS AND *girls, friends and animals of all ages!*" a voice boomed in the blue darkness. "*You are about to experience the most marvelous, prodigious, miraculous, stupendous show to ever visit the Pacific Northwest. Welcome to Bartholomew's World-Renowned Circus of the Incredible!*"

The audience burst into wild applause and a live orchestra at the front of the stage started playing. At the same time, there was a loud BOOM and the spotlight appeared, shining on a cloud of red smoke. A tall, slender, and elegant man in a red suit and a black top hat stepped out from the fog, a cane raised over his head. I narrowed my eyes.

Bartholomew.

I was sitting so close I could see his pale, smooth skin and the light glinting off his dark hair. My blood began to boil, just seeing him looking all smug and important. And to see the audience respond to him like they thought he was so great! They had no idea what he really was. The Count from who-knows-where, who sold his soul to the devil, who practiced black magic, who robbed museums, and who forced people to perform against their will.

Boy, they wouldn't be applauding him for long.

What followed was a huge fanfare around him. He stood still in the middle of it, directing it all while elephants and a whole slew of clowns and performers marched and jumped around the ring.

"Clowns freak me out," Lloyd leaned over and whispered. "You can never tell what they're really feeling."

I nodded. *Same with murderers,* I thought.

I scanned the performers for my mom but didn't see her. At the end of the little parade, Bartholomew pointed his cane at a box on the stage and flames suddenly shot out of it, followed by four tumblers.

"Behold, the phenomenal, sensational, spectacular, and wholly singular magic of the human body!" his voice boomed, filling every corner of the tent.

We watched what looked like identical nine-year-old quadruplet contortionists twist their bodies into knots while balancing on chairs and each other.

After that, we "beheld the magic of the flame" while a man breathed fire (*snore*), and watched "the magic of the beasts" which was a man wrangling three enormous tigers balanced on giant rubber balls. We were so close we could see the tigers shedding. After each performance, clowns came out and did funny skits for the little kids.

But the scariest was Sharkman's routine, which was just before intermission. Even though I'd seen him before (and yes, hit him over the head), him being there really freaked me out. I was so close to the circus that I knew who the bad guys were just by sight.

They introduced him as a *bizarre, baffling, bewildering, perplexing, and peculiar fluke of nature.* But I remembered what Nero had said about him—it was mostly implants. He was in a shiny gray bodysuit, his dorsal fin sticking out and they'd somehow attached a fake shark nosepiece to his face. Even though I knew he was just a man in a permanent costume, knowing he would be backstage when I was trying to find my mom was *terrifying.*

His stunt was diving. There was a large, clear tank of water and a ladder and high dive above it. Just seeing the high dive gave me horrible flashbacks.

"That guy's a real piece of work," Lloyd whispered to me, interrupting my thoughts. I nodded and we clapped politely as Sharkman did some okay dives from really high up, like the stuff you see at the Olympics. But honestly, Will could probably do better.

AS THE FIRST HALF WOUND down and the circus broke for intermission, my heart began thumping like a drum. It was time to make the phone call. Time to ditch Lloyd and his mom. Time to get this show on the road.

"Some circus, eh?" Lloyd said loudly, leading us through the noisy crowd to the concessions.

"Yeah," I agreed. "It's really good."

"I especially like the tumblers," Beverly was saying as we got to the front. "Say, when is your mom—?"

"I waited way too long to pee," I blurted out. "Gotta find the restroom!" Without saying anything more, I dove into the crush of people before Lloyd or his mom could follow.

Let's do this, I told myself, trying to psyche myself up as I shouldered my way to the entrance.

The sun had gone down since the circus started and I left the grounds under the cover of... well, I guess Eli wouldn't call it dusk. It was too late at night for that. Twilight, maybe.

I went to the phone booth I'd staked out earlier, just across the street from a gas station. I looked behind me, making sure Lloyd hadn't followed, that he wasn't going to eavesdrop on the call... and take out a knife from his jacket and...

I shook my head. Couldn't think about that. Must not think about that. I let out a shaky breath, picked up the receiver, and dialed.

"911, what's your emergency?"

I hesitated for a long moment before I spoke. Once I did this, it couldn't be undone. "I want to make an anonymous tip," I finally said. "I just saw this guy—the murderer from the wanted posters. Lloyd... I mean *Dan* Lloeke. He's at the circus tonight."

There was some clacking on the keyboard. "And how sure are you that it's him?" the man asked.

"Rolling Stones tattoo, right forearm," I said with certainty.

"Where are you located?" he asked.

"Bartholomew's Circus, near the park downtown. The intermission is ending, so you should probably get here fast." And with that, I hung up the phone.

My body felt heavy. I'd done it. It was out of my hands. Things were going to start happening now. I could feel it.

You better hope this works, Spartacus.

With this cloud hanging over me, I raced back to the circus and to the edge of the concessions, spying on the place where I'd last seen Lloyd. Luckily, there was no one left there except for the concessions people. No Lloyd. No Beverly. They must've gone back to the seats.

So far so good.

The lady selling popcorn saw me and called out, "It's about to start—hurry up!"

"Oh, no!" I yelped, faking concern as I sprinted by her and down the hall.

But I wasn't going back in. It was time to find Mom and then wait for the fireworks.

I RUSHED ALONG THE CURVING hallway that led along the outside wall of the tent. I could hear music playing and Bartholomew's voice announcing the next act. All the curtains leading back to the seats were drawn shut.

I kept going all the way to the end of the corridor, still not a soul in sight. I finally came to the end of the corridor and was met with a canvas and plastic door. It was marked STAY OUT! CIRCUS PERSONNEL ONLY.

As though that would be enough to stop me. Not now.

I pushed through the canvas door and found myself in another long, dark, and curving corridor. The hall had a steel ramp that seemed to spiral up and around the side of the tent, back behind the stage.

At first, I could hear the circus going on to my left, the audience laughing and *oohing* and *ahhing* as the music rose and fell. But the ramp twisted and turned and I went up one set of metal stairs and down another. It wasn't long before I was all disoriented.

I was about to start panicking when I heard a comforting voice in my head. *Don't panic,* it said. *You can do this.*

It sounded kind of like Eli's voice. And I trusted him.

Finally I heard people ahead. I crept along the curve to see a stage entrance on my left. Clowns and performers bustled up and down a ramp to my right. Some were changing costumes as they raced down the hall, others had on headsets and were cuing entrances and lights and effects.

It would have been pretty cool to watch—that is, if I wasn't in danger of being caught.

I could have turned back, but I already knew what was back there: nothing. If I wanted to find my mom, I would have go through them and find out where the people were coming from. But standing at the edge of the activity, I felt a nauseating wave of déjà vu. My forehead broke out in sweat under its face paint. It was just like sneaking into the sideshow—and that had turned out so well.

But there are a hundred performers here, I reminded myself. The sideshow only had twenty. And this time I knew I was in the right place. If I just acted like I belonged there, I'd blend right in. Besides, with my face painted, even if they discovered me, they wouldn't know I was *me*.

So I closed my eyes and counted to three. When I opened them and saw the first gap in the foot traffic, I merged into the chaos.

Just keep moving. Just keep moving.

What with the circus music and jostling amongst the performers and the tech people, it felt really surreal—like I didn't exist. Everyone was so focused on the show that I didn't even get a glance as I hustled past the stage entrance.

I caught a quick glimpse of Bartholomew in front of the audience but I immediately ducked my head, telling myself to keep moving.

Then, in what felt like a few seconds, everyone suddenly thinned out. It was like I'd just swam through a school of fish and they'd all darted away. I looked around in alarm, only to see they'd scrambled to take their places onstage—some were even climbing the scaffolding above.

As I sped down the ramp on the other side, I met a couple stragglers straightening their green tutus as they booked it for the stage, but neither stopped to ask me what I was doing.

For a circus with so much to hide, they didn't seem to have much security.

The ramp curved down until I was walking on grass again, in another long corridor of canvas. With all the performers hurrying from this side of the tent, I knew I didn't have far to go.

The sides of the corridor were lined with colorful metal doors a few feet from the ground, metal stairs leading up to them. I scratched my head for a second before I figured out that they were the doors of the trailers arranged around the tent.

The trailers that housed the performers.

I was almost there!

I tried not to run as I passed by them, looking at the names next to the doors. I saw one labeled DR. HEISLER. *The plastic surgeon maybe?* Scary. I hurried past.

The fourth door I passed said BARTHOLOMEW in big gold letters. And the very next one said ATHENA.

Mom.

Heart pounding, I glanced around to make sure I was still alone. Then, I knocked on the door.

I waited for all of about three seconds before pulling it open and throwing myself inside.

I HATE TO ADMIT I cried when I saw her, so I won't.

"Mom, I know it's a surprise to see me—" I began but Mom jumped up from a chair before I could even close the door behind me, smothering me in a hug.

"Oh my god! Spartacus!" she said into the top of my head, squeezing me tight. I think I was as shocked as she was.

"What are you doing here?" she exclaimed, pulling back to look at me. She looked at the orange and red makeup smudges I'd left on her black shirt. "What's that stuff on your face?"

"I had to see you," I said, forgetting my speech and suddenly so overwhelmed that my voice was trembling. I couldn't believe I'd made it. She was there. She was real. She was all right. She wasn't handcuffed or beaten up or anything.

"Oh, come here, my baby," she said, pulling me back and holding me again, not seeming to mind the paint.

After a minute she let me go and walked me over to a huge leather couch. We both sat down and I looked around. The trailer was awesome, with a kitchen and a decent-sized bed. There was even a large walk-in closet in there, stuffed with colorful costumes.

"Look at you in that suit," she said in that adoring way that had always embarrassed me. Hearing her now made me realize how much I missed it. "You're growing into such a man, and it's only been a few months."

"It's been *ten* months," I murmured, not looking at her.

"Has it?"

I was looking at the closed door that must have led to a bathroom when Mom gently turned my face toward her.

"Spartacus," she said, pausing to breathe and then starting again. "Your dad told me you'd run away and I didn't know what to think. I—well, I was afraid you'd been kidnapped."

I almost laughed out loud, but instead I just sputtered.

"You were afraid *I'd* been kidnapped?" I said, maybe too loudly. But she didn't know about Will, about the postcards. I didn't even know if she knew about the museums.

"And then I heard Finn saw you in Albuquerque. At least then I knew you were alive! What were you thinking?" She looked at me with her dark eyes in that way that always made me feel like I'd done something wrong.

"I'm sorry, Mom, I didn't mean—" I started to explain, but she cut me off.

"Spart, if you wanted to come see me so much, we could have planned it out," she said, slightly scolding. "You and Will could have come up to see me together."

Then I shook my head. This was no time to play the role of the silly child. I leaned in close to her so that no one could hear through the door or the walls.

"I came here to get you out," I said. "I thought *you* were the one who was kidnapped!"

"Me?" she said, and then she was laughing.

"*Shh!*" I said. "With the house the way you left it, and Will sending, well, sending these postcards—" I paused. This was going to take too long. I changed my angle, telling her everything in a flood. "Look, I know Bartholomew won't let anyone leave once they're in the circus. I know that he's stealing from museums."

"What are you talking about?" Mom said in her normal-volume voice, pulling away. "The mess at the house was obviously from my audition. I didn't get a chance to—"

"Keep your voice down," I flinched. "I know about Santa Fe. I know about Prizrak and how he got locked in a safe and died in Chicago. I know about the streetcar and Abraham Lincoln's china."

Mom stood up, eyes wide, and shook her head. "Who told you this? How about we get that makeup off you and—"

"I figured it out. Mom—I know about everything. You don't have to pretend with me."

I watched as she crossed over to her vanity, pulled out some wet wipes, and sat back down next to me. She looked nervous, with that crazy kind of smile she'd get sometimes when Dad would go on one of his angry rants. Maybe these were the signs of Stockholm syndrome? Maybe she was afraid to admit that she needed help.

"Pretend?" Her laugh was thin and tight, as she tried to wipe my face. "Let's stop talking like this and—"

"Mom!" I interrupted, pushing her hand away. "Look, maybe you don't know about it. Maybe they're doing the jobs without you."

"*Doing the jobs!*" she exclaimed. "You—you are so *nutty*. Whoa, look at this bruise, honey. What happened?" I pulled the wipe out of her hand and threw it on the floor.

"Mom, you have to come with me. *Now.*" I was so angry I was shaking. "Even if you don't believe me. Just trust me."

I got to my feet, slow and determined and held out my trembling hand. Frustrated tears welled up in my eyes. I'd known it was going to be hard, but I was totally unprepared for finding her like *this*. Why wasn't she listening to me? She was just sitting there, shaking her head, mouthing the word *no* over and over again.

"I don't know what's wrong with you, but please just trust me." I took hold of her hand and tried an encouraging voice. "Maybe you're scared. But you don't have to be. I've called the police. They're going to show up and then you can tell them what you know."

"The police?" she said in a low, low voice.

"Yeah. I told them everything." It was a little white lie that I thought would help. If she *did* have Stockholm syndrome, this might help her feel more safe.

"What do you mean, *'everything'*?" came a man's voice from inside the room. My heart sunk as I turned to see a tall, pale man step out of the bathroom. In his hands was a large top hat.

Bartholomew.

I flinched when I realized what that meant. *He'd been there the whole time.* But, wasn't he just onstage? Somehow he'd snuck into the trailer faster than I had found it!

Bartholomew came over and stood right next to my mom. She didn't shudder, didn't shrink away. In fact, she didn't even seem to be scared at all...

"I, I—uh," I had no words. I was dumbfounded. I was speechless.

Bartholomew up close was much scarier than Bartholomew in the ring. He really did have a smooth face, like they said. Smooth, shiny, and ageless, pulled tight like a fish... I couldn't even guess how old he was. He could have been twenty. He could have been as old as my grandparents.

"Pleasure to meet you, Spartacus," said Bartholomew, with a half bow and a wide, easy smile on his face. But it was a clown's smile, almost like he'd painted it on. I didn't think for a second that it was real—it didn't reach his eyes. And his accent was different than his performing voice. It was a strange accent I'd never heard before. "I've heard a lot about you."

I stayed quiet. Bartholomew leaned down, studying me closely.

"Tell me," he said in a calm voice. "Did you really call the police, Spartacus?"

"Yeah, I did. They'll be here any minute."

"What exactly did you tell them?"

I stared him in the eye, trying my hardest to look confident, like someone who had just called the police and had nothing to worry about. Then Bart stood up and looked at my mom.

"No," he said to her, shaking his head. "He didn't."

I thought I saw my mom relax and let out a big breath.

Then Bartholomew laughed a big laugh, with my mom laughing a smaller one.

"Spartacus, I remember what it was like to have so much imagination," he said in his deep, melodic voice. "I really do. When you're young, it seems like everything is big and mysterious and everyone's plotting something, doesn't it? But, Spartacus, we're not stealing anything and nobody was kidnapped and nobody in my circus is trapped. Your mom is staying here because she wants to be here. She's an amazing performer and we're glad to have her. There's nothing more to it than that."

I glared at him.

"Sweetie," said Mom. "It's true. I shouldn't have run off without talking to you first. I'm sorry, I was...impulsive.

But no one is trapped. No one's holding me against my will. I can leave anytime I want."

"Fine," I said. She was either completely in the dark about the museum stuff or else she was too afraid to say anything in front of Bartholomew. But I couldn't stop my stupid mouth. "What about him stealing museum art? Did he tell you about that?"

"What are you talking about?" asked Bartholomew, that painted-on smile back on his face.

"You know. The Georgia O'Keeffe Museum. And all of the other places. The streetcar? Abraham Lincoln's china? That dinosaur skeleton?" And then, just to see if there was any reaction, "The gold scarab from Mexico?"

Mom blanched, but Bartholomew laughed. "I heard about the O'Keeffe museum. I don't know the other ones. But what makes you think we were involved with any of that?"

"Every time you visit a city, something gets stolen."

"Trust me, Spartacus: we haven't stolen anything," he said. The tone of his voice sounded so reasonable that I blushed. "You're overreacting. Things get stolen in big cities all the time and you never hear anything about it. Just because we've been to some cities and they've had a few things go missing isn't proof of anything."

I knew I should just keep quiet, but I couldn't help talking back to him. "But what about the woman who looks just like Mom?" There was no way he could explain that.

"You mean Charlene? We do look alike," Mom said, her eyes and voice soft. "But maybe you just wanted her to be me so badly that you imagined we looked more alike than we really do."

Was it possible I'd made a mistake about that? There was *no* way. She'd looked just like Mom. Hadn't she?

"But what about Zacharias Prizrak?"

"You know how rumors are, Spartacus," he said. "Prizrak used to work for me. But he was a criminal. He got in trouble and, yes, he had an accident while he was committing a crime. I know people have blown that out of proportion. But trust me that it was entirely his doing, not mine. I can't be blamed for the actions of everyone who works for me."

Bartholomew had a way of looking at you that made it hard to look away. Those big dark eyes set in that pale face were almost... mesmerizing.

I shook my head and took a step back. "Mom, they say he's violent. He's vicious. He's sold his soul to the devil. He even fixed the Tour de France!" I practically shouted this out, just releasing all my suspicions in one stupid rush.

Bartholomew smiled like he felt sorry for me. "Have you been visiting IHateBartholomewsCircus.com?" He didn't wait for me to respond, he just nodded and smiled. "That's a fun website, isn't it? Would it surprise you to know that I put that website up myself? Would it surprise you to know that we make those rumors up? For some reason people like to believe in mysterious, dark things. And that's what our circus is all about. Giving people what they want."

"It's true, Spartacus," said my mom. "That's just a thing to get people interested in the circus and make it all seem more mysterious than it is."

I felt like I was sinking slowly, slowly into quicksand. Not that I'd ever been in quicksand, but that's exactly how I thought it would feel.

Bartholomew looked at his watch, then glanced at Mom. "We do have to get onstage in a second, so we'll have to continue this conversation after the show." He and Mom exchanged a strange look. I couldn't tell what they were thinking.

"And really, Spartacus," Bartholomew continued in a calm voice. Calm as a clam. "You have to admit it all does seem a bit strange, doesn't it? You have to admit that maybe you've been a little immature about all of this, Spartacus. We all want to have a big adventure once in a while, but really, Spartacus, the world isn't as big a place as you think it is. It's a calmer place. It's a much more boring place, really. It's a much more peaceful place, really, Spartacus."

There was something about the way he talked. I couldn't put my finger on it. He kept saying my name over and over and his voice had a weird lulling quality that made me think of my mom when she used to read to me in bed.

That was it. His voice made me tired. Or maybe I was already tired. I had been awake a long time and I suddenly felt all of those hours I'd been up.

My mom started to say something—"I'm really happy here, Spartacus, you have to—" but Bartholomew shushed her gently.

"Maybe you need a nap, Spartacus," said Bartholomew. "A nap would really be good for you. After all you've done. All you've traveled. A nap in this comfortable trailer that your mom finds very comfortable, too. When we get back, we'll talk about this a little more, but right now I imagine sleep sounds very good, don't you agree?"

Yes, I did. He was right. I wasn't sure why I'd been so angry and upset a few minutes ago. Taking a nap seemed like a reasonable idea. I would wait for them to get back and we could figure things out then. It was silly to get so upset.

I stretched out on the couch and closed my eyes. My head was swimming. How could Bartholomew and the circus be doing all the stuff I thought they were? It didn't make any sense, did it? I'd gotten it all wrong from the start. Will had written the coded postcards, not Mom. Mom wanted to come here. She was happy here. I had been so stupid to think she needed rescuing. I'd been very silly the whole time.

But then Zeda's face floated into my mind. Like one of those real-life pictures that you get in your head right before you drift off to sleep. Zeda's pretty face. Telling me that nobody trusted Bartholomew. Zeda and Nero and Remmy and Zeda's dad—they all hated Bartholomew, didn't they?

Zeda. I promised Zeda I'd help Matilda. Matilda. Where was she again?

My mind wasn't working right. I didn't know why, but I knew I needed to snap out of it. I did something that always worked in the movies. I hauled off and gave myself a big cracking slap across the face.

"Aaah!" I cried out, sitting up. That did the trick. I was fully awake.

What the heck had happened?

Mom and Bartholomew were gone. I didn't even remember them leaving. One second I was standing there, listening to Bartholomew defend himself, and the next I was waking up on the couch.

Strange.

I went to Mom's vanity and wiped the rest of the paint off my face, thinking about absolutely nothing at all—until the roar of the audience outside brought me back.

Did Bartholomew hypnotize me?

I stared at my bruised and scratched face in the mirror and felt the remaining fuzziness disappear. I'd read rumors online that Bartholomew had the power to do that to people—but that was on the IHateBartholomew website, which he and Mom insisted was fake.

I shook my head, my brain feeling thick and slow. I put my head in my hands, rubbing my temples. I didn't know what to believe right then. It really did seem absurd that a circus would be involved in the museum robberies.

But all those places had had stuff stolen while Bartholomew's Circus was in town. That was too big of a coincidence, wasn't it? And the scarab. Eli and I knew the scarab was stolen. Mom had even looked funny when I mentioned it.

Another cheer from the audience.

Time was passing and the circus was still going—*but for how much longer?* Lloyd and his mother were still in the audience, probably wondering where I was, if I was okay. And the cops would be here any moment to arrest Lloyd.

I only had one choice. I had to get to the police and tell them everything I knew about the museums and Bartholomew. If it wasn't true and I really had been wrong about everything, they could sort it out. If it was true, they could help me save my mom.

When I went to the door, though, it was locked.

I shook the handle, fiddled with the lock, and tried the handle again. It wouldn't budge. I should have been able to open it from the inside—I mean, it was basically the door to a large motor home. But it was stuck shut, which meant they had locked me in from the outside. If they were innocent, why would they lock me in?

They?

Yes. They.

I could just barely remember it, but right before they left, I'd caught a glimpse of Bartholomew taking Mom's hand to lead her out. Bartholomew and my mom, as thick as thieves.

I barely made it to the toilet before I threw up.

I felt cold and clammy as I paced the length of the trailer like a caged animal, trying to find a way out. There wasn't a phone anywhere to be found. It wasn't long before I picked up the chair in front of the vanity and tried to break the windows. They didn't break, though, just as I'd thought. It's like they were made of shatterproof glass. Maybe bulletproof? Figures a criminal mastermind would have those in his girlfriend's trailer—just in case she snapped out of it and got the idea to leave him.

Girlfriend. That's what the situation was, wasn't it? Bartholomew and my mom were a couple. Together. "An Item." She was with him and knew all about everything. But then again, there was also that trick with the hypnotizing. I was breathing hard through my nose. There was still that teeny chance, that last shred of hope, that Mom wasn't a criminal. That she was hypnotized by him. That she was still my mom, the one I remembered.

I shouted loudly in frustration and kicked the wall. *What now?* I thought. *What's left? Just wait until Bartholomew comes back and puts me in a bank vault? Wait until—*

Just then the door swung open silently. I had just enough time to dive behind the corner of the couch to hide, thinking it was Bartholomew again or maybe Sharkman. No one came inside, though. A few seconds later I heard—

"Ryan?"

CHAPTER 23

THE VOICE SOUNDED FAMILIAR. I peeked out over the couch. *It was Will!*

"You got the door open!" I exclaimed.

"Ryan!" he blubbered, running to me and collapsing like a giant, stubbly, after-shave-soaked baby. "Oh my god, Ryan, I thought you were dead. I thought that I'd killed you."

"Thank goodness you're here," I exclaimed, patting him on the back. "We've got to get out of here." I tried to pull away but he just kept hugging, kept sobbing.

"I did it. I sent the postcards. It was just a joke—I never thought you really believed it."

"I know all this," I pleaded, pushing him away so he'd look at me. "I figured it out forever ago. But you have to believe me. We need to get out now!"

But he just kept talking.

"I saw this morning that the circus was in Portland and thought this was my only chance to get to you. I sold my iPod to get bus fare and—"

He wasn't stopping. And, in an instant, all the anger about the postcards and the pool and his general awfulness boiled up inside me. I knew it wasn't the right time, but I couldn't help myself. Right mid-sentence, as he blubbered away, I hauled off and smacked him right in the kisser.

Even though it felt good, one look at his shocked, sad, crying face and I knew that this was all the revenge I would ever need. The World of Fartcraft was safe for all eternity.

"I'm sorry," I said quietly, rubbing my stinging fist.

"I deserve it," he said, calm now, putting his hand to his jaw. "I deserve much worse. Pretty good punch. Wait... why were you locked in here? And why are you wearing your suit?"

"I'll tell you all about it—but first, we have to get out of here, okay?"

I ran down the trailer steps, Will right behind me. Will showed me the "lock," which was a large crowbar they'd jammed into the doorframe.

I shivered.

Nobody normal uses crowbars. People only use them when they're serious about breaking something—or hurting someone. I was done playing around. It was time to get out of this funhouse hall of mirrors. Mom didn't want to come with me. I wasn't going to save her. Not tonight. I had to make it to the cops and tell them what I knew.

We headed for the back of the circus.

"So why were you locked up?" Will asked, huffing beside me. "And why are we running away?"

"No time for that," I said. "Just know that you can't trust anyone here. They all—"

That's when two large guys walked around the corner, right in front of us. They both had black shirts that said SECURITY in white letters across the chest. Will crashed right into one of them, getting knocked to the ground. Will was a big guy, but these guys were much, much bigger. One of them knelt and pinned Will down. The other took a few steps toward me. I had no choice but to turn around and run in the other direction.

"Get off me! My mom works here!" I heard Will shouting behind me. That wouldn't help at all, I thought. It didn't sound like they were hurting him. Not yet, anyway.

"I'll get help!" I shouted over my shoulder. The other security guard was right behind me, breathing hard, coming at me like a freight train.

I passed by the trailers again, running toward the backstage area. As I neared, I saw a group of performers getting ready to go onstage. One of them was Sharkman. The group looked up when they saw me running toward them at full speed, the guard right on my heels.

"Stop him!" yelled the guard.

Sharkman held out his hands, but I zoomed to the right, out of his reach. I was running alongside the heavy, red curtain—the one that bordered the stage. I tried to run back the way I had come, parallel to the stage, but there was a bunch of metal scaffolding in my way. I spun around and saw the security guard and Sharkman inching toward me, saying things like "Don't worry, we're not going to hurt you," which I did not believe for a second.

I was officially cornered.

I didn't have any choice.

With my heart pounding in my ears, I got down on the floor and rolled right under the curtain.

Onto the stage.

Other than the spotlight centered on Bartholomew, who was sitting astride a big white cannon a few feet away, the stage was dark. I recognized the cannon immediately as the one my mom did her act with.

Bart glanced at me immediately and he froze for all of 1/16th of a second—it was so quick that no one else noticed, but I sure did. I didn't dare back up because I could hear Sharkman cursing right behind me, on the other side of the curtain.

I froze. My breath stuck in my throat.

I was trapped.

I was done for.

I was dead.

I didn't think anybody in the audience had seen me yet, since I was on the very edge of the spotlight. All the focus was on Bartholomew, who continued to speak as though I wasn't there.

"I would like to present to you the most awe-inspiring, stupefying, petrifying, horrifying, electrifying, and death-defying event of the evening. This act will amaze, astound, and astonish you. You're about to behold an unbelievable, unimaginable, unutterable, miraculous, spectaculous, and all around cracktaculous feat of wonder!"

Are those even words? I thought. But I sensed that Bartholomew was stalling, giving me the chance to go back under the curtain. But I wasn't going anywhere, not with what was waiting for me on the other side.

That's when I noticed something a few feet away. It was a small, orange megaphone, the kind a performer would yell through to make their voice boom. It must have just been for show, though, because Bartholomew had a microphone.

That's when I got an idea. It had only partially formed in my head, but I shrugged my shoulders. I had to do *something*. I couldn't just stand there. Besides, if you can't go backwards, you might as well go forwards.

I STEPPED FORWARD DELIBERATELY INTO the circle of light, toward the megaphone and the middle of the ring. I could sense the audience notice me, but I couldn't see them because of the lights in my eyes. I could see Bartholomew, though. He looked down at me from his perch on the cannon and fear flickered in his eyes. Just that tiny flash made me feel more comfortable. If I hadn't seen it, I'm not sure I would have been brave enough to face him like I did.

I picked up the megaphone and then planted my feet, glaring up at him.

"I say," boomed Bartholomew. "If it isn't the newest member of our performance troupe—and the son of our own Human Cannonball, Athena! Young Sir Spartacus. Let's have a round of applause for him, shall we?"

The crowd clapped politely. They all thought that this was part of the show! Wow. Bart didn't miss a beat, did he?

"Were you scared for your mom?" Bartholomew asked, still playing his role. "It's only two hundred feet. I promise, on my honor, you will not become an orphan! What do you say—should we bring out the Flying Athena?"

The crowd began to cheer, which was good because it took me a few moments to find my voice. I put the megaphone to my lips and started to speak, not even knowing what I was going to say.

"Excuse me. Before you start," I said, my amplified voice making me jump. I turned toward the audience. "I'd like to tell everybody what kind of things Bartholomew does in his free time."

"Oh, dear, now, child, don't... uh—don't go sharing *that* information," he said, scrambling off the cannon and moving a few feet toward me. But I was ready. I dropped the megaphone and pulled out the paraffin and torch from my pocket. When Bart took another step forward, I lit the torch and then blew a huge fireball toward him. I thought it might have burnt his eyebrows, it was so big. Zeda would have been proud.

The audience cheered and Bartholomew balked and ducked back behind the cannon.

"Is this the roast of Bartholomew?" he quipped. The audience laughed.

That infuriated me. My torch was still burning as I grabbed the megaphone again.

"No, it... it's a game," I stumbled.

"I like games," he said, peeking from behind the cannon. "Can we play hide and seek? You can go hide first."

"No... we're—we're going to play Truth or Dare."

"Is this family friendly?" he asked, and everyone laughed again.

"Depends," I said, speaking slowly and loudly through the megaphone. I had to make sure everyone heard this. "Do you think stealing from museums is 'family friendly'? How about hypnotizing people? Or locking kids up in trailers?"

There was scattered, confused applause from the audience and one person shouted out, "I hate Bartholomew's

Circus!" Some other people chuckled. *Those idiots!* They thought this was part of the show! What could I possibly say to make them believe me? It all sounded so ridiculous when you said it out loud.

But Bartholomew's eyes blazed.

"I think somebody's broken out of the loony bin," he said pointedly.

"Truth or dare?" I shouted.

There were some snickers from the audience. I happened to look out and catch Lloyd's eye, in the fifth row. He didn't seem to be laughing. He was leaning forward in his seat, like he was watching a very close tennis match that he had money on.

"Oh, dare, I guess," said Bartholomew after hesitating.

"I dare you to come out from behind that cannon," I said, my torch's flame still flickering.

"Truth be told, I'm afraid you'll toast me like a marshmallow."

"No, I won't do that. Not if you stay away from me."

I caught movement out of the corner of my eye and saw that there were police officers in the audience. There were four of them, edging up the aisles. *They'd actually come for Lloyd!* For once! As long as they were around, nobody could hurt me or Will. This might work out after all.

I looked back to Bartholomew as he stepped out from behind the cannon and faced me from ten feet away. The orchestra gave a large *ta-da!* that made the audience chuckle and clap.

"That was an easy dare," he said. "Now your turn. Before they come and take you away. Truth or dare?"

What was he talking about? Take me away? He was still stalling, trying to distract me. I saw the cops had already passed by Lloyd's row, though, and were moving toward the stage. Maybe they had seen the security guards grab Will and were coming to intervene. Either way, I was safe.

"That's not how *my* game works!" I said, with renewed confidence. "True or false—you stole Abraham Lincoln's china?"

"What on earth are you talking about?" he laughed, looking nervously at the cops. "Are we playing Clue now, too? You have the rules all wrong."

I snickered a little myself. He was trapped and he didn't even know it.

"What about a dinosaur from Philadelphia?" I shouted. Even though my knees were shaking, I took a few steps toward him. "Did you take that, too?"

Now that I was closer, something about him looked a bit odd. His hair wasn't as dark as I remembered. And his eyes—his eyes didn't have that same hypnotic effect that they had in the trailer. I thought about Not-Mom and something clicked.

"You seem to have lost your steam, child," he said, eying me as I eyed him. "Have the voices in your head turned off for a second?"

"No. It's just—I don't think you're the real Bartholomew," I said. Because he wasn't. This man was a good six inches shorter. There were wrinkles around his eyes. His skin wasn't as smooth as the man's in Mom's trailer.

"You know what happens when you stop believing in Bartholomew," he said and, with a snap of his fingers, the band started to play a distorted version of "Stars and Stripes Forever" and the cops sprinted up onstage.

But they were after *me*.

One glance was all it took for me to see that these weren't real cops after all—their mime-faces proved it.

I dropped the megaphone and moved away from them. The clown cops formed a semicircle and started closing in on me. I got my paraffin and torch ready. Then the clowns rushed me and I found myself running around the stage, blowing fireballs at them while the orchestra blared zany marching music. Every time I fell or a cop tripped, a cymbal crashed.

It was total madness. Not-Bartholomew had turned me into part of the show. No one in the audience had believed a single thing I'd said.

I could tell after a minute or so that the clown cops weren't really trying to chase me. They were just putting on a goofy act. But I knew if I let myself get caught, they'd just drag me backstage and I had a feeling they weren't going to be too happy about all of this.

When my torch's flame went out, I chucked it at one of the clowns. It caught him square in the neck and he cursed under his breath before flashing me a lunatic smile.

"All right, coppers!" shouted Bartholomew through the megaphone I'd dropped. "Enough pussyfooting! Let's take him away!"

The cops formed another semicircle and cornered me near the back of the stage. They moved slowly toward me, making little fake grabs at me as they closed in. There was nowhere to go except up. The scaffolding behind me stretched up to the rafters. Maybe if I could get up there, I could stall until someone figured out that I wasn't part of the show. Or until the real cops came for Lloyd.

I started climbing and the music picked up speed, sounding as tense as I felt. Everyone in the audience *ooohed* and *aahed*.

Bunch of stupid sheep!

Below me, I could see that the clown cops had started to climb up, following me. I climbed faster, reaching a catwalk high above the stage. I tried shouting, but no one could hear me above the crowd and the music.

I didn't see how this could end well at all.

CHAPTER 24

BUT HERE I AM AT the beginning again. Well, the beginning of the end. There was even a fat lady singing—literally. She'd come out with the rush of performers who'd stormed the stage, adding to the confusion. She was warbling along with the orchestra, but she was the least of the chaos.

Strobe lights flashed, jugglers appeared. The tech people backstage let loose some paper birds on strings that began swooping through the audience, dropping confetti. Kids were squealing, adults were guffawing. Everyone was so entertained, they forgot all about the boy in trouble. They'd never seen such an apparently well-organized mess. Then again, neither had I. Maybe I was missing the hilarity, though, seeing as I was too busy escaping a mob of deranged clown cops.

After climbing a sixty-foot scaffolding and falling ten feet to Sharkman's diving board, I was officially cornered again. Clown cops above, below, and climbing. Sharkman in his tank. The audience was my only hope, but my throat was sore from shouting and I was only getting harder to hear. But it didn't really matter. Nothing in the world would have shushed that mass. They thought this was all just part of the show and, by the grin on Not-Bart's face, he knew it, too.

His grin got even wider when the first person in the audience shouted, "Jump!"

They call it déjà vu, but it's more like déjà *vomit*. Suddenly I was back in Brenville all over again, reliving that horrible nightmare.

What is it with me and diving boards? At least this time I had my clothes on. Even in the serious situation I was in, my face reddened thinking about how everyone had stared at me when I got up out of the Brenville Pool. When everyone saw what had happened and they went silent as death.

The clowns were about ten feet below the diving board and gaining. They would be up to me in seconds, and then they would grab me and haul me backstage and that would be all she wrote. No one would ever hear from the Zander brothers again.

What is it that you do when you're being kidnapped? If… if you're getting kidnapped, you throw a fit. You make a lot of noise. That's what they told us when we were young.

"You let anyone who is nearby know that something strange is happening," Dad had told me when I was little. *"Even if they can't stop them, they'll remember. They'll remember what happened, and maybe it'll help find you."*

But I couldn't make noise! I'd tried that and no one could hear me.

I looked down and saw Lloyd looking up at me. He was the only one who looked like he wasn't fooled. But even if Lloyd could read my lips, it didn't really help having an about-to-be-arrested murderer on your side. Speaking of which: Where were the cops?

Behind me, the first clown had reached the top of the diving board ladder. Maybe it was just his makeup, but his grin was terrifying.

If everybody would just shut up, I could tell them that none of this was an act!

Then everything fell into place. In one second, I knew what I had to do.

I took a deep breath and did it. Really. I didn't back down, I didn't give up.

I. Did. It.

In one swift move, I dropped my pants... and my boxers.

Spartacus Ryan Zander, once again, naked for the world to see.

The gasp from the crowd felt endless. Hands flew up in front of kids' eyes. Old ladies swooned. Kids' mouths dropped and little girls giggled. The music screeched to a halt, ending in an oboe squeak, but then that was it.

The whole circus had fallen into silent, gaping, motionless horror as I stood there, my suit pants around my ankles, my button-up shirt barely covering my rear end, a red blush covering my entire body. Yes, my entire body.

But.

But.

But the clowns on the ladder backed off. Sharkman stopped swimming. Not-Bartholomew's eyes bulged from his fake Bartholomew face. He looked like he might have been even redder than me. The stage was mine.

"I'm sorry," I shouted into the silence. "I don't want to offend you all, but I need to say something and I need you to listen. What I said was true. Bartholomew's Circus has been stealing from museums. Tonight I think he's planning on taking silverware from the Portland Art Museum. He locked me in a trailer but I got out. He's even got my brother backstage. Bartholomew's Circus is evil—and it's not just made-up stuff on some website. Please! Call the police!"

The silence was so thick I thought I was going to choke on it. I felt tears getting ready to pour out of me, so I pulled up my pants and secured my belt.

And, because I couldn't think of anything else to do, I launched myself off the diving board in an Olympic-worthy half gainer into the water tank below. After being naked in front of a thousand strangers, it didn't even seem that difficult.

The first thing I saw when I surfaced was the angry face of Sharkman, glaring at me with his black eyes from across the tank. Luckily, he stayed on his side.

"You stole my act, kid," he whispered. "Get out of my pool before I eat your face."

I didn't wait to see if he was just talking tough or if he meant it. My suit made it hard to swim, but I got up the ladder and pulled myself out, dripping, onto the stage. The whole tent was so quiet you could hear the water sloshing in the pool and the dripping of my suit. I stood in front of the spotlights, not sure what was going to happen, when the music gave a large *ta-da!*

"How about that?" boomed Not-Bartholomew, his voice cutting through the awkward silence. He looked at me like I was some vile thing he wanted to stomp, but he also held his arm out to me like I was his son. I felt myself being nudged over there by one of the clowns and I stumbled forward. I tried not to flinch as he put his arm around me.

"That was a little experimental entertainment we're working on," said Not-Bartholomew, his hand pinching the back of my neck so hard I thought he was trying to do some sort of Spock move on me and make me pass out. "He's wearing a body suit, though, folks, so don't worry! We wouldn't really... Crazy stuff, huh?" Not-Bartholomew kind of faded off, at a loss for words.

The crowd was still uncertain and quiet. Then Not-Bart leaned down and whispered in my ear, "Look to your right. Offstage." Instinctively, I looked.

It was Will. The two security guards were holding him where the audience couldn't see him. Will looked at me with scared eyes. He looked like he'd been crying.

"If you ever want to see your brother again," Not-Bart hissed down to me, "you will take a bow. Like you mean it."

I was *so close*. So close to exposing Bartholomew. So close to getting Mom back. All I had to do was say a few more words to the audience and everyone would believe me.

But I couldn't let them hurt Will. Even if he was the worst brother in the world, he was still my brother. I glanced offstage again, but the guards had already dragged him away.

And so I took a bow. It was a stiff bow and I wasn't smiling, but I did it. At that, the crowd laughed awkwardly and clapped politely, but there was no cheering. Not like before. I thought I saw someone pull out a cell phone and start to dial, but I wasn't sure—it might have been a trick of the light.

Within a few seconds, the circus music started up again and a few of the clowns play-fought with me as they led me backstage, into the dark.

THEY BARELY HAD A CHANCE to push me behind the curtains before I was tackled to the ground. Clowns, fake cops, Sharkman... the gang was all there. It was like, suddenly, I was not just one scrawny kid, but some kind of superhero that required massive strength to contain.

"Please, don't do—*mmmph*," I was about to say "this" when someone shoved a scarf in my mouth. The scarf tasted like face paint, making me gag.

This was not good. Will and I could both be dead before the cops arrived. Or we might simply "vanish." Maybe the plastic surgeon would make a double of me and they'd be able to play off everything I'd done as part of their routine.

I turned my head and saw Will through the wall of clown cops surrounding me. He had a security guard on either side of him and had already been gagged. I took a little pride in the fact that Bart's people thought I was a bigger threat than Will, who was twice as big as me and ten times as mean. Then I noticed another clown—how many clowns does one circus need, anyway?—pull out a length of rope. Were they going to hang me? String me up?

But no, they just started wrapping me in it.

I'd never been more relieved to be tied up in my life. I would have breathed a sigh of relief had I not been gagged. *You won't get away with this,* I thought, remembering the exact phrase I'd used when Nero and Robin had tied me up on the bus. I'd be out of that rope the moment they left us alone.

But then again...

If they put Will and I in one of those trailers, we'd never get away. My mind began racing with all the horrible possibilities. Being fed to the tigers. Being locked in an air-tight safe. Being dumped in the river...

I went as pale and cold as a dead fish as the fake cops spun me around, wrapping me with so much rope you could have made a rope bridge out of it. But I remembered what Nero and Robin had taught me: puff yourself up, push your arms out.

"You know, Bartholomew might have something to say about all of this," Sharkman snarled, while standing over me.

Once I was wrapped like a cocoon, they dragged me over to where Will was.

"Take them somewhere and lock them up," ordered Sharkman. Then he smiled at us coldly, exposing his razor-sharp teeth. "Or maybe we should just feed 'em to the animals..." Will's eyes darted around frantically, and Sharkman laughed.

"Everyone else, back to your places—we've got a show to finish."

FOUR CLOWN COPS CARRIED ME and half-pushed, half-dragged Will down a set of metal steps, around a corner, and into some kind of dimly lit animal staging area. Beside me, Will was doing his best to fight back. It's hard to do much damage when your hands are tied.

Each pen was separated by a short wall of canvas to keep the animals from seeing each other. As we approached the tiger pen (they appeared to be asleep, but even so, they were huge and absolutely terrifying), a feeling of dread settled over me. They weren't really going to feed us to the tigers, were they? I relaxed a tad when we continued past the tigers and then tensed again as I saw a giant, floor-to-ceiling cage with two slow-looking elephants.

"You like our rubber cows?" one of the clowns said, jabbing Will, who grunted in response. "Maybe we'll let you feed one, later."

"Feed you *to* one!" Another clown laughed.

But we kept going until we reached the last cage in the row. It was empty and I recognized it: it was Matilda's.

I was shoved in first, Will second.

"Mmmph!" Will grunted as he tripped over the lip of the cage and landed on his knees. It was a tight fit, but there was just enough room for the two of us.

"Might as well put this to use," said one of them. "I hate to think of where that crazy animal is, though. Just running around somewhere?"

"Yeah, gives me the creeps, too," agreed another.

Funny how I freed Matilda and now I was locked in her cage. I hoped her escape had been more successful than ours.

The tallest clown shut the door and locked it. That's when I remembered I had the cage key in my pocket. What with the ropes and that key, we'd be out of there the moment they left. I tried my best to look depressed, for the clowns' sake, so they wouldn't know.

"Hey, honestly, kiddos," said the tall clown, looking serious. "We were kidding about feeding you to the animals. Finn just wanted us to scare you. This is just until the show's over. Then I'm sure Bart'll have a nice long talk with you and then send you on your way."

"Or something like that," said a shorter one. The tall one shot him a dirty look. But with that, the four clowns were gone.

Will immediately started rolling around, trying to get untied. I counted to thirty before moving, just in case the clowns were still around. After that, I wriggled into action just like the sideshow had taught me. I slipped my shoes off and... well, I'm not meaning to brag, but I was out of that rope in, at most, two minutes.

I staggered to my feet, sweating, aching, rope burned—but free. I pulled the wadded scarf out of my mouth and spat on the floor a few times, trying to get the taste of clown paint off my tongue. Then I knelt down and pulled off Will's gag.

"Ryan?" he asked, coughing. "How'd you do that?"

I grinned at him in the dim light. "It wasn't *that* much rope, Will." I started patting down my damp suit pockets but couldn't find my pocketknife—or the screwdriver—anywhere. Maybe I lost it when I dove into the tank...?

"Seriously, Ryan," Will was saying. "You got out of that so quick!" He seemed to be waiting for an explanation.

I sighed. "Well, I met a bunch of sideshow performers in Albuquerque and—"

Will just stared at me in shock. "Wait—Albuquerque?"

"Yeah, Albuquerque," I said.

I helped him to his knees so I could start working on his knots—which was no easy task. He must have struggled quite a bit when they were tying him up because the knots felt like rocks under my fingers.

"Spartacus?" Will said, "what the hell is going on?" He looked so confused I had to laugh. When I thought about it from his perspective, the whole thing must have made zero sense. Him finding me locked up, him being grabbed by security, me getting naked and jumping off the high dive.

"I'll tell you everything once we get out of this cage," I said. Even if Will was still tied up, we could still run out the back of the circus.

I started digging through my suit pockets while Will just stared at me like I was crazy.

"What are you doing now?" he asked.

"I have the key to this cage, somewhere," I explained. "Zeda gave the key to me so I could break out Matilda—she's the monkey this cage belongs to—"

"What the heck are you talking about now? *Keys? Monkeys?*" But he was looking expectantly at me while I checked my jacket pockets again. "Well? Where is it?"

But then I remembered. The key was in my jeans—which were in my backpack.

Which was with Lloyd.

"It's with the murderer. In my bag."

"The *murderer?*" Will practically shouted. "*What are you talking about?*" All this was obviously getting to him.

I put my hands on the bars of Matilda's cage and shook them as hard as I could. They were solid as a rock. We weren't going anywhere. I slumped down next to Will and sighed.

"I've got a lot to tell you," I said. "And I guess we have the time for it now."

THEN I DUMPED EVERYTHING ON him—the places the circus had been, the museums that had been broken into and robbed, the picture of the person breaking into the art museum and how it had looked like Mom. I told him about Mom's double and Sharkman, and how Bart had hypnotized me and how he and Mom had left holding hands.

"And then they locked me in that trailer and that's where you came in," I finished. It was a relief to tell someone everything. I'd kept it all in my head for so long, it had started driving me a little crazy.

"Wow," he said, his mouth open. I could tell he was impressed with the story, and with me, and I grinned in spite of our situation. "I just can't believe you did all that alone. Geez, Ryan!"

"Well, I tried to get you to come with me, but then you pulled that swimming pool joke and—"

"Wait—you really thought I did that on purpose?" Will turned to look at me.

"Well, didn't you?" I scoffed.

"I would *never* do something like that to you," he said, and he looked so upset, I felt like *I* was being a jerk. Geez, how the tides had turned. "I mean, I might play a lot of jokes on you, but I'd *never* do that. Maybe I shouldn't have given you those big shorts, but I swear I didn't know they'd come off like that. You've got to believe me."

Seriously? Will didn't do that? I just sat there in shock. Did I really make a mistake that big? But, with all the other stuff he'd done, I couldn't blame myself for thinking the worst.

"But I guess I can't blame you for really hating me," he went on, reading my mind. "Even without that, I guess the postcards really were over the line. Well, along with everything else. I'm really sorry."

I stood up and tried Will's ropes again, only because I couldn't handle Will being so serious like this. Even though he was apologizing, seeing him so contrite made me uncomfortable.

"I don't hate you," I said. "Just… if we get out of here, can you try to treat me like an equal?"

"I can try," he said, then, "I mean, I will." He strained to turn his head to look at me, like he wanted to make sure I got that last part. This was the most serious talk we'd ever had.

There was a pause, then, "I can't believe you got caught so easily by that guard," I teased. "What happened back there?"

"You know what *I* can't believe?" Will asked, catching my tone. "*I* can't believe you dropped your pants again—but this time on purpose!" He tried to turn to see my reaction, but I was biting my lip, ignoring him. "Seriously. Who does that? You're a maniac. That took, well… there's no other way to put it. That took serious *balls.*"

"Let's… let's just never bring it up again, okay?" I asked. Will snorted.

"Agreed."

WE'D FALLEN INTO A COMFORTABLE silence (well, as comfortable as you can be crammed into a cage waiting for certain doom), when we heard what could only be described as the voice of an angel.

"*Spartacus?*"

I jumped to my feet and grabbed the bars, but couldn't see anyone yet. But when I heard her call out a second time, I found myself falling in love all over again with Zeda Marx.

"Zeda?" I called out.

"*Spartacus!*" Closer now.

"At the end! On the left!" I shouted. I whooped. I couldn't believe it.

"Are they friendlies?" Will whispered, like we were in a spy movie.

"They're friends of mine. From the sideshow."

Then Zeda came around the corner with Nero at her side.

"Here they are," she said, running. "See? I told you he was in trouble."

"I am *so* glad to see you guys," I exclaimed. Zeda reached in and grabbed my hand. Will raised his eyebrows at that but didn't say anything.

"What are you guys doing here?" I exclaimed. "How—how did you find us?"

"Lucky, I guess," said Nero, looking grim. "You lose the key?"

"Yeah," I said. Zeda nodded and pulled a large ring of keys from her purse and began trying one after another.

"Who put you in here?" asked Nero.

"A bunch of clowns," Will said bitterly, getting to his feet. "Tied us up—Ryan got out of it like a pro, though."

I beamed at the compliment, but Nero's face stayed a dark cloud.

"I'll admit it. I didn't believe you, Zeda. I really didn't. But seeing you guys in here..." he trailed off for a moment, as he closed his eyes in thought. Then he set his jaw and nodded. "We'll put an end to this. I promise. Zeda, you sure you got the key?"

"Positive. Just... well, gotta find the right one." She tried another, but it still didn't turn.

"We have to hurry," said Nero. "They're getting to the end of the show. Here, turn around, put your hands through the bars." Will did as he asked and Nero took a long razor blade from his pocket and began slicing through the ropes.

"How long have you guys been here?" I asked, suddenly nervous about my appearance onstage. I hoped they hadn't seen my... well. My thing.

"We just got here," said Zeda, continuing to sort through the keys. I breathed a sigh of relief. "We heard them playing 'Stars and Stripes' from across the lot—circuses only do that when there's trouble and they want to create a diversion."

"No kidding," I said, remembering everyone rushing out from backstage.

"I made Nero come with me and—" Zeda paused, looking up from the keys. "Where did you stash Matilda?"

"Oh, Matilda. About that. She sorta—"

But before I could break her heart, Nero put his hand up, shushing me.

"We've got company," he said.

"Who's back here?" a voice bellowed moments later. Will and I cringed, but Nero actually smiled.

"I'll be right back," he said. "Stay here."

"Wait!" I hissed, but Nero stepped out of view. Zeda looked unconcerned as she quietly continued trying keys.

"Nero's not a very big guy," she whispered. "But he knows aikido. He can fight anyone."

We couldn't see Nero's fight because of the animal pen wall, but we heard a scuffle and some *oofs* and *thwacks* and panting.

"Got it!" Zeda whispered, as the key in her hand clicked in the lock. I burst out of the cage, ready to help Nero (or run), but at that moment, he came back around the corner, rubbing his hand. Will was still partly tied up and I had to help him out of the cage. We peeked around the corner and saw two guys on the ground.

"Are they *dead?*" I squeaked. Nero smiled.

"Unconscious," he said."

"That was—what?—like twenty seconds?" Will asked, his eyes round. "For *two guys?*"

"What can I say?" said Nero, smirking. "Security is really lax around here."

Nero finished untying Will and we were all about to head down the corridor when Nero's hand went up again.

"Wait," he whispered. "Get back by the cage. Out of sight."

Will, Zeda, and I ran back behind the canvas, hiding. We went quiet, listening as footsteps stopped just a few feet away.

"Well, if it isn't Nimrod," said a man's voice. Even though I couldn't see him, when I heard his voice, my blood went as cold as the Brenville Pool in January.

It was Sharkman.

I watched Zeda's face go pale

"They hate each other," she hissed, her eyes shining. "This won't turn out well." She darted back behind the cage where she could move the canvas and peek. Will and I followed suit.

"*What is that?*" Will asked, horrified, seeing Sharkman clearly for the first time.

"That's Finn," I said darkly.

"What are you doing here, Sword Boy?" Sharkman was asking Nero.

"I don't want any trouble," Nero said. "Just came to gather up a few things that belong to us and then I'll be out of your... well, I was going to say hair, but..."

"Can't let you do that," said Sharkman, ignoring Nero's comment and taking a step toward him. "The boy is none of your concern."

Will's grip tightened on my shoulder.

"So since when have you been snatching kids?" Nero said, putting on an innocent act. "I don't think the sideshow got the memo that that was the new gig."

"I *said*, this doesn't concern you," Sharkman repeated, stepping forward again.

"I'm not leaving without him," said Nero.

"You're not leaving *period*."

And with that, Sharkman lunged at Nero. There, in front of our eyes, they were wrestling and fighting on the ground.

I'd never seen a real fight before. And I definitely didn't want to see one again. Especially one with a guy who's half shark.

"Piece of ocean trash," Nero growled, punching him in the stomach, but Sharkman got the upper hand by biting Nero on the arm. Nero cried out in pain. Will and I found ourselves struggling with Zeda, who was trying to get to Nero.

"You can't go," I pleaded as she flailed at Will and I.

Then we heard a dull crash and footsteps running away.

When we peeked around the wall again, Nero was lying motionless on the ground—and Sharkman was gone.

"Nero!" Zeda cried out in a small voice, running for him. Will and I followed and with so much blood pumping in my ears, I could hardly hear. When we got to Nero, he was breathing but unconscious. There was a shovel on the ground next to him and a rising goose egg on his forehead.

"That *monster!*" Zeda shrieked, jumping to her feet. Before we even saw it happening, she was sprinting down the corridor after Sharkman.

"Go stop her!" Will commanded, already pressing on the bite wound on Nero's arm. "I'll make sure he's okay—and Ryan?"

"Yeah?"

"Be... be careful, okay?"

I nodded. "You, too. And watch out for clowns."

Will smiled wanly.

And with that, I took off after Zeda.

As I raced after Zeda, I could hear Bartholomew's booming voice finally announcing Mom's human cannonball act. The grand finale. His voice rumbled through the tent.

"Bartholomew's Circus is proud to present the unbelievable, unmatchable, phenomenal incredible, and the world's only female cannonball—Flying Aaaa-theee-naaa!"

But of course, it wasn't Bartholomew—it was his double. Not that it mattered at that point.

Zeda was fast but I was faster. I caught up to her as she rounded a corner. Sharkman was silhouetted just ten feet in front her—and she was still moving toward him at a dead run.

I had no choice. I tackled her.

We hit the ground behind a support post hard, rolling over a few times. Against all odds, she hadn't shrieked out loud when I hit her. She glared at me and while I didn't know what *she* was thinking, *I* was sending telepathic signals to Sharkman: *Don't turn around. Don't turn around.* Luckily, the sound of Not-Bartholomew speaking to the audience covered up any noises we'd made.

"You are about to witness the most exceptionally-extraordinary, impressively-inconceivable, death-defying act appearing in any circus anywhere in the world!"

I peered out from behind the post. Sharkman was crouching down, maybe ten feet away from us. He'd pulled out a flashlight and was looking down... what was that, a hole? No, wait. It wasn't a hole. Was it... was it the *sewer?*

He was only there a second before my mom appeared, coming up from below. Up a ladder from a dark sewer.

"Isn't she onstage?" Zeda asked in the tiniest whisper.

I shook my head. I knew that *this* was my Mom. "*Her

double is onstage," I whispered back. But if Not-Bart and Not-Mom were onstage, what were the real ones doing?

In a flash, it all made sense. The doubles. The museums. The circus. It was all one big alibi. One big front. If their doubles were onstage, that meant *they couldn't be considered suspects.* It also meant that Bart and Mom went out—*during the show*—to loot the museums. It was genius. It was diabolical. And it made sense. Every bit.

Zeda saw the realization on my face, but there was no time to tell her what I'd figured out. Sharkman was actually pushing my mom back into the sewer.

"*Get down,*" Sharkman growled at her. "Your son's ruined everything." She started to say something, but he actually put his hand on her head and pushed her underground.

I waited a beat before getting to my feet, this time with Zeda pulling on my arm, protesting, but I shook her off. She followed and we both peered down into the darkness. I was certain it was the sewer—there was a manhole cover right next to me.

If only I had my flashlight!

But I couldn't wait. Of all the possible reasons Sharkman could have for shoving Mom back down, not one that came to mind was good. He'd sounded angry.

Really angry.

I started to follow them but Zeda seized my shoulder. "You're not going down there without me."

"You need to get help," I insisted. "Make sure Nero is okay and then get help. Just tell them where I've gone."

"No, please," she begged, her eyes large and scared. "I won't let you go alone."

"Look, if I don't go now, it might be too late. Don't—don't follow me!" I said resolutely. I mean, *really* resolutely. I don't think I'd ever been more resolute in my life. Zeda even took a step back.

Mom needed my help. That was all I knew. That was why I'd gone through all of this. If I didn't help her now, or at least make sure she was all right, what was the point of me even coming?

I gave Zeda one last look before climbing down into the sewer.

CHAPTER 25

IT WAS AS DARK AS a sealed bank vault at the bottom of the ladder. It smelled musty, but not like... well, not like poop, like I'd imagined it would. I couldn't see, but you know how you sometimes have a sense of space, even when you're in the dark? It felt more like a tunnel than a room. I put my hand out and found a brick wall but in every other direction seemed to be an even darker dark. I didn't dare leave that wall, so I stood there, straining my ears and eyes for *something*. My chest felt desperate and tight as I willed something to happen.

But there was nothing.

Don't panic, Spart—they didn't just disappear. Just give it a second.

I felt blind and deaf. It was like I was struggling to use senses I didn't have. But then... to my left. Something, in the blackness. It was a sound. Something heavy being dragged—and then, something... like a *tinkling*.

I took three slow, deep breaths and then inched along the wall. The tinkling grew louder, and then there was a light buzzing. No, not a buzzing. *Voices*.

Sticking flat to the wall, I began to make out something in the dark. It started as a dim glow with an edge, as though it were a light shining around something. As I got closer, I saw I'd guessed right. It was a long tunnel and, maybe a few car-lengths ahead of me, it turned to the left. The light and the voices were right around the corner. As I got closer I started to make out the words.

"...falling apart up there... so stupid!" That voice was Sharkman's. And the tinkling sounded like they were setting a table or doing the dishes.

"...let's use our civilized-people words." That was Bartholomew—I'd recognize his calm, low voice anywhere.

"...knows everything. And then I came across Nero snooping around in the back—I took care of him, but not before he took out Ed and Louie. I think the place is crawling with—"

"Nero?" Bart interrupted. "Why does that name sound familiar?"

"From the freak show. I think they—"

"Finn, I don't pay you to think," Bart said. "Did you *think* it was a good idea to use *cloth* sacks to hold actual silverware? As in actual, honest-to-god sharp knives?"

Silverware. They'd done it! They'd stolen the silverware from the Portland Art Museum, just like I'd guessed! It took all my will not to peek around the corner. But as my eyes adjusted, I could see their shadows on the far wall. They looked like they were picking stuff up from the ground.

"Well no, I didn't think about it," Sharkman said in his rough growl. I heard more clinking. "I'd just assumed that the stuff was old and wouldn't be that sharp."

"Your assumptions have led to mint condition, 15th century Elizabethan silver flatware spread all over the ground."

Ah! They were picking up the silverware!

"It doesn't matter," said Sharkman. "It's over. We need to just leave it and go."

"You're always so quick to tuck your little fin and run," said Mom. *Mom said that?* I couldn't believe what I was hearing. "Think we have enough time to return it?"

"We don't have a choice," answered Bartholomew with a sigh. "If your son's strip show happened like Finn said it did—that's going to make people remember what he said about us and the museum—shine a light over here, Finn. But if they don't find the silverware missing, they've got nothing on us. Except Spartacus's story and a bunch of circumstantial evidence. And that's if they even decide to look into it."

There was silence and the clinking of silverware, when Mom spoke up again. "The streetcar was easier than this."

"We didn't have to return the streetcar, did we?" said Sharkman. "And all because of your kid."

"Lay off, okay?" she retorted. "You think I wanted him to show up? Think I invited him?"

I turned my face away from the corner and pressed my head to the wall.

I know it sounds naïve and stupid, but up until then, I'd still been clinging to the idea that Mom was an unwilling participant in this. That Bartholomew had hypnotized her or threatened her to get her to stay. I hadn't prepared myself for the possibility that she was really, truly a thief herself. I was trying to come up with some way, some idea to explain away what I'd heard. But, as if to drive it home, Mom went on.

"After we return the silverware, we'll entertain Spartacus. There's nothing we can't explain. He'll end up doubting himself. He'll go home. Then we'll only have to lay low for a few months, and everything will blow over. It'll be like it never happened."

I felt sick listening to her talk to these maniacs like she was one of them.

"Indeed," Bart agreed. "I think that's our only option at the moment. And dear, your most inconvenient child aside, I do have to hand it to you. These—what are they? These Chinese Tunnels?"

"Shanghai Tunnels," Mom corrected him.

I squeezed my eyes shut. *This isn't happening. This isn't happening.*

"They are quite a bit nicer—and cleaner—than the sewer. Good find."

"We'll have to come back to Portland and try this again," Mom said.

She couldn't be in on this. *But she was.* And now that I knew it, did I really want to bring her down right along with Bartholomew? Now that I saw she was every bit as guilty as he was?

No.

I was done.

I was officially done chasing after my mom.

I was, without out a doubt, no longer on a rescue mission. I had to get out of there, while I still had a chance to save Will and Zeda and Nero and myself. Bartholomew couldn't find out I'd heard everything they'd just said. That would mean they'd really have to get rid of me.

"I think this is the last piece," Sharkman was saying.

Then—a noise, coming from the dark to my right. A rat maybe? Or was it the scrape of a shoe?

"Hey, what was that?" asked Sharkman. I held my breath and shrunk back.

Then, even though I couldn't see Bartholomew and the others, I saw their flashlights swivel in my direction. And that's when I saw another, smaller shadow appear on the wall.

It was Zeda. She'd run right past me… and right into the middle of them.

"Who is this now?" Sharkman exclaimed. "Kids are friggin' everywhere!"

Why did she follow me? Why couldn't she stay put?

"It *is* a circus," Bartholomew said pointedly to Sharkman. "But please, miss, you are… ?"

"I… I was looking for someone," I heard her small voice say anxiously. "I'll just… um, be going."

She'll be okay, I told myself. Mom is there. She wouldn't let anything happen to her.

"No, no, by all means, stay," snarled Sharkman.

"Hey! Let go of me!" Zeda cried out.

"Finn!" Mom exclaimed.

I couldn't just hang back around the corner and listen any longer. I peeked around the corner and there they were, all in black: Mom and Bart, three large duffel bags at their feet—and Sharkman holding Zeda by the arm. He'd apparently lost one of his black contacts in the scuffle with Nero, which made his eyes look all lopsided and even more terrifying. Bart was stepping forward and pulling Sharkman back by his collar.

"That's not how we do things," Bartholomew said through clenched teeth.

I breathed a sigh of relief as Sharkman let go of Zeda's arm. Her face was pale and unreadable as Bart put his arm around her thin shoulders.

"Besides, it's not necessary, is it?" Bart said, as much to Zeda as to Sharkman. "She's just a girl, Finn. We'll just keep her with us until we find out what's going on. Sometimes it's good to have a little bargaining chip."

Then Bart took out what looked like a walkie-talkie and began fiddling with it.

"Hey, I recognize you," said my mom, crossing over to Zeda. She actually reached out and raised Zeda's face so she could see it better. "Yeah! You're from the sideshow, too. You... you're the fire-breathing girl, right?"

"Nice to meet you, too, Athena," Zeda said icily. Mom dropped her hand away, while Zeda rubbed her face. "We always knew you people were doing something funny. I can't believe you're really Spartacus's mom. What kind of mother—"

"You know Spartacus?" my mom asked. I cringed. Why would Zeda say that?

Mom returned to Zeda, looking her in the eye.

"What do you know about my son?"

"I know he took on all sorts of danger to try to help you," Zeda said, and I actually blushed. "And you sure don't look like you're doing him any favors."

"I love my son. You don't know anything about him *or* me."

"Both of you—shut up," said Sharkman. "I don't want to hear that kid's stupid name any more."

"Shhh... All of you," Bart said before speaking into the walkie-talkie: "What's happening up there?"

There was a static-filled pause before the crackling answer came.

"Everything has gone down the toilet. Grand finale went off without a hitch, but for some reason that sideshow is out front, performing—so now the audience isn't leaving, they're just milling around. And we lost the two kids from the cage—door was just wide open. I thought—"

But Bart turned off the walkie-talkie and pushed the antennae down with a snap.

"Oookay," said Bartholomew coolly to Zeda. "I believe a certain line of civility has officially been crossed. Trespassing. Breaking and entering. Et cetera. Finn—as you were."

There was a slight nod to Sharkman and he lunged immediately at Zeda, grabbing her by the throat. This time, he had a gun in his hands.

"Ow!" Zeda cried out in pain and fear.

Oh-no-oh-no-oh-no...

"All right, fire breather," Sharkman said. Still holding Zeda's neck, he put the gun to her stomach. "You tell me every single thing you know right this instant."

"He's bound to get a fair bit angrier," Bartholomew said to Zeda. "So I would start talking if I were you."

Why did I bring her into this? Why didn't I just go get help with her and leave Mom? My fingers dug into the wall, my mind racing.

That's when Mom stepped forward, looking concerned.

"This isn't right," she said to Bartholomew. "This isn't what we do." I breathed a small sigh of relief—she wasn't completely rotten to the core. Bart just shook his head slightly at her, though, like everything was under control.

"I don't know anything!" Zeda shrieked as Sharkman smiled, all his pointy teeth inches from her face.

I'd never felt more helpless in my life. *Think Spartacus!* What should I do? What *could* I do? I was about to just jump out and pummel someone (a lot of good that would do) when my eye caught something shiny on the ground.

It was a fork. A large, heavy-looking fork.

Mom had only trained me with knives, but what was the difference when you got right down to it? Without a moment of hesitation, I stepped out, snatched up the fork, and flung it as hard as I could.

It landed square in the middle of Sharkman's back—where it stuck.

"*Argh!*" he cried out, his hands going to his back, dropping the gun. Zeda was in shock and didn't move a muscle, staring at the three of them in horror.

"Who threw that?" Sharkman demanded. "*Who threw that?*"

Bartholomew picked up the gun—and the flashlight.

"I believe I can answer that," he said, shining the light on my face. "Here's our young hero now. Nice aim with that fork. I might have an opening for a knife thrower…"

I squinted back at him, trying to look taller and braver than I was.

"Spartacus!" Mom and Zeda both exclaimed. Zeda rushed over to me and almost crushed my arm in her grip. She was shaking like a leaf. Then again, so was I.

"Am I ever glad to see you," Zeda said.

"You're going to pay for that, kid." Sharkman sneered at me, throwing the fork to the ground. Bart looked at him and then at the fork. Sharkman scowled before picking the fork back up and putting it in his duffle bag.

"So you two know each other, I take it," Bart said, gesturing wanly with the gun at me and Zeda. It was them versus us, facing off in the tunnel. "Certainly making some interesting friends on this trip, eh?"

324

I glowered at him. When Mom tried to take a step toward me, Bartholomew held out his arm and stopped her, sighing heavily. "You don't quit, do you Spartacus? I normally like that quality in a person."

"You can't keep getting away with this," I said, but I was only talking to my mom. I had to reason with her. "Everyone knows about the robberies now."

Zeda nodded in agreement, but otherwise remained silent.

My mom looked sheepish, like she was embarrassed to be talking. "Spartacus, they're not robberies. Robbing is when you take something by force or threaten or harm people to get what you want. We just steal things. We never hurt people."

"Could have fooled me," I said, glaring at Sharkman, who glared right back.

"There's an exception to every rule," Bart sighed. "Finn is who we use when there is, well—an exception."

"I guess that includes putting me and Will in a cage?" I demanded.

"Will?" Mom asked, looking bewildered. "He's here, too? What cage?"

Sharkman scowled at her. "Your *other* son showed up. We had to put them both in a cage to keep them out of the way."

Mom shot an angry look at Bartholomew. "What did I say about my kids?"

He held up his hands innocently. "I swear to you, Athena. I knew nothing of this."

After a long moment, Mom's shoulders relaxed, and she nodded. "I believe you."

I shook my head in a mixture of disbelief and annoyance. "*Really,* Mom? Cages? You're okay with that?"

"I'm sure the cage was just for a little while. To keep you both safe," she said.

"What kind of mother are you?" Zeda finally exclaimed, but Mom ignored her. So much for her liking my first girlfriend.

"You still haven't told me—*why* are you doing this?" I asked in desperation. "How can you work with these people? This isn't you!"

"You don't understand, sweetie," she said. "It *is* me." She opened her mouth to say more but I interrupted, trying to bargain with her.

"Look, if we could get all the silverware returned, like you said, the police wouldn't know you robbed—I mean stole stuff and you could come back home, like it never happened, right?"

She shook her head, not like a "no" to the question, but like in a you'll-never-understand way. It was the expression she wore when she was breaking bad news—the type of bad news that wasn't going to change.

"Spartacus," Bartholomew said. "I'm sorry to say, but the time for returning the thieved items has come and gone." He pulled the walkie-talkie out again, keeping the gun trained on us. "Our other show, on the other hand, must go on."

"How is it up there?" he spoke into the radio.

"It's crazy. People everywhere," came the fuzzy answer.

"We can deal with that. Got any heat?" he asked. I realized he meant police.

"Not yet," came the answer.

Geez, what does it take to get a couple of cops to show up around here? With accusations of grand theft and kidnapping, a reported sighting of a wanted killer, *and* a display of (very) public indecency, you'd think at least a couple officers would be kind of curious!

"Perfect. We're going to leave everything in the back yard, and go with Plan X. Copy? Plan X as in x-ray."

"Copy that. We have her up and running; meet at point W, as planned."

Was that his escape car? I was confused. He was speaking in some weird code. Zeda looked just as puzzled as Bart put the radio away. He smiled his plastic smile at us. "Sorry kids, but the intermission is over." He directed us toward a metal ladder conveniently located just a few feet away. "If I've guessed our location correctly—and I'm quite sure that I have—this exit ought to put us in the perfect position."

Sharkman went up the ladder to remove the manhole cover.

"After you, children," he stood aside and waved us ahead with the gun. Zeda climbed up ahead of me and I followed. Bart spoke as we climbed up. "I have to say, I'm very sorry to lose the circus. The American children will be so disappointed, and I admit, I will be, too. It was a great gig while it lasted."

When we got to the top of the ladder, I saw that we were in the empty main tent. The lights were mostly out, except for one of the spotlights. Mom's cannon sat in the ring but the audience was gone.

There was no one up there except Sharkman, looming over us. No one to see us, no one to save us.

Zeda's eyes met mine. *What are they going to do?* they asked. I shook my head. I didn't have a clue. Bart and Mom emerged from the tunnels and Zeda took my hand and squeezed it. I couldn't believe I'd gotten her into this! We were both as good as dead—and there was nothing I could do about it.

And then—something strange happened...

Bartholomew tucked the gun into his jacket pocket.

"You're lucky you told so many people, Spartacus." He paused, pursing his lips. "Your little burlesque routine on the high dive was—well, it was something else. I cannot imagine any other way you could have gotten yourself out of that situation."

I blushed, but I wasn't sure if it was because I was flattered or embarrassed. Zeda looked at me, raising an eyebrow.

Bart continued: "You're a worthy adversary. I won't underestimate you in the future."

"So you're going to let us go?" Zeda blurted out what I didn't dare to ask. I cringed. I didn't think wanted to hear the answer.

But he surprised me. Again.

"Yes," Bartholomew said before leaning forward, his face going very smooth and calm—and horrifying. "But Spartacus, remember this—*never* forget this: I'm giving you a rare opportunity that I don't give anyone. Ever. Don't make me regret it."

I swallowed hard, my chest heaving with fear and relief.

This was it. This was really it. It was over. I was never going to see my mom again.

But then she spoke up.

"Give me a minute," she said to Bart. "I can catch up. I'll meet you in… in the middle."

Bartholomew considered her for a moment before touching her cheek softly. Mom reached up and held his hand while I silently gagged.

"You have five minutes," he said gently. "That's all I can wait."

CHAPTER 26

BARTHOLOMEW AND SHARKMAN STRODE OFF through the curtains and I turned to Zeda.

"Wait here?" She nodded and gave me a hard hug.

Mom put her hand out to me. I took it, confused about what this meant, what was happening. As we walked toward the stage, I saw there were tears running down her face.

"I'm a terrible mother," she said in a shaky voice. I wanted to comfort her, and say she wasn't... but it would have been a lie and I didn't have any energy left for lies.

It didn't matter that I didn't say anything, though, because she went on. "I do love you, but I've also got some issues, bigger than you or your father or brother. Problems in my head."

I started to protest but she put her hand up.

"You have to let me speak," she said softly. "I know how you feel about me. You love me. I know that. But you don't really know me. To you I've always been just *Mom*. But that's not who I am. I mean, that's not all I am.

"I stayed as long as I could," she continued. "And when I got the chance to join Bartholomew—well, I didn't know *this* was the kind of adventure I wanted. But now that I have it, I wouldn't trade it. Not for the world."

Then I asked the obvious question. Call me naïve.

"Not even for Will and me?"

She shook her head and I looked away, tears blurring my eyes.

"I know you'll both grow up to be clever and brave young men," she said. "I've always known that. You especially."

I didn't like her talking like this. It sounded like a good-bye. The kind of goodbye that means things will never go back to the way they were, ever. I knew I didn't want to hear the rest. I wanted to run away from her, even after I'd worked so hard to find her.

"But you can't just go," I whispered, the tears starting to flow. I rubbed them away with my suit sleeve.

"I can. And I will miss you, baby, but you have to stay with your family." Mom tried to put her arms around me but I pushed her away.

"My *family?*" I shouted. I couldn't help it. I was shaking. "You're leaving me with Will and Dad—'*my family*'? They don't understand me and I don't need them! Will makes my life hell and Dad doesn't even care. Did I tell you that Will made me think you were kidnapped? What kind of rotten family is that?"

"But they *are* your family," she said, tears in her eyes, too. "And you won't get another one. You'll have friends

330

and adventures, but you'll only have one family that's your own blood."

"But you threw your family away," I said. "How could something so important be so easy to walk away from?"

"It was different—*I* was the one who didn't deserve *you.*"

I turned around and stared at the cannon while she spoke in her low, breaking voice.

"Your dad was there for you when I wasn't. Even when I was home, you can't lie to yourself and say I was a good mother then. Your dad and your brother, they love you, in their own way. *That's* your family, like it or not. I'm only me, and I left. And while I was there, what did I do for you except give you a name?"

"Great name, too," I muttered to myself.

"I gave you that name for a reason, Spartacus. Because when I was pregnant with you, I had a feeling that your life wasn't going to be normal. Or easy. I wanted you to be strong—a lot stronger than I felt. And look at you now. You are. In every way. You've become stronger than I ever hoped you'd be."

We stood looking at each other for a moment before she put her arms out again. I fell into them. "You were the only thing that made it good," I whispered into her shoulder. "And now you're leaving me again."

"I'm sorry," she whispered, rocking me. "I'm so sorry. I do love you. Remember that."

She was still holding me like that when we heard the crash of doors flying open all around us. We looked up and saw that there were cops—real cops this time—standing at every entrance.

"Time to go," she said, pulling away.

I couldn't tell if they were police, FBI, SWAT, National Guard, or what, but they were closing in. Zeda, who was on the other end of the tent, ducked down behind the seats.

"Put your hands where we can see them!" a man barked. He was actually wearing a bulletproof vest and a helmet. I threw my hands in the air, but Mom—well, Mom didn't listen.

In an instant, she had scrambled up the backside of the scaffolding next to us and then, like she was some sort of ninja, she leapt at the canvas tent and slid down it, using a knife to slice a hole as she went. Cold air immediately came rushing into the tent.

Yup. That was my mom.

"Get on the ground, lady! Get on the ground!"

They moved in closer, but still, she ignored them. I watched helplessly as she wheeled the cannon so that it faced the hole she'd made. She picked up the helmet from the ground next to the cannon and pulled it on her head. Before I knew it, she'd popped herself into the barrel.

"Ma'am? Ma'am! I said, don't move!"

Then her head reappeared. "A little help, Spartacus?" she asked, as casually as if she were asking me to help her zip up her dress. But her eyes were pleading.

It was funny. She still kind of looked like Mom in there, the mom that made me green-dyed pancakes and who taught me how to play Gin Rummy. She *was* my mom, and when it came down to it, I'd rather have her free somewhere in the world than locked up in a cage like an animal.

"What do I do?" I asked.

"Just turn the key there, and press the button," she said. Then, "You make me very proud, Spartacus."

I didn't know if she meant I *had* made her proud or I *should* make her proud, but I didn't have time to ask.

She dropped down inside and I turned the key and hit the button.

In reality, a circus cannon makes very little noise. Without the fake fuse, fireworks, and explosion, there's nothing really to it. There was just a pause and then the hollow *thwack* of compressed air. We all watched as she shot through the hole in the wall.

It was the first and last time I ever saw my mother perform.

The cops stared at where she had blasted off, then cursed and took off for the front of the tent. Zeda and I raced out after them. We found everybody in the park outside, facing the river—and I mean everybody. It looked like no one from the audience had left. It was total chaos.

Yet again.

Zeda and I pushed to the front of the crowd where we saw strange lights low on the water, like they came from some kind of short, black boat. We could see the silhouette of someone helping my mother out of the water.

"Meet you in the middle," she'd said to Bartholomew. Of the river.

"Do you see that?" exclaimed a cop.

"I do, but I don't believe it. What is that?"

"I think... I mean, it *looks* like the submarine from the children's museum across the way," answered someone else. "But that thing doesn't run, does it?"

"Got it up and running," Bart had said on the radio. *"Plan X."*

"You know," said Zeda, turning to me. "I have to hand it to her. She may be terrifying and—honestly?—kind of a bad mom, but she sure knows how to make an exit."

I had to smile in spite of myself.

"Zeda, I am so, so sorry about all of this," I said, turning serious. "I didn't know that—"

I was about to embarrass myself by blubbering, begging forgiveness, but I was saved by one of the SWAT-looking guys who'd been in the tent

"Spartacus Zander?" he said, tapping me on the shoulder.

"Yeah?" I answered sheepishly. He took me by the arm and led me to a park bench. Zeda followed.

"Don't move a muscle," he said as I sat down. "Just stay right there, okay?"

Zeda and I looked around. The place was absolutely crawling with people. The sideshow had really done its job, keeping everyone there. I could see their bus across the way, strung with lights, but there were too many people to actually see what was going on.

But in the foreground, there were police cars, fire engines, and ambulances. It was what I'd been hoping for all along. They'd finally come—too late, I guess. But at least everyone would finally know the truth. I watched as the police rounded up the circus performers and tech people Bartholomew had left behind. Some were just being questioned, but I saw quite a few being loaded into waiting squad cars.

"What a circus!" Zeda said. I wasn't sure if she was surprised at what kind of circus Bartholomew ran or at all the confusion.

"Why did you follow me?" I asked her.

"I couldn't let you go down there alone," she said, exasperated. "You shouldn't have run off after them in the first place."

"No, no," I answered. "Not in the tunnels. I mean to Portland. Why are you here? *How* are you here?"

Zeda gave me an awkward smile. "I talked the sideshow into coming and performing after the show. The people always meander when there's a second show. I assumed it would be too much chaos for Bartholomew to really try anything."

"So everyone knew what was happening?" I asked.

"Well, I told them what you said. But I don't know how many of them actually believed me. You heard Nero. Even he thought it was crazy until he saw Will and you in the cage. But the rest, no matter what they thought, wanted the chance to stick it to Bartholomew. The sideshow always annoyed him—what? Why are you looking at me like that?"

I guess I was grinning a bit too widely at her. But I couldn't help it. "You did that for me? Why?"

Zeda's cheeks flushed. "Well, I couldn't let you do all that yourself. I mean, we're friends, right?"

I think we were about to have some big romantic, mushy scene, but my dumb brother chose to interrupt at that exact moment.

"Ryan!" he gasped, running across the grass toward us. Zeda and I jumped back from each other, embarrassed. He sat down next to me, oblivious to the perfect moment he'd just ruined, his face shining with excitement. "You guys okay?"

"Yeah. You?" I asked.

"Fine. I'm fine. Nero is fine, too," he told Zeda, pointing over to an ambulance out in the street.

"Nero! I need to see him," Zeda said, getting up. She and I exchanged an awkward look. "I'll see you in a bit, okay?"

I just nodded and watched her disappear in the crowd, in utter disbelief.

She liked *me. Sure, she'd kissed me before, but that was just about—*

Then Will interrupted again, this time snapping his fingers in my face.

"Hey, Casanova!" He was giving me a sick grin. "What was all that about, eh? Did I interrupt something?"

"Shut up," I said, but I couldn't keep the corners of my mouth down.

Luckily, a paramedic arrived to check on us, so he changed the subject.

"Was that Mom who blasted out through the tent? Into the river?"

I nodded. The paramedic was trying to be professional but I could tell she was listening. She gave me an ice pack to hold against my knee.

"Where's she going?" Will asked.

"All I know is that it's not Brenville," I glowered.

Will stared at the river with a weird expression. Sadness, maybe? Or longing? I'd never really thought that Will even missed Mom, but the look on his face pretty much proved that he did. I could tell he wanted to say something, but he must have pushed it down, because he stayed quiet.

"What happened after we left?" I asked, trying to get him talking again.

"Oh, yeah, I forgot to say thanks *so much* for coming back to help," he said sarcastically. "I had to carry Nero outside to the sideshow, but by then all the cops and ambulances were arriving. Hey—are those my *shoes?*"

I was trying to explain when I heard a familiar, booming voice.

"Got another one for you!"

It was Lloyd, coming up from the riverbank—and he was dragging a squirming, but pretty much defeated, Sharkman behind him. I couldn't believe my eyes. *What was Lloyd doing?* I tried to slouch down so neither of them could see me but the paramedic squeezed my wrist.

"Try to sit still, please," she said while dressing a cut on my arm.

By the looks of both Lloyd and Sharkman, there had been another epic fight—but apparently Lloyd had won. Sharkman had a bloody nose and it looked like his fin might have been crooked. Two police officers rushed over and handcuffed him. As he was heaved past us, though, he saw me sitting on the bench. The look he gave me chilled me to the bone. Even the paramedic flinched when she turned and saw him.

"You don't know how many people you've crossed, you little rat," Sharkman snarled. "This is bigger than Bartholomew now! *Way* bigger!"

One of the cops was about to say something when Will stood up, his chest thrust out.

"*Shut your goddamn pie hole!*" Will hollered. "*No one threatens Ryan, you got it?*" And before Sharkman could say anything else, the cops threw him in the back of a squad car.

I stared at Will, like I'd never seen him before.

"What?" he said sheepishly. Then he saw my expression change. "What?" he asked again, only this time it was nervous. There was no time to explain to Will about Lloyd. But what was he *doing* here? A killer surrounded by cops and not batting an eyelash—it was ridiculous!

"Never thought I'd get bit by a shark on dry land!" he joked, limping toward us and dropping on the bench next to me.

"H-hey, Lloyd," I stuttered, watching him pull up his pant leg to show a bite mark on his calf.

"You have any antiseptic for this?" he asked the paramedic.

Oh, god, don't leave us alone with him, I pleaded with my eyes, but the paramedic nodded and jogged over to one of the ambulances.

"Guess Bartholomew had had enough of his fish friend," he said. "I heard him on the bank of the river, shouting for them to come back."

"So you fought him?" Will asked.

"Let's call it a citizen's arrest," he winked, before putting out his hand. "I'm Lloyd, Spartacus's friend. I gave him a ride from Bend to Boise a few days ago, for the funeral."

"Right. The funeral…" Will said slowly, shaking Lloyd's hand but looking at me. "I'm his brother, Will."

"I think he told me about you," Lloyd said. Will looked confused.

"Where's your mom?" I asked.

"I sent her home in a cab when I realized things were getting too out of control," he said. There was a long pause before he said it. "That was some mess you were in, Spartacus."

"No kidding," I managed. I mean, there wasn't anything I could really say about it at that point, was there? It was exactly that: a mess.

"I kinda knew you were in trouble, even before you called about seeing the circus," Lloyd continued. "Something just seemed *off.* And when you didn't come back after the intermission? And then, of course, there was your *performance…*"

My face went red just at the thought of what I'd done in front of… oh god, thousands of people. I'd probably relive that moment in nightmares for the rest of my life. "It wasn't supposed to turn out like that," I said.

"I wouldn't think that would be part of your plan," Lloyd said wryly. "That's what made me call the cops."

"*You?*" I asked, incredulous. "*You* called them?"

"Who wouldn't?" he countered. "You laid it all out on the line. And I mean *all* of it."

It didn't make any sense. Why would he…? He'd put his own freedom at risk for *me?*

At that exact moment, a man in a brown suit appeared next to us. I thought he was there for me but he spoke to Lloyd instead.

"Dan Lloeke?" he asked. One hand showed a badge and the other was on the butt of his gun. My stomach dropped and Will's mouth gaped open. It was the last piece of my plan, falling into place—too little, too late. I felt guilty and my gaze went to my lap.

"Oh, hey, Jerome," said Lloyd easily. "Nope. I'm still Lloyd. Busy night, huh?"

What? I looked up and saw Lloyd holding out his arm with the tattoo while the guy with the badge inspected it with a penlight.

"You have no idea," answered the officer, putting the penlight away. "I'm glad I'm only here to see you—the rest of this looks like a bureaucratic nightmare."

"No doubt," Lloyd chuckled.

"Sorry to bother you again," said the officer. "Have a good night." He turned away and got lost among the other emergency workers.

"What was that?" I ventured, looking from Lloyd to the cop and then back at Lloyd, completely confused.

"We-ell, since you've shared your family secrets," Lloyd said. "I might as well share mine. Remember when I told you I had a rotten big brother, too?"

Will shot me a dirty look but Lloyd went on.

"Dan Lloeke is my brother—my twin brother. And Dan... well, let's just say he's done some awful things that we're all paying for."

"Your twin," I repeated slowly.

"Yep," Lloyd said, looking at me thoughtfully. "Jerome," he waved in the general direction of the crowd, "and I do this pretty regularly."

Oh god. I knew I was giving myself away, but I didn't care. "But the shaved head—" I stuttered.

"We both went bald in our twenties."

"And the tattoo—"

"Same band, different songs."

"And... and the face."

"Twins," he said again. "Identical."

Will just sat there in disbelief, trying to sort everything out from the pieces he was hearing.

Lloyd waited for me to respond, trying to hide a smile.

I was quiet for a few moments before I spoke up. I had to come clean.

"I called the police," I said. "I saw your—Dan's—wanted poster after you gave me the ride, and... well... I really needed to get the cops here. I'm so sorry..." I trailed off.

He waved his hand dismissively. "Happens all the time."

AFTER LLOYD DRIFTED OFF AND Will went to fetch my backpack, I had my first moment alone to just breathe. I felt like I'd been going at a hundred miles an hour since... well, since forever. I saw Zeda and the sideshow through the thinning crowd and she waved at me. I was smiling, waving back, when I remembered. I'd been going a hundred miles an hour since I lost Matilda.

Matilda.

I couldn't believe I'd forgotten about her.

I am the worst pseudo-boyfriend ever.

Ignoring what the police had said about staying on the bench, I raced over to the first fireman I saw.

"I need a ladder. My... well, my *pet* is up in a tree and she's... she's really important."

Zeda jogged over to me while the fireman fetched a ladder. "What are you doing off your bench?" she teased.

"I didn't get the chance to tell you earlier," I began, my shoulders slumped. "Matilda—well, she got out. earlier..."

"Oh, no!" Zeda clapped her hand over her mouth. "I forgot about her!"

"She might still be in the last place I saw her, though," I said trying to sound hopeful, but I couldn't hide how dejected I felt. "I'm so sorry."

"It's not your fault," she said, surprising me by pulling me into a tight hug. "You tried."

She was trying to be strong but I could tell she was also trying hard not to cry.

Will appeared with Remmy and Robin and we all walked along with a sniffling Zeda as I led the firemen over to the funnel-cake stand.

"That old monkey has got enough sense to survive anywhere," Remmy was trying to comfort Zeda. Then he turned to me. "And don't look so glum, kid. That Great Responsibility we talked about doesn't mean you have to be a superhero."

"But it was just one monkey," I moaned. "How could

I not hold on to a single, tiny monkey?"

"Spiderman, as far as I know, never had to babysit an aye-aye," Remmy said. "And, monkey or no monkey, I sure think you've done more than your fair share of the hero work in the past few days."

"I agree," said Robin.

"Me, too," sniffled Zeda, squeezing my hand again.

"Ditto," said Will.

I looked around at the tired but hopeful faces and blushed. There was nothing I could say. I think they understood.

We watched as the firemen leaned their ladder against the scaffolding and Zeda called out: "*Matiiiilda. Matilda? Here girl!*" She was wringing her hands so tight it was hard to watch.

I really, really hoped she was still up there. It was so dark and everything had been so crazy and loud. She had to be scared, being in a strange place, away from Zeda and the sideshow. They were the only family she had.

She just *had* to be up there.

"Don't worry, Ryan," said Will, seeing my shining eyes. "It'll be okay."

The five of us stood there, looking up into the dark tree branches, hearing the fireman rustle about. And then his voice rang out in a frightened yell:

"AAAAYEEE!"

Zeda clapped her hands, jumped up and down shouting "Matilda!" then hugged me tightly. Relieved, I looked over Zeda's shoulder at Will, who was giving me the thumbs-up.

Funny how it all turned out, this reuniting families business. Zeda got Matilda, and I got Zeda... and Will.

Will was pretending to make out with his hand.

I snorted.

Well, at least it was something.

EPILOGUE

AFTER THE POLICE WERE THROUGH talking with us, the sideshow offered to give Will and me a ride to Brenville. I won't ever forget the look on Dad's face when he saw us getting out of that crazy sideshow bus. At first he was angry with everyone, and yelled at me and Will and even Remmy and Robin. But he calmed down after they explained to him how I'd pretty much single-handedly brought down Bartholomew's Circus and International Crime Ring.

Then I couldn't get him to shut up about it. It was embarrassing. It didn't help that the story was all over the Oregon news. It even made the national news. By the end of the first week, everyone in town had heard, and I couldn't avoid the whispers of people saying, "Did you hear what Spartacus did?"

The Sideshow of Curiosities and Mayhem stuck around Brenville for a few days—they even did a few performances in the pool parking lot. It seemed like the whole town came to watch them at least twice.

The show was every bit as incredible as Remmy had said it was. I thought Zeda's fire breathing routine was the best part, but then, I admit I was probably a little biased.

But even though I was something of a hero, Dad didn't think that completely made up for my running away. Will came up with a deal, though, where he'd share in my grounding. That way I'd only be grounded for the rest of the summer—and not the rest of my life. It was pretty nice of him. But then, it was pretty nice of me not to bring up the whole Will-sending-me-postcards story to Dad. I think, after all we'd been through, we had a newfound respect for each other.

It took maybe two weeks of transition, but Will never called me Poop Lip again. Neither did anyone else—except for the guy at the gas station, but he'd always been weird. Unfortunately, everyone thought the logical replacement for Poop Lip was Spartacus. I would have preferred to go back to just plain Ryan, but I guess anything is better than Poop Lip. And, seeing as not a single person brought up the pool incident, I suppose that was about as good of a trade as I was going to get.

As for Eli, he was grounded for even longer than *I* was. I figured I was going to owe him for a long time to come, but he never complained or blamed me. In fact, when Dad sent me over to apologize to his parents, Eli greeted me with a triumphant smile and a couple of enthusiastic high-fives. "We totally brought him down," he said, and I grinned back.

Then his parents sent him up to his room. He gave me a thumbs-up as he backed his way out of the room. His parents just shook their heads. And if his parents weren't happy with him, they wanted *to strangle* me. I had to sit at the Carson dining room table and get chewed out by his father *and* mother, each of them speaking over the other in their rush to call me "reckless" and "irresponsible" and "out of control."

It was a strange summer, to say the least.

Eli and I weren't allowed to talk until school started. Of course, we *did*, we just had to be sneaky. We met at the fence a lot that summer, me slipping comic books and candy to him from the "outside." We also emailed strange new posts we found on IHateBartholomewsCircus.com back and forth. Someone was still updating the site. The posts had gotten more and more outrageous, including ridiculous stories about the circus's temporary hiatus and exile to Eastern Europe. Even though we were fairly certain Bartholomew was the one updating the site as part of his evil plans, I couldn't help checking it. It was as addictive as ever. And it made me feel like I was staying connected to Mom.

Mom.

I heard from Mom less than before, but it's not hard to understand why. Her postcards were postmarked from places like Latvia and Estonia. She said they were still "performing" (whatever that might have meant), but she never mentioned where. I guess with Interpol after you, you can't be too precise in your postcards. I'm sure they were all being read before they got to me, anyway.

It's kind of hard facing the fact that the world is sometimes nothing like you think it is. I could make a mile-long list of things I'd gotten wrong—everything is so much easier to see in retrospect. Sure, it's easy to say I made mistakes because I was just a kid who didn't know any better. But if I learned anything from the whole experience with Bartholomew and my mom, it's that you can't ever be too sure about anything.

Just look at Will. I thought he was evil, without one redeeming quality, but after he realized what a crappy brother he'd been... everything changed. Will became, well, actually *cool*. We even started having fun together.

And then there was Dad. I'd always looked at him as the enemy, the one who practically drove Mom off. But what Mom had told me was the truth. He *had* stayed with us after she'd taken off. Sure, he was a big grump for a long time after she left, but, looking back on everything, I couldn't really blame him. Dad was someone who'd loved and lost, but he was dealing with it the best he could. He loved me and Will, though. And he was trying. Especially after I came back, I could see he was trying. So I tried. When he suggested I join the swim team in the fall, I actually humored him.

And my mom? Well, she wasn't the person I thought she was. To say the least.

For a long time, lots of people would ask me about her. Teachers, kids, Eli, Zeda. Especially Zeda; she always grilled me for details. Whenever we saw each other (which was never enough), or talked on the phone (which was as often as we could), she'd have a hundred different questions for me.

"Do you hate her? Do you love her and hate her at the same time? Can you ever forgive her? What would you do if you saw her again?" Tough questions like that.

But it's complicated. I always think about what Lloyd told me later when I asked him what it was like having such a messed-up brother.

He said, "You can hate what your family does, but you always have the choice to still love them like family."

I guess that's how I feel about Mom. I don't like what she's doing, but I don't have a say in how she leads her life, do I? If I could stop her, I would. Honestly, just thinking about her and Bartholomew out there, together, makes me so mad sometimes. But I know that I still love her, and I always will. And I still haven't given up hope that she might get tired of her dangerous life and come home someday. If she does, well, I'd take her back, no questions asked. I can't say the same thing about the cops or Dad, though. Even after all she's put me through, she's still my mom.

And I love her.

And that's one of the only things I'm sure of.

MEET YOUR BOOKMAKERS

RAINTOWN PRESS
PORTLAND, OREGON

RAINTOWN PRESS IS PORTLAND, OREGON'S premier independent press dedicated to publishing classic and original literature for middle grade and young adult readers.

PORTLAND SERVES AS THE PERFECT backdrop for a press dedicated to young readers — the diversity of culture, literature, and landscape here encourages us to be strong, autonomous, and even outright rebellious. There is a spirit of independent thinking and innovation paired with perseverance and tenacity among the people of the Northwest. Through the drudgery and gray skies, we not only survive, we thrive. We view the wet days we endure as being custom-made for reading a good book—or in our case, making one. To that end, we say close the umbrella, and

LET. IT. DRIZZLE.

MEET THE AUTHOR

MOLLY E. JOHNSON STARTED OUT writing sports for her small-town newspaper in Sisters, Oregon—that is, until they discovered she knew nothing about football. She went on to write sarcastic movie, restaurant, and art reviews for her college newspaper. After barreling through a B.A. from Linfield and an M.A. from Portland State, she then barged (and blogged) through a year of teaching English to some of the coolest kids in China. She now works as a copywriter in Portland and lives with her cat, Achilles. She spends her free time reading, writing, learning, and lying through her teeth every chance she gets. She has seen Spartacus thirteen times.